BY ALL MEN'S JUDGMENTS

a novel

Brad Cotton

First Prinia Press Printing, April 2014.
10 9 8 7 6 5 4 3 2 1

Library and Archives Canada Cataloguing in Publication

Cotton, Brad, 1977-, author
    By all men's judgments / Brad Cotton.

ISBN 978-0-9919724-2-5 (pbk.)

    I. Title.

PS8605.O8847B9 2014   C813'.6   C2014-902086-4

Author Website: www.BradCotton.com
Twitter: @bradcott0n
Facebook: facebook.com/bradcotton

For Stephanie and Riley

"Have you heard of John Dillinger, Mr. Bishop?"

"Of course I have."

"What about Bonnie Parker, Clyde Barrow?"

"Yes."

"George Kelly?"

"Him too."

"Jesse James?"

"Yes."

"What about George Nelson?"

"Outlaws, all of them."

"Indeed."

"Famous ones."

"Ah, yes. And why are they famous, Mr. Bishop?"

"Because of their crimes. Because of what they did, of course."

"Undoubtedly that's part of it. But why are they still famous today? Why do we even know their names at all?"

"I would imagine because they stood out from the average person. Because their stories were exceptional."

"Exceptional indeed. But that's not why we know their names today. All things considered, there were many exceptional people in those times whose names we do not know. In fact, probably many outlaws just like the ones I've mentioned."

"So why is it that we know their names, Mrs. Meacham?"

"Well, Mr. Bishop, the reason we still know the names of those outlaws in particular is that they got caught."

Chapter 1

Charleston, South Carolina. 1995

"Could you open the window a little, dear? I'd like to look outside."

Madeline did as her grandmother requested and pulled open the shutters to expose the sky.

"That's better," Liza said with a sigh.

She lay in her bed, where she now spent the better part of her days.

"Is there anything I can get for you?" Madeline asked the old woman.

"No, thank you, dear. I don't think I'll be needing anything for a while."

Liza spoke with a delicate twang. Her Southern drawl had once been as thick as honey, but living in the North as a younger woman had deprived her vowels of a sliver of their charm. The one-time roundabout A's and I's had become more sharp and to the point.

Liza turned her head on the pillow and looked out the window. The sun began to emerge from behind a puff of white cloud and shone a ray onto her pale, weathered face. She closed her eyes and felt the warmth on her cheeks.

"He's coming today, you know," Liza said, her eyes still closed.

"Who is?" Madeline asked, folding the knitted blanket that had fallen off the end of the bed.

"What do you mean, 'who is'?" Liza asked, opening her eyes and looking down her nose.

"Right. The writer. Yes, Grandma, I know he is."

"He should have been here by now. He's late."

"I'm sure he'll be along any time now."

"Would you stop fussing already," Liza said with quiet vigor.

Madeline placed the folded blanket at the end of the bed. She looked up at her grandmother and smiled.

"Come sit here with me," Liza requested, patting the bed.

Madeline did as her grandmother asked.

"Now what did I tell you about running yourself ragged?" the old woman said. "I don't need anything more than what I have right here. You just mind yourself for a while. Why don't you go freshen up? There's a gentleman coming."

"What's wrong with how I look?"

"There's nothing wrong with how you look – nothing at all."

Liza put her hand on top of Madeline's. Madeline looked down at her grandmother's thin, furrowed skin.

"I just want you to tend to yourself," Liza continued with a smile. "You're driving me mad with all this attention."

"And who is this man again?" Madeline asked, knowing full well the answer.

"Nathaniel Bishop. He writes for the paper. I told you this just last night."

"I forget these things. You know that."

"Yes, well, I have a feeling you try to forget."

"And whose son is he?"

"Well I'm sure he's someone's son, but I don't know the name of his mother."

"Then how did you —"

"Prudence Goodholm, God bless her heart, swears up and down that he is the finest writer in Charleston. He's the son of one of her silly friends. Now get! Get on with you."

Once again Madeline did as her grandmother asked, but not before leaning over and kissing her forehead.

"Good writer or not, it's impolite to be late," Madeline said before taking her leave of the room.

"I find it remarkable how you manage to dislike someone before you've even met them," Liza said into the openness.

Her voice was not strong enough to carry into the hallway.

Liza turned her head and looked out the window once more. The sun was hiding behind a passing cloud. Closing her eyes, she took a deep breath and held it in her lungs. It was a warm summer's day, and so far it was a good one.

Liza was soon enveloped by the quietude and began to doze off.

"How about this?" Madeline asked, holding out the bottom of the yellow sundress she had put on.

"You look beautiful," Liza said. "A perfect flower."

"I found it in Mom's old closet."

"I know you did. I'm the one who put it there. You look just like her, you know."

"I look just like you, Grandma."

There was a knock at the front door.

"That'll be him," Liza said. "Go and let him in, dear."

Madeline headed down the stairs in no hurry. She reached the front door and opened it. The man standing there looked nothing like what she had expected. He was tall and slender and young. He looked right into her eyes and smiled.

"Hello," he said. "I'm Nate Bishop."

He reached out his hand.

"Madeline."

Madeline shook the man's hand.

"Come in," she said. "Grandma is expecting you."

"I'm sorry I'm late. I don't know the area very well."

"You're not from around here, then?"

"Minnesota, actually. There are parts of Charleston I still haven't seen. This is one of them."

Nathaniel entered and Madeline closed the door behind him.

Nathaniel's hair was longer than that of most men she knew. He wore blue jeans and a T-shirt under a sports jacket. The jacket was thick and made of tweed, with colorful specks of thread interwoven into the gray. His brown leather shoes looked like they had long since seen their best days. He carried a small leather bag across his shoulder.

"Grandma is upstairs," Madeline said.

"After you," Nathaniel offered, holding out his arm.

Madeline began to climb the staircase. She stopped on the third step and turned to face the stranger.

"Can I ask what this is about?" she asked.

"You mean you don't know?" Nathaniel said.

"I don't."

"Then your guess would be as good as mine."

"So you're not here for the newspaper?"

"Not that I know of. Didn't you ask your grandmother?"

"I did, but she likes to have her secrets."

"I see."

Madeline and Nathaniel held their gaze on one another.

"Her room is right up here," Madeline said, breaking the silence.

Madeline led Nathaniel into her grandmother's room. Liza was sitting up in bed, looking spry, her white sleeping gown newly preened.

"Grandma," Madeline said, "this is Nathaniel Bishop."

"Ma'am."

"Nathaniel, this is Liza Meacham."

"Let's have a look at you," Liza said.

Madeline moved out of the way so her grandmother could have a clear view of the man.

"Handsome," Liza said. "Younger than I would have thought, though. You must be only a few years older than my granddaughter here."

"I couldn't say, ma'am."

"I'm certain of it," Liza assured.

"Can I get you anything?" Madeline asked. "A drink of water?"

"I'm all right for now, thank you," Nathaniel replied.

"Why don't you get comfortable, Mr. Bishop," Liza offered. "I'm looking forward to speaking with you."

"Oh. Well... certainly."

Nathaniel looked around the room for somewhere to sit.

"Why don't you take that chair right there? Pull it here, beside me."

Nathaniel crossed the room and picked up a wood and wicker chair from in front of the woman's vanity table. He placed the seat down beside the bed, precisely where Liza had requested, and put his bag down beside the chair.

"Madeline, why don't you join us as well?"

"You want me to stay?" Madeline asked.

"I do... if that's all right with you, Mr. Bishop."

"It's fine with me," Nathaniel said with a smile.

"I'll get another chair," Madeline said, disappearing instantly from the room.

"So how do you like Charleston, Mr. Bishop? I understand you're from up north."

"I like it. Some of the finest people you'll meet."

"Indeed."

Madeline returned with chair in hand. She placed it beside the window, on the opposite side of the bed from Nathaniel.

"Is everyone comfortable?" Liza asked.

"Sure," Nathaniel said.

Madeline nodded in agreement.

"Good," Liza said, stroking down the bed sheet on her lap. "Now you're probably wondering why I asked you here, Mr. Bishop. And I intend to tell you. But would it be all right if I asked you a few questions first?"

"I don't see why not."

"What do you think of my granddaughter here?"

"Grandma!"

Madeline was clearly flustered.

"She's… very pretty," Nathaniel answered.

"It's okay, dear, I'm only being playful. I'm sorry, Mr. Bishop. I didn't mean to embarrass you. I'm old, you see, I sometimes forget my manners."

"It's fine," Nathaniel said, smiling again.

"Tell me, Mr. Bishop," Liza said, "if I were to share privileged information with you – say, reveal something that might still be of interest to some – could I trust you to keep it a secret for some time?"

"I don't think I understand," Nathaniel said, after a moment's delay.

"If I were to reveal sensitive things to you, could you guarantee me that you would not speak of them or write about them until the time came that I said it was all right to do so?"

"I suppose I could do that… if I'm understanding you correctly."

"Good."

"That is, of course, unless what you tell me could lead to someone being harmed or a crime being committed, or something like that. I believe I would have an obligation in those cases to inform –"

"Everything I mean to share with you happened a very long time ago, Mr. Bishop. I can assure you of that. The story cannot bring harm to anyone. There is nothing more to do with it now than to tell it."

"Well, then, I don't see why I couldn't agree to keep it to myself."

"Until the time comes that you will do with it as you wish," Liza added.

"Ma'am?"

"You are a writer, Mr. Bishop. Is that not true? You are not here for your handsome good looks alone. There will come a time when you will write about what I'm going to tell you. You are here to listen to my story. Once I am done telling it, it will be yours to write about."

"I see."

"As long as my granddaughter agrees that what you write is truthful and accurate."

"Me?" Madeline asked.

"That sounds fine," Nathaniel said.

"And as long as you do not print a word of this story until you receive word from me that the time has come for you to do so. Can you agree to that?"

"I think I can," Nathaniel said.

"Grandma," Madeline interjected, "why me?"

"Who better, dear? You'll be here to listen as well. And I trust no one more."

"But I don't know anything about what you're going to tell, or –"

"You know the difference between truth and lies, do you not? Surely I raised you well enough for that."

Madeline smiled.

"I've read your writing in the papers, Mr. Bishop," Liza said.

"That's good."

"I don't care for most of it."

"Oh."

"What I mean to share with you is unlike anything you have written about before."

"Well, I've always taken well to change, ma'am."

"Do you think you might have it in your constitution to write an entire book?"

"That all depends, ma'am."

"On what?"

"On how long your story is."

"It covers enough events to fill at least one full book."

"Well, then, Mrs. Meacham, I can certainly offer to do my best."

Liza looked the young man dead in the face.

"Yes, well, I think that will have to do, then, won't it?" she said. "So if we are all in agreement, I don't see why we shouldn't get started. If that's all right with you, Mr. Bishop."

"Do you mind if…"

Nathaniel fumbled around in the pockets of his jacket, finally pulling out a digital voice recorder.

"Do you mind if I record our conversation?"

"Not at all."

Nathaniel pressed a little red button on the small machine and placed it on the bedside table. He took out a yellow notepad from his bag and removed the cap from his pen.

"Whenever you're ready, Mrs. Meacham."

Liza took a deep breath.

"Have you heard of John Dillinger, Mr. Bishop?"

"Of course I have."

"What about Bonnie Parker, Clyde Barrow?"

"Yes."

"George Kelly?"

"Him too."

"Jesse James?"

"Yes."

"What about George Nelson?"

"Outlaws, all of them."

"Indeed."

"Famous ones."

"Ah, yes. And why are they famous, Mr. Bishop?"

"Well, because of their crimes. Because of what they did."

"Undoubtedly that's part of it. But why are they still famous today? Why do we even know their names at all?"

"I would imagine because they stood out from the average person. Because their stories were exceptional."

"Exceptional indeed. But that's not why we know their names today. All things considered, there were many exceptional people in those times whose names we do not know. In fact, probably many outlaws just like the ones I've mentioned."

"So why is it that we know their names, Mrs. Meacham?"

"Well, Mr. Bishop, the reason we still know the names of those outlaws in particular is that they got caught."

Nathaniel smiled. A moment of silence passed.

"Have you ever heard of Joseph Tilley?" Liza asked.

"No ma'am, I can't say that I have."

"And you?" she asked Madeline.

Her granddaughter shook her head.

"I'm not surprised," Liza said. "Well, I'm going to tell you the story of a man named Joseph Tilley. It's not likely one you've heard, as it all happened much before your time, of course. It's a good story, one that must be told from the beginning if it's to be told right.

"Now, my memory isn't what it used to be, so you'll forgive me if there are parts of the story that are less complete than others, won't you? And, though I'll do my best to retell it in its entirety, there are certain aspects that will need to remain untold, at least for the time being.

"Now the names I'll be using will not be real, for obvious reasons. Likewise, you won't find most of the places I speak of on God's good earth."

"Ma'am," Nathaniel interrupted. "How will I be able to confirm the story if none of the names or places are real?"

"Oh, the people and places are real, Mr. Bishop. They're very real indeed. They'll just be called by different names for now. And I can assure you, for whatever it may be worth to you here today, that everything I'm about to tell you is true. In due time, I have no doubt, you'll find a way to confirm that."

"Grandma," Madeline said, "is this about Grandpa?"

Liza smiled widely at Madeline.

"I didn't know him very well," Madeline said to Nathaniel. "I was only ten when he died."

"I think you knew him well enough," Liza said. "Well enough to know his character, don't you think?"

"I suppose so."

"Anyway, I have a feeling Mr. Bishop will help you down the path to discovery. Won't you, Mr. Bishop?"

"I can do my best."

"See? Just like I told you."

Madeline was intrigued. She had never known her grandmother to be so mysterious, to be so unforthcoming that she left Madeline wanting, with no justification beyond an appeal for fortitude. She was curious. She was curious and excited at the prospect of learning about her grandfather. He had never spoken of his past and even shied away from the topic when it arose.

"You were saying…" Nathaniel offered.

"What's that?"

"You were going to tell us about Joseph Tilley."

"Indeed I was, wasn't I?"

Chapter 2

Logan County, Oklahoma. 1914

The first twelve years of Joseph Tilley's life were like those of any other young boy in rural Oklahoma. He went to school. He helped his father around the farm. He minded his mother and always did what was asked of him.

Being slight of stature, Joseph couldn't help his father as much as he would have liked with the daily labors. Joseph's father would instead dispatch the young boy elsewhere on the farm to tend to smaller jobs, leaving the men to do their work. Joseph wanted to help more, but he knew his first duty was to obey his father. He didn't dare speak back to his father, not because he was afraid of the man, but because of how much he loved him.

Joseph's father was a quiet sort. He went about the humble business of feeding his livestock and tending his crops with not so much as a whisper of complaint. All his life he had wanted nothing more than his small farm and a large family with which to work it. After Joseph's early and violent arrival into the world, however, Joseph's father had learned that his wife would be unable to bear him more laborers for his fields. But Joseph's father never made the boy feel guilty for spoiling his mother's insides, nor did he make mention of more children from that day forward, not to anyone.

Joseph's mother was a beautiful woman. For a year after Joseph's birth she lay weak and sickly in bed. Like Joseph she was slight, and she too was not strong. When she became well again, she was able to return to her duties as homemaker and helper and obedient wife to her husband. She too made no mention of the need or desire for more children after Joseph was born. She instead loved her only child as if he were two or three or more.

In the summer Joseph's mother would sit upon the porch of the farmhouse and sew clothing for the family. The dexterity of her fine fingers made her a talented seamstress. Joseph would often sit with her and watch her hands swiftly weaving in and around the pieces of fabric. He especially liked to see how the ends of his mother's brown hair would turn a light auburn in the summer sun as it disappeared in the distance at the end of the day.

When not with his mother or father, Joseph would venture out into the woods that surrounded the farm. He loved the outdoors. As soon as he was old enough to go off on his own, he did so, and very often. Not having any brothers or sisters meant Joseph had to manufacture his own adventures. He had a favorite spot in the woods just behind his house. It was a small clearing by a stream.

One time on a summer's day, a day like any other, Joseph came upon a short fishing line and hook caught on a rock. The stream's delicate current threatened to drag it away, but Joseph quickly nabbed the line for himself. He attached the thin string to a branch he liberated from a birch tree nearby. The still live and limber arm of wood provided a comfortable hold and ample give. At the age of nine Joseph taught himself to fish against the stream's shore.

In a small cave beside the stream, Joseph had over time fashioned for himself a formidable hideout. Beside his rocky fort Joseph built fires, and within the cave he hid treasures he found on his hikes and drew plans and maps with white chalk on the five-foot-high walls. On livelier days, to Joseph the cave was Fort Joseph, a refuge from the attacking Cherokee or Chickasaw nearby. No one but Joseph knew about his cave, and Joseph liked it that way.

When Joseph was called back to the farm, his mother needed only to yell from the edge of the woods and he would come running. Across the sparseness of the Oklahoma wilderness, even her delicate voice could carry the one hundred yards or so it took to reach Joseph's ears.

Joseph spent much of his childhood in the woods behind the house. It could be said that the earliest years of Joseph Tilley's life were good.

It was three days after Joseph's twelfth birthday when life on the Tilley farm changed forever. Changed not by an act of the Tilleys themselves, and not by the hand of God or by the will of other powers that be. Three days after Joseph's twelfth birthday, the Tilleys' lives were altered evermore by just one man.

It was a Monday in May. Joseph remembered that it was a Monday because on Mondays his father would work on the farm alone. After school Joseph came straight home to help. That day he helped his father feed the horses, a job often prescribed to one of the farmhands when they were around. Joseph was pleased to help his father, and once the job was done, he went looking for his mother to inform her of the deed. Joseph found his mother lying on her bed.

"Momma?"

"Hi there."

"Momma, are you okay?"

"I'm just feeling a little tired, Joseph. I'll be okay."

"Can I bring you something? Maybe you want some water?"

"No, no, that's fine, thank you. I have to get up and find something to make for dinner."

"Is it your stomach again, Momma?"

"I'll be fine, Joseph. I just need a minute."

Joseph's mother had bouts with problems of the stomach. She never spoke of it, but Joseph had discovered some time before then that the problems had arrived just after he had.

Joseph left his mother to rest. But he wanted to do more for her. He got it in his mind that he was going to do more.

He made his way out the creaking back door of the house and headed straight into the woods. Joseph's father saw the boy running from across the field and waved his arm high in the air.

Joseph breached the woods and soon reached his cave. Once inside the hideaway, he packed his small brown satchel with a penknife, a compass, some twine, an old tobacco tin full of worms, and a black rabbit's foot for good luck. He also grabbed his trusted fishing rod. He began to make his way upstream toward the open pond in the distance.

Joseph followed the stream for a few hundred paces, all the while looking down in hopes of spotting a fish or two making their passage to larger waters. Joseph held his fishing rod at the ready, a worm hooked and poised to be swallowed.

The stream gurgled and rolled, making a soft, soothing noise as it lapped against the rounded rocks. Joseph saw a shadow move along the bottom of the water up ahead of his position. He picked up his pace and scurried up to the spot.

There was nothing there when he arrived. It was just the shadow of the leaves overhead.

A small rustle came from the ground on the other side of the stream. Joseph's eyes darted. He hunched down low. Another rustle, this time louder. Joseph followed the noise and soon came upon the location of a gray hare sniffing at the base of a tree. Joseph ducked down the side of a small hill behind him. Leaning against the protective, grassy incline, he reached into his satchel and took out his knife. He looked on the ground for a stick suitable to his needs. Finding nothing of use, Joseph quickly untied the line from his fishing rod, pulled out his twine, and tied the knife to the branch's end. Joseph was going to spear the hare and bring it home to his mother.

Joseph emerged from the side of the hill with the stealth of a tiger. He remained low to the ground and kept as quiet as he could. The hare had since moved from its original position. Joseph moved toward the area where the animal once was.

A rustle came again. Joseph's ears perked.

Another noise, this time even closer. Joseph readied his spear. He could easily hurl the spike across the narrow stream and kill the animal in one clean shot. The rustling began again, but this time it sounded different to Joseph. The noise was heavier, and it was accompanied by the sound of cracking twigs. Joseph halted his progress. He knew that the small hare couldn't be the one making that kind of noise. Joseph's gaze moved up the hill on the other side of the stream. At first he wasn't sure if his eyes were playing tricks, but as the figure got closer, there could be no doubt that it was an animal much larger than the one he was hunting.

Joseph scurried back down the small knoll and dropped back to the ground. After a few quiet moments he lifted his head just enough to see what kind of animal had scared away his family's dinner. As the noise continued to approach, Joseph began to feel fear. Surely a small penknife on the end of a fishing pole could not stay something making that harsh a noise.

The figure appeared. It was an animal very different from what Joseph was used to seeing in the woods behind his house. It was a man.

He was walking through the woods, heading toward the pond. Joseph ducked back down as far as he could so as not to be spotted. He raised his eyes to the ridge carefully.

He noticed that the man was walking strangely; he was limping. Was he hurt? Perhaps the man was injured, and lost.

Joseph perked up his head, thinking he might help, when the form of another man appeared and frightened Joseph back down. The second man was following behind the first. He was walking with no limp at all.

The two men soon crossed in front of Joseph's position. Joseph held his breath as they came close on the other side of the stream. They passed him by without caution and headed off to his right. Joseph could have begun to make his escape, but he did not leave.

Joseph couldn't help but follow the two men, slowly, quietly, along the valley under the sightline of the hill's peak. He crept along like a hunter, making certain to stay at least fifty paces behind the two men. His curiosity wouldn't let him turn away.

Joseph followed the men until both stopped walking. They'd reached the edge of the open pond. The man with the limp stood against the shore and looked out at the dark blue water. The second man stood behind him, motionless. Neither said a word to the other. Joseph didn't dare get any closer. He could tell that the first man was indeed injured. His pants had been ripped off halfway down on one leg. His shin and shoe were covered with blood.

The injured man got down on one knee and leaned in toward the pond. He cupped his hands together and filled them with water. He used the water to wash away the blood. He tapped his fingers lightly against the skin of his leg. The man then took another scoop of liquid from the pond and put it to his lips. To Joseph it looked like the man was praying. The injured man wiped his wet hands against his hips and, with much difficulty, rose to his feet. The man looked out across the pond once more. He then turned slowly toward his escort. The two men were facing one another.

The second man raised a pistol and without hesitation pulled the trigger and put a bullet into the injured man's head.

The sound shook Joseph's body. He had never heard a gunshot like that one before. The violent sound echoed across the opening of the pond. It rang through Joseph's ears. It lingered in the air.

The wounded man wilted and dropped to the ground like a pile of mud-soaked clothing. His head hit the edge of the pond and made a small splash that rippled outward. Darkness flowed into the water from his body.

Joseph was filled with fear. He stared at the man lying in the water, hoping he would move a limb, or even just a finger. The man did not move.

Joseph's eyes turned to the man holding the silver piece of metal by his side. The man looked odd. From his vantage point Joseph couldn't say why exactly. From where he hid, Joseph couldn't make out many distinguishing features of the man with the gun. All that stood out to him were the red suspenders he wore.

The man with the gun took a few steps forward and knelt down beside the man he had just shot. He put his hand into one of the dead man's pockets but came out with nothing. He reached into another pocket and pulled out his wallet. The man with the gun put the wallet down on the ground. He put the gun down on the ground beside it. The man then gathered several rocks and placed them in every lodging place he could find in the dead man's clothing. In his pockets, in his socks, even down into his undergarments.

Joseph watched, stunned and motionless.

The man with the gun grabbed the ankles of the man he had killed. He turned and began to walk, dragging the body along the ground. He entered the water, pulling the body with him. He glided into the water until he was up to his waist, where he turned and pushed the dead body outward into the pond as if he were shoving a boat to sea. The body began to float away slowly, gently, peacefully.

The man with the gun began wading back to shore. He did so with a watery stroll so casual that one might think he was merely returning from a leisurely swim. He waved his hands over the water, enjoying its coolness. He rubbed his hands together and scratched off remnants of dirt and blood. He looked as though he didn't have a care in the world.

Then he stopped.

The man perked his head and began to look around the shore of the pond. He stood, still as a statue, shifting his eyes.

He turned his head, little by little, from side to side. He lowered his neck to see below a hanging tree branch. It was as though he sensed a presence.

Joseph ducked down, and though he was sure the man would not be able to see him, he could feel his heart beating ever more heavily in his chest. It was time for Joseph to go.

Joseph slid gradually farther down the hill and into the narrow valley.

"Hey!" he heard the man yell.

Joseph ducked behind a tree. He waited. After a few moments he poked his head around the trunk. The man in the water was looking off to his right but was instantly attracted to the boy's movement. The man's head snapped over and his eyes instantly locked with Joseph's.

The man in the water said nothing. After a moment's pause he simply began to lumber through the water in haste, and with purpose, splashing and pumping his arms through the air.

Joseph had been spotted. He didn't hesitate any longer. He jumped out from behind the tree and ran as fast as he possibly could.

He bounded over fallen branches and over rocks. He dodged trees and bushes like a fleeing deer, keeping his eyes straight in front of him, sure to mark his path ahead. Joseph's legs and feet were moving faster than they ever had before, or at least that's what it felt like as his satchel bounced up and down off his hip and back. Joseph sucked in the air and spit it back out again.

Only a few hundred yards more and he would reach the cave.

Joseph ducked inside the boy-sized opening of Fort Joseph and scurried to pull branches and leaves to cover the hole. He threw his satchel down and fell to the ground at the back of the darkened hideout. He clung to the rocky wall as if he were hoping it would envelop him, saving him, sucking him in and hiding him from the world. His heart thumped. His stomach turned. His mind raced over a single thought as his eyes stared at the opening of the cave: *God save me, God save me, God save me.*

Minutes began to pass, though each felt like more. Joseph's young lungs began to recover. Air filled his chest and his breathing returned to a normal pace. Not enough time had passed to be safe, though, he thought. Not enough time for the man with the gun to run by, or get lost, or even give up looking.

"Joseeeeeph!"

Joseph's eyes burst open. The voice of Joseph's mother lilted through the woods.

"Joseph, come on in now!"

Joseph held his breath. He dared not move or make a sound. Joseph knew that he had five or so minutes before his mother would call again, or even worse, send his father to call instead.

Only once had Joseph not returned to the house after his father had bellowed. It had been an error Joseph was certain to never make twice. But Joseph dared not move. Not then.

God save me, God save me, God save me.

Chapter 3

Joseph's rigid grip on the wall of the cave began to loosen. He didn't know how much time had passed, but if the man with the gun had been close behind him as he ran, he surely would have reached the cave by now. Outside the cave there was silence. Not a sound had been heard since the call of his mother's voice had wafted through the trees many minutes before.

Joseph crawled toward the opening of the cave on his hands and knees. He moved as quietly as he could. He reached the breach, brushed away some branches, and peeked out his head ever so slightly.

He saw nothing.

He passed his eyes across the area. There was no one to be seen. He had lost the man with the gun, or at the very least, the man with the gun had lost him.

A few more moments passed. Joseph's head poked out of the cave like a prairie dog up from his hole to sniff for food. His mother was expecting him.

Joseph sprung to his feet and darted through the woods toward the house. He didn't run with as much fear this time, but he ran with similar purpose. When he pierced the edge of the woods and felt only grass beneath his feet, Joseph's stomach sank. He was out in the open, visible, vulnerable.

Joseph reached the back of the farmhouse. He pressed his back up against the hard wooden wall. He scanned the precipice of the woods. If the man with the gun had seen or heard him, he would no doubt spring forth at any second.

The man did not spring.

A thud came from inside the house. Joseph turned his head.

No sound followed.

Could it be? Joseph wondered.

Joseph felt a pang of fear unlike anything he had known before. He inched his way across the wall of the house, never removing his back from its touch. He reached a spot with a window overhead. Ever so slowly, Joseph knelt down beside the back porch and took hold of a tin bucket. He placed the bucket upside down below the window. He carefully mounted the overturned container, holding on to the wall for support. He steadily unbent his knees and began to rise. Joseph's eye's reached the bottom of the windowpane. He peered inside.

There, motionless on the floor of the kitchen, was Joseph's father, a knife handle protruding from below the nape of his neck. He wore a thick necklace of blood that led down to a blanket of red upon which he lay. Just above Joseph's father stood a man. The man's back was turned, but Joseph could plainly see his red suspenders. The man's arm was around

Joseph's mother's neck. He held her up against his body like a shield. The man's gun was pressed to her head.

Joseph jerked his head down away from the window. He stood atop the tin bucket, shaking.

"Shut up," the man with the gun said. "Shut up or I'll pull this trigger and put a bullet in your brain."

Joseph's mother whimpered.

"Say one word, lady, and I swear it."

Joseph couldn't help but look up through the window once more. The man turned slightly and Joseph got a look at his face. Joseph noticed one more distinguishing mark, something the man could not take off at the end of the day like he could the suspenders. The man who held Joseph's mother at the end of his gun was missing the better part of his left ear.

On the side of his head, where a full ear should have been, was merely a hole with a lobe and some mangled skin above it. The top of his ear was sheared clean off. It was plain to see that the man hadn't been born that way. Where the top of his ear should have been were scars. The man with the gun had tried to grow his hair long enough to conceal the missing ear, but his thin, greasy mane did a poor job of it.

"Stop moving. Stop moving, lady!"

The man with the gun pressed Joseph's mother up against the kitchen counter.

"I'm just waiting for the little one," he said.

And just like that, Joseph's mother ceased to whimper. She became eerily calm. It seemed a strange sight to Joseph.

"Don't do it. Don't do it, lady, I swear…"

The man tightened his hold on her neck.

The woman's eyes had found Joseph's. Mother and son locked gazes through the window. She smiled at him the slightest of smiles, before her face grew grim.

She took a deep breath.

"JOSEPH RUUUUUUU –"

The man pulled the trigger.

The last thing Joseph saw before he ran like a lighting bolt back into the woods was the sight of his mother's blood slapping against the kitchen cupboards.

The sun was going down and shade was beginning to overtake the woods behind the house. To Joseph the path to his cave was so familiar that he needn't look down, not even once. Joseph weaved his way back through the trees.

He reached the cave. He grabbed his satchel. He leapt into the shallow stream, stomping in the center before emerging on the other side of the ten-foot width. His feet were wet and cold. His legs were heavy. But he did not stop. Joseph ran through the Oklahoma woods and didn't look back.

Chapter 4

"Did that really happen?" Madeline asked.

"Of course it did," Liza said. "That's not something I would joke about, is it? It was a terrible thing."

"No, of course."

"Mrs. Meacham," Nathaniel said. "You said that Joseph ran off into the woods after the gunshot."

"I did."

"Where was he going?"

Liza took a good look at Madeline. Then she looked over to Nathaniel.

"Would you mind if we picked this up again tomorrow?" she said. "I'm getting quite tired."

"You feeling okay?" Madeline asked.

"Fine, dear. I'm fine. I would just like to get a bit of rest now."

"That's no problem," Nathaniel said. "I can come back tomorrow afternoon, if that suits you."

"That suits me fine, Mr. Bishop."

Nathaniel reached over and shut off his voice recorder. He placed it and his writing pad back into his bag.

"I can show you out," Madeline offered.

"Thank you."

Nathaniel got up from his chair.

"Thank you for coming, Mr. Bishop. I'll see you again soon."

Madeline led Nathaniel from the bedroom. She let him pass through the door and then closed it behind them.

Nathaniel was standing at the front door of the house, about to take his leave.

"Do you mind if we talk for a minute?" he asked.

"No," Madeline said. "I don't mind at all."

Nathaniel put down his bag.

"Off the record, of course."

"Would you like a cup of tea?"

"That would be great, actually, thanks."

Madeline led Nathaniel to the kitchen. He sat down at the table while Madeline filled the kettle.

"Have you always lived in Charleston?" Nathaniel asked.

"I have."

"But you haven't always lived with your grandmother."

"No. I moved in here to help a few months ago."

"Is she... sick?"

"She's not in the best of health. Some days are better than others."

Madeline placed the kettle on the stove. She came to sit with Nathaniel at the table.

"What do you make of her story so far?" Nathaniel asked.

"What do you mean?"

"Well, I mean you're her granddaughter. Have you ever heard anything like it before?"

Madeline thought for a moment.

"Mr. Bishop –"

"Nate."

"My grandfather died when I was very young. He was a quiet man, especially about the past. I don't think I ever heard him talk about his youth, or his family."

"What was his name?"

"William Meacham."

"I don't suppose you know where he was born?"

"He was born in Oklahoma. That I know. But like I said, I was young when he died. I went off to college some years later, and his past never really came up again. Until now, of course."

"I see."

"Why do you ask?"

"I don't know. It doesn't seem so strange, I suppose, all that happening back then. Do you think it's strange?"

"You're doubting the story is true."

"No, no," Nathaniel said, "I didn't say that."

"Mr. Bishop –"

"Nate."

"I know my grandmother. Perhaps not as well as my mother did, but I would say I know her well enough to tell you that she wouldn't make up a story like that. She simply wouldn't go to the trouble. Not in her state."

"Okay," Nathaniel said. "I can see that."

The kettle began to hiss. Madeline rose from her chair and removed it from the stovetop. She poured the steaming water into two mugs, the string of a tea bag slumped over the side of each.

Madeline placed a mug down in front of Nathaniel and took her seat at the table once more.

"I suppose…" Madeline said. "I suppose if something like that happened to you when you were that young, it wouldn't be a story you spoke of very often."

"That's a good point."

Nathaniel took a sip of his tea. Madeline smiled and took a sip of her own.

"So where did you go to school?" Nathaniel asked.

"Barton."

"Ah. An NC girl."

"And you?"

"Northwestern."

"I was an English major," Madeline admitted.

"We have something in common, then."

"I don't know about that. I was more of a reader."

"Do you have a favorite author?"

"Well, that's like asking someone to name their favorite music, isn't it? I guess if I had to pick… I'd probably say Flaubert."

"Really?" Nathaniel said. "I mean, there's nothing wrong with Flaubert – don't get me wrong. I think I've even read one of his books."

"He's not the most well-known."

"A romantic, though, right?"

"You could say that."

"So tell me, Madeline –"

"Maddy."

"Tell me, Maddy, what do you do in Charleston, besides help care for Mrs. Meacham?"

"Right now that's my only job."

"Did you do something before?"

"I did."

"Am I being too forward?"

"No, that's all right. I was a waitress."

"I tended bar for three years after school," Nathaniel offered.

"I've thought about going back to school, but then Grandma needed help, so…"

"I think it's great what you're doing. I never knew my grandparents."

"I might go back one day… to school. Who knows?"

"Who knows, indeed?"

Nathaniel lifted his mug and took one more sip.

"I should be going," he said.

"You can stay and finish your tea."

"I would, but I have work to get finished if I'm going to be coming back here tomorrow."

"Okay. I'll show you out."

Back at the front door Nathaniel picked up his bag. He looked up the stairs to Liza's bedroom door.

"I'll see you tomorrow, then?"

"Tomorrow."

Madeline opened the door and let Nathaniel out. He made his way down the path and onto the sidewalk. There he offered a wave and then carried on down the tree-lined street to his car.

Chapter 5

1916

Joseph's mother had a cousin in Kansas. His name was Bryson Bladwell. Bryson had a wife, Erma, and three children: Mona, the eldest at nineteen, and her two younger brothers Myron and Paul. Myron was seventeen, Paul was fifteen.

By the time Joseph was brought to their home, he was nearing his fourteenth birthday. Two years had passed since the man with one ear had killed his parents. For those two years Joseph didn't dare return to the farm. He lived on his own in the wilderness, often scavenging for food and shelter in small towns when the woods couldn't provide. The outdoors gave respite, and he often found solace in the quiet, dark nights alone by the banks of the narrow river he had come to know so well. Joseph sat under the stars and wondered what the next days would bring. He would think about his home, he would think about his school, he would think about his mother and father, and he would think about the man who had pulled the trigger and taken it all away.

Joseph became expert at living off the land. His once novice fishing skills improved greatly. His ability to make shelter grew impressive, as did his knowledge of the local wildlife. The lay of the forest had become second nature to him; it had become his home.

When Joseph was thirteen, more than a year and a half after his parents' murder, it was a small-town sheriff who finally caught up with him. Joseph was held for sixty-four days in a local jailhouse for stealing a shirt and some food from a general store. The theft was a minor offense, but neither the sheriff nor the town mayor knew what to do with Joseph once they had him in their custody. The deputy sheriff, a man named Alfred Winter, took a quick liking to the boy and made it his duty to look after him during his stay.

Joseph slept in a jail cell under the watch of Deputy Winter. Alfred would bring him corn bread and soup and whatever leftover dinner he could gather from his table. After the first week of incarceration the iron door to Joseph's cell ceased to be locked. When drunkards or outlaws were brought to the jailhouse, they were not placed in the same cell as Joseph but instead were put in the only other cell, beside his. Deputy Winter would hang a blue sheet to separate the scoundrels from the youngster.

Joseph quickly grew to appreciate the jailhouse for the minor luxuries it afforded: a mattress, regular food, and protection from the weather. When on the sixty-second day of his incarceration Deputy Winter showed Joseph a response letter from cousin Bryson Bladwell, a part of Joseph was saddened by the news that this unknown relation had agreed to take him in.

It was the next night that Alfred Winter took Joseph home to meet his wife. Mrs. Marie Winter cooked him supper and gave him some clothing that had once belonged to her youngest brother. The clothing fit Joseph well.

It was Alfred who delivered Joseph to his cousin's home in Kansas. He drove the boy up on a weekend himself.

"Alfred," Joseph said along the drive.

"Yes?"

"How come you don't have any kids of your own?"

Alfred looked Joseph in the eyes. He turned and gazed out the windshield and into the distance.

"I never did tell you, did I?" he said.

His stare remained fixed on the road ahead.

"I did have a child, once upon a time."

"You did?"

Alfred nodded.

"A daughter."

"What happened?"

"She died soon after I got back."

"Where were you?"

"I was in the army, in the war. She was just a baby when she died."

"Was she sick?"

"Not when I left," Alfred said. "Came down with a fever one night. Mrs. Winter took her to the doctor, but he couldn't do much to help her. She died at home a few days later. Doc said it was just God's plan."

Joseph didn't know what to say, so he said nothing.

When they arrived at their destination, Alfred walked Joseph from the car to the front door of the Bladwells' house. As he approached the door of his cousin's home, Joseph felt low. He realized then that he would indeed miss the company of Alfred Winter. He would miss the stories he shared, the books he brought him to read, and the mere presence of the man sitting silently as Joseph fell asleep at night in the unlocked cell. Joseph thought about telling Alfred the truth about what had happened to his parents, that he had seen them murdered, but something inside him made him keep the story to himself.

"This him?" Erma Bladwell said from the doorway of her house.

She folded her arms as if the mere look of the boy was a disappointment.

The woman wore an apron and held a wooden cooking spoon in her hand. She glared at Joseph as if he were someone coming to collect her taxes.

"You must be Mrs. Bladwell," Alfred said.

"I must be, mustn't I?"

"I'm Deputy Winter, ma'am, and this here is Joseph, your cousin."

Erma gave Joseph another look over.

"My husband's cousin. Ain't got nuttin' ta do with me."

"Either way, ma'am, here's the letter from your husband stating that you agree to take him in. You are about the only family of his we could find."

Erma took the letter from Alfred. She didn't try to read it but instead stuffed it into the pocket of her apron.

Erma was not a clean woman. She was missing teeth, and the ones she did have were brown or crooked. Her hair was knotted and dirty and went off in various directions. The dress she wore under her apron was so faded that the pattern on it was nearly impossible to make out. And Erma didn't smell like a woman should smell, at least not to Joseph.

"Well," Erma said, "what you waitin' fer? Get on in if yer gonna."

Joseph was not glad to be at his cousins' house. He had met only one of them so far, said not a word, and it seemed he was already disliked.

"Goodbye, Joseph," Alfred said as he stuck out his arm.

"Goodbye, Alfred," Joseph responded, shaking his hand.

"Best of luck to you."

"Thank you."

"Ma'am," Alfred said to Erma.

Erma said nothing in return.

Alfred made his way back to his car and drove off down the long dirt road that led up to the secluded house. Joseph watched him go.

"Yer cousins 're out back," Erma blurted. "Leave yer things and go on out there."

Joseph's possessions consisted of only one small bag filled with a few articles of clothing. He left the bag by the front door and did as Erma directed.

The sound of the creaking back door reminded Joseph of the one back home at the farmhouse. He looked up at the hinges on the wooden frame. They didn't look familiar to Joseph, but nonetheless they were easily his favorite part of Kansas thus far.

"Hey!" a voice rang out.

Joseph looked across the grassy field and saw two boys in the distance. One of them waved an arm in the air to notify Joseph of their location. Joseph walked out to the pair.

"You Joseph?"

Joseph nodded.

"I'm Myron. This here is Paul."

"Hiya," Paul said.

"So you're our cousin, huh?"

On Myron's shoulder rested a hunting rifle.

"Guess so."

"Got caught up with the laws, didja?"

"I guess so."

"So what happened? How come you ain't got no parents?"

Paul elbowed his brother.

"Aw, stuff it. You don't mind, do you, Joseph?"

"They died," Joseph said.

Myron took notice of Joseph's stare.

"You like it, huh?"

Myron took the rifle from his shoulder.

"Winchester .30-30. Can take a deer down two hundred yards away."

Joseph wanted to hold the gun. He wanted to feel the wood and metal in his hands.

"You know how to shoot?" Myron asked.

"I dunno. Maybe," Joseph said.

"Well come on, then. No better time to learn than now."

In the distance Joseph could see the outskirts of a wooded area. He liked the thought of being among the trees again and followed Myron and Paul as they headed out toward the forest.

At the breach Joseph could smell the aromas of the woods. Having spent the last few months in the jailhouse, he had forgotten how much he loved the odor of leaves and grass and trees. The three boys entered the woods, Joseph following obediently along.

"Here," Myron said as they reached a clearing.

He handed the rifle to Joseph.

"Go on. Out there."

Myron pointed out into the distance. Sitting atop a downed tree trunk nearly fifty yards away were four tin cans. The shards of light that poked through the holes in each made it clear that this was not the first time they had been shot at.

"Go ahead, kid. What you waitin' for?"

Joseph lifted the gun to his shoulder. He closed his left eye and peered down the top of the rifle with his right. Joseph tried his best to line up one of the cans between the sights, but when he pulled the trigger and the weapon jerked upward toward the sky, it didn't matter where he'd aimed.

Joseph took a moment to collect himself. A successful shot or not, Joseph felt a rush of excitement the likes of which he hadn't ever known.

"Just squeeze the trigger," Paul said. "Slowly, like you ain't in no hurry at all."

"Put the butt against your shoulder, like this," Myron said.

He abruptly set the gun up against Joseph's chest. He lifted Joseph's elbow into the air.

"Like that," he said.

"Aim for a middle one," Paul instructed quietly. "That way if you miss and hit another, no one's the wiser."

He gave Joseph a pat on the arm.

"Now take in a breath and don't let it go."

Joseph closed his left eye. He peered down the sight. He took in a lungful of air and held it in as Paul suggested. He could feel his heart thumping.

"Just squeeze," Paul reminded.

Joseph pulled the trigger, and with a hollow sounding clank one of the cans went flying from the log. A rush of blood went straight to Joseph's head. He felt a tingling in his hand and in his arm.

Shooting was something Joseph took a liking to right from the start.

"See?" Myron said. "Easy as pie. Now watch this."

Myron yanked the gun from Joseph. He pulled it up to his shoulder and with three consecutive shots exterminated the remaining cans from atop the log.

"Now that's how you shoot," he said.

Myron turned to Paul. They both held out their fists.

"One, two, three," they said in unison.

Paul held out two fingers, Myron held out one.

"Ha!" Paul said. "Your turn."

"Nah," Myron said, "it's Joseph's turn,"

"My turn for what?" Joseph asked.

"To go and pick up them cans, that's what."

"Myron, look," Paul whispered.

Paul pointed up to a small black lump in a tree at the edge of the clearing.

"I got it," Myron said.

He lifted the gun to his shoulder.

"Let Joseph do it," Paul suggested.

"He can't hit it."

"I can," Joseph insisted.

Myron peered over at his cousin.

"I can do it," Joseph said.

With little enthusiasm Myron lowered the rifle and handed it to Joseph.

"This'll be good," Myron said.

"You see it?" Paul asked. "The squirrel in the tree there?"

"I see it," Joseph said.

"Just like the can."

Joseph lifted the rifle to his eye. He took another deep breath and held it in his lungs. He squeezed the trigger and let go the shot. A thud echoed out in the distance. A bird flew out from a tree nearby.

"You did it!" Myron exclaimed. "It's tree bark for dinner tonight," he said, laughing.

Joseph had hit a tree dead center in the middle of its hefty trunk. The sound of the shot had been more than enough to frighten off the squirrel.

Myron snatched the gun from Joseph. He reached into his pocket and pulled out some bullets.

"You need practice, kid," he said as he began reloading the weapon.

"Give me another try," Joseph said.

"Go fetch those cans and maybe you'll get another shot."

Joseph looked over at Paul, who shrugged his shoulders. Joseph darted off toward the log in the distance in search of the tin cans.

Chapter 6

It was beginning to get dark outside when the three boys arrived back at the house for dinner. Joseph followed his cousins in through the creaking back door. There, already sitting at the table, were cousin Bryson and his only daughter, Mona. Erma was still at the counter preparing the food.

"Well, lookee here," Bryson said. "You must be Joseph."

Bryson got up from his chair and approached the boy.

"A lot smaller than I would have thought."

Bryson lifted Joseph's arm in the air.

"You must get that from yer pa. Put 'er there, boy."

Bryson held out his hand. Joseph took it in his.

"Not much of a grip on ya either," Bryson said. "No matter, I s'pose. Don't know what you'd be needin' it for anyhow."

Bryson Bladwell was filthy. His hands were nearly as black as the soot-covered clothing he wore. His once blue coveralls were nearly worn through in certain parts, and the buttons that had originally been there to fasten them together had long since been replaced by strange looking metal pins. His mustache was long and covered both his lips when he wasn't speaking. His hair, just like the rest of him, was black and greasy and unmaintained.

"I see you met the boys already," Bryson said. "And, that there is Mona. She's yer cousin too."

Joseph looked over to the table. Mona didn't even so much as turn her head to look at him.

"Sit down now," Erma said.

She placed a steaming pot of brownish yellow stew in the middle of the wooden table and began ladling out portions.

"Better listen to her, if ya know what's good for ya," Bryson said, winking and patting Joseph on the back.

Bryson took a seat at the head of the table. Joseph waited for everyone else to sit down before taking the lone chair remaining, beside Paul. Bryson pawed the loaf of bread and tore off a hefty chunk with his soiled hands. He passed the remainder to Myron, who sat at his right side. Myron took his share and then passed it to Paul. Paul tore a piece for himself and, before passing it across the table to Mona, made sure to take a slab for Joseph too. Erma filled Joseph's bowl with stew last.

"You go to school down there in Oklahoma?" Bryson asked.

"Used to," Joseph said.

"Well, Paul here goes. I suppose you could go with him. Less'n you ready to go right to work, that is."

"What kind of work?"

"Mona works in a clothing shop in Buford, 'bout five miles away. Can't imagine you could do that."

Bryson laughed.

"He's too small to work at the yard," Myron said. "Leave him with Paul."

"He can come to school with me," Paul said.

"Don't y'all be worryin' 'bout what the boy is gonna do," Erma said, taking her seat at the table. "There's plenty to do 'round here if he be lookin'."

"Woman, you sit around all day on your be-hind," Bryson said.

"Is that so? Well then who made this food you're eatin'? What would you know anyway?"

"I know what I know."

"Say, Pa," Paul said, "you should see Joseph here shoot. He's a right clean shot. Steady hands for someone his size."

"Don't be wastin' your time out there in the woods with these two, Joseph. Learn yourself a trade while you can," Bryson said.

Joseph took a spoonful of stew. He nabbed what looked like part of a potato and some sort of brown, stringy meat. He looked at the food. He expected the worst, but when he took it in, he was pleasantly surprised. It seemed the raggedy old woman was actually a fine cook. She had at least one redeeming feature, if it could be considered that.

After dinner Erma showed Joseph to a small room beside the kitchen. It looked more like a closet than a bedroom, but it was to be Joseph's lodging nonetheless. The furnishings consisted of a small cot and a tin kerosene lamp resting on the floor beside it. There was a small, dusty window about the size of a book above the cot. The room had a strange smell. Joseph couldn't put his finger on it exactly, but it wasn't a pleasant odor.

On the first night Joseph wanted to leave his room. It wasn't until the house was dark and still, though, that he opened the door and wandered out. He crept out the back door of the house and sat on the small stoop. He looked out at the woods and up to the stars.

"Thought I heard somethin'," Paul said, creeping out from the shadows.

Joseph was startled at first but made out the figure of his cousin quickly. Paul was smoking a cigarette.

"I didn't know anyone was awake," Joseph said.

"Yeah, well, I don't sleep so good sometimes."

Paul took a drag of his cigarette.

"Can I try that?" Joseph asked.

"What, this?"

Paul handed the self-rolled cigarette to his cousin. Joseph took a puff and blew it out.

"You gotta suck it into yer gut. Like this, here."

Paul took the cigarette from Joseph and offered a demonstration. He handed it back to him for another try. Joseph pulled the smoke in, the white paper crackling ever so slightly, and immediately began to cough it up. Paul laughed.

"It burns," Joseph said, finally catching his breath.

"That's the point."

Paul took the cigarette from Joseph.

"So what did happen to your folks, anyway?"

"They died."

"They sick or somethin'?"

"They were murdered."

"You don't say."

"A man came into the house and killed them both."

"Did you know him? The man that killed 'em?"

Joseph shook his head.

"What happened to him?"

"Don't know. No one found him."

Paul tossed the cigarette down to the ground and crushed it under his boot.

"No matter, I suppose, right? Ain't gonna bring yer folks back now, anyhow."

Joseph looked out to the woods.

"So you say you wanna go to the school with me, huh?" Paul said.

Joseph shrugged with indifference.

"You kiddin'?" said Paul. "I ain't goin' to no school. Haven't gone since last spring. No good that place'll do ya."

"So… what do you do, then?"

"Well, you'll see, woncha? Just don't be tellin' Pa. I don't need him puttin' me back to work with him. There are better ways to make money than shovelin' shit all day."

"Like what?"

"Like what, what?"

"You said there are better ways to make money?"

"Sure are. Plenty o' things for smart folks like you and me to make a buck."

"So… like what?"

"I told ya, you'll just have to wait and see. So you want a piece?"

Joseph didn't know what "wanting a piece" meant, but it seemed that cousin Paul was the only one willing to offer a hand.

"Sure. Yeah, I want a piece."

Paul pulled out a small sack and began rolling another cigarette, spinning one up in mere seconds. He rolled a second and handed it to Joseph. He then struck a match and lit them both. Joseph took a puff and sucked it into his lungs. The smoke tickled his throat on the way down and made his chest feel warm.

"That's the way to do it," Paul said.

Joseph blew the smoke out into the air.

"When will I get to shoot the gun again?" he asked.

"We'll shoot plenty. I got me a pistol hidden away too."

Joseph pictured the man with one ear. That was the first time he had seen a pistol. He had since seen more, the latest being the one Alfred Winter carried around on his hip.

"Can I shoot it, your pistol?" Joseph asked.

"Maybe one day you can. But first you gotta make me a promise, cousin."

"What's that?"

"You gotta make a promise on the souls of your ma and pa that you don't tell no one not one word of what goes on or what you see out there with me."

"I promise."

"Now think about it before you answer. Think about what I'm askin'. You gotta keep them lips sealed tight. You can't say a word, not to no one, ever."

Joseph took the mandatory moment to think.

"Well, who do I have to tell?" he said.

Paul smiled.

"The less people that know yer business, the better."

"You mean your brother doesn't know anything?"

"Myron? He knows I'm up to no good, but he don't know what goes on. He's too busy with his work and Missy Tithering anyhow."

"What's that?"

"*Who's* that? Missy's the girl Myron's tryin' to get in with. That fool's been after her for years. If old man Tithering ever catches him around his place, it'll be the last thing Myron ever does, too."

Paul took another pull from his cigarette. Joseph followed his lead.

"Meet me back here tomorrow in the morning," Paul said. "We'll head off ta 'school' together."

Paul and Joseph threw their cigarettes down onto the ground. Joseph got up from the step and crushed his out under his shoe, like his cousin. Paul headed up to the door.

"Oh," he whispered, "and you can call me Buck. All my friends do."

"Buck?"

Paul lifted his shirt and displayed a series of tiny scars across his stomach.

"Took a buckshot a few years back. Got up and walked away from it, I did."

"You got shot?"

"Don't look surprised, Joe. These parts, lotta people get shot time to time."

Chapter 7

1995

Nathaniel sat at his desk in the office of the Charleston Post and Courier, clicking away on his computer. He was looking through old Oklahoma daily newspapers. Nathaniel pulled up the death notices. For as long as he looked, he found nothing that matched the last name Tilley. Nathaniel looked through the Kansas papers too but found nothing that pointed to a family called Bladwell.

Nathaniel picked up the phone and dialed a number.

"Is this Madeline?"

"It is."

"It's Nate calling."

"Hi, Nate."

"I'm meant to come by your house a little later today, but I was wondering…"

"Do you need to reschedule?"

"No, no, nothing like that. I was just wondering if you could meet me somewhere beforehand?"

"Oh. Well, I suppose I could."

"Okay, great. Let's make it somewhere near you."

"There's a coffee shop on the north end of the street. We could meet there."

"How's four o'clock?"

"That would be fine."

"I'll see you at four, then."

Madeline was already sitting at a table when Nathaniel arrived at the coffee shop. He looked at his watch. It read ten to four. Nathaniel sat down across from Madeline.

"Hi, Maddy."

"Nate."

The waitress saw Nathaniel come in and came by the table.

"I ordered a tea," Madeline said.

"I'll have what she's having. Thank you."

"Is everything okay?" Madeline asked.

"Yeah, sure. Everything is fine."

"What did you want to meet about?"

"I couldn't find anything on a Mr. and Mrs. Tilley being murdered in Oklahoma."

"You looked?"

"I did a little digging, nothing too extensive. My concern is that we'll have to have something to corroborate the story somewhere along the line if we're claiming it to be true."

"It's not a newspaper article, Nate. It's a story, like you said. Why must we claim it to be true at all?"

"Because if it is true, like your grandmother says it is, it would be a much bigger deal. We're talking about people dying, and who knows what else."

Madeline thought for a moment.

"Just give it some more time," she said.

"I guess I'm just looking for something I can hang my hat on here."

The waitress came by with Nathaniel's tea. Madeline smiled and took a sip from her cup.

"Grandma is eager to see you again."

"Is she?"

"I think it gives her something to look forward to. Seeing you, telling the story."

"You said she's not sick, but… I have to ask."

"She's old, Nate. She's old and proud. She gets out of bed from time to time, but mostly she doesn't have the strength for it."

"I hope I'm that with it when I'm her age."

"Her mind is still sharp, like a razor. It's her body that's giving out."

"Can the doctors do anything?"

"She refuses to go back to the doctor."

Nathaniel laughed.

"That doesn't surprise me."

"Yeah, well, last time she went the doctor just told me to take her home and make her comfortable."

"Tell me what you know about your grandfather."

"What can I tell you? He was also proud. He worked hard and came home to his wife every night. From the way

Grandma talks about him, you would think he was Superman or something. He could do this and do that, and fix this and build that."

"What did he do?"

"Construction, mostly. He started as a day laborer and worked his way up. All those newer houses in the neighborhood, he built them. Him and his company."

"So he had money?"

"Some. Well, enough. When he died there was enough to look after Grandma. He wasn't rich, but he also didn't seem to spend much. Of course, how much does a ten-year-old really notice?"

"Were you close?"

"I wish I could say I remember. I know I loved him. And I know he loved me."

"And your mom?"

"Mom died a few years after Grandpa."

"I'm sorry."

"Now *they* were close. He loved her more than anything. Even at ten I noticed that. She never told him she had cancer. She was afraid it would break his heart. Once he passed, she seemed to get worse quickly. She didn't suffer much, though, all things considered. She went quickly in the end."

Madeline looked down into her cup of tea. Neither she nor Nate said much more on the topic.

"You're still coming over, right?" Madeline asked into the silence.

Nathaniel took a final sip from his cup.

"Of course."

Chapter 8

1924

The years of Joseph's stay at the Bladwells' would be among the toughest of his life. The daylight hours seemed to go by well enough. Paul, whom he now called Buck, took him to meet Gumpy the day after their talk in the back yard. Through Gumpy they found a way to make some good money and learned a trick or two about life outside the law in Kansas. Joseph would escape with Buck to the woods to shoot cans and paper targets every chance they got. He became exceptionally good at it, and he loved that time more than anything else. The days went by quickly, and Buck and Joseph grew closer. Joseph was becoming wiser in the ways of the world and learning much else too from his experienced older cousin.

What made those years the hardest for Joseph was what happened at night, when all was dark and quiet in the house. From time to time, and wholly too often, cousin Bryson would find his way into Joseph's small room to make an unwelcome visit.

Joseph was too small and too weak to fight off his strange advances. On the first few visits Joseph was so frightened that he didn't know what to do even if he could have done anything. These visits went on for nearly two years. Once a month or more Bryson would come home drunk and wobbling and wander into Joseph's room. He would lie down beside Joseph and kiss and touch his body. On a few occasions Bryson would take Joseph's hand and make him touch him back. The further details of Bryson's visits are among the grimmest details of the story, and ones that Joseph swore to never speak of again.

It was following the events of one particular night, after Joseph had turned sixteen years of age, that the visits stopped. Joseph had grown, gotten wiser and more hardened, but most importantly Joseph had gotten stronger.

On this night Bryson came home covered in soot and stinking of whiskey. He stumbled into Joseph's room as he had done on many nights before. But on this night Joseph was waiting for him. Bryson hovered his face above Joseph's. Joseph's eyes remained closed, though he was not asleep. Bryson's breath sullied the air pungently, and Joseph couldn't hold back any longer. Joseph opened his eyes, lunged forward, and plunged a kitchen knife into Bryson's right thigh with a grunt.

Bryson exploded in screams, his hands gripping the knife's handle where it protruded from his leg.

Erma came rushing in to see what all the commotion was about. If Erma hadn't liked Joseph before, she certainly despised him thereafter. No words about what happened needed to be shared that night or in the days that followed. As dim-witted as Erma might have been, even she knew what had been going on after that.

Bryson never came back into Joseph's room again, though Joseph never stopped sleeping with a knife under his pillow, just in case.

Years passed, and Joseph was now in his early twenties. It had been two years since both Mona and Myron had married and left the house for good. Three years had passed since Bryson had gotten sick and died from black lung. Only Joseph, Buck, and Erma remained in the house.

Myron married Missy Tithering and moved to California, where Missy's father had started a prosperous clothing business. Mona, who never did say more than two words at a time to Joseph, married a local man named Phillip Weathers. In two years she had given birth to three babies: a set of female twins and a sickly, slow-witted boy who required all of her attention. Erma detested Phillip, and she and Mona hadn't spoken a word since their wedding, a wedding that Erma failed to attend.

Erma had become a sad and nasty old lady. She barely left the house, and when she did, she often didn't bother to wash herself or change her clothes. It was a popular belief in town that since her husband died and her older children moved on, Erma Bladwell had slowly begun to lose her mind.

Two things had remained constant in the time since Joseph had arrived in Kansas: Joseph and Buck were nearly inseparable, and Joseph never lost touch with Alfred Winter.

Alfred, now sheriff, would send one letter and one book each month to Joseph. It was a tradition started when Alfred first met Joseph in the jail cell and handed him *The Adventures of Huckleberry Finn* to help him pass the time. Joseph loved the books Alfred would send, and upon completion would write back to Alfred to tell him all his thoughts on the stories. Though the pair hadn't seen each other in years, aside from Paul, Alfred Winter was Joseph's closest and most trusted friend.

"You ready?" Buck asked.

Joseph was standing in the clearing of the woods behind the house, a black handkerchief wrapped around his head, covering his eyes.

"Are you?" Joseph said.

Buck yanked the handkerchief from Joseph's eyes and Joseph turned quickly. With five successive shots, Joseph hammered down five red tin cans scattered in various positions in the distance.

"Too easy," Joseph said, lowering the rifle to his side and leaning on it. "At least make it a challenge next time."

"Yeah, yeah. Next time I'm gonna hide one of them cans. You'll go dizzy tryin' to find it."

"Want me to set 'em up for you?"

"Nah, we gotta go. Gumpy'll be waitin', I'm sure."

"Let 'im wait."

Joseph raised the rifle to his chin in one swift motion. With a single pull of the trigger he sent one of the cans he had already knocked off its perch spinning up through the air in the distance.

Buck and Joseph trekked through the woods. They reached a hill about half a mile inward and followed a small dirt path that a stranger would not immediately recognize as such. At the top of the hill was a congregation of thicket and bush so dense it would be nearly impossible to wade through if one didn't know the specific route. The pair reached a wooden structure in the middle of the brush. Black smoke gushed from the roof.

Some would call the Volstead Act a rancid blemish on the history of the United States, but those who made a living off its back might have called it a blessing. Soon after Prohibition was passed in 1919, Buck and Joseph had found the big-time opportunity they were looking for. They were already skilled at making moonshine and selling it to a few acquaintances, but the two-man operation had since given way to something much more lucrative.

Buck had arranged a deal with Charles "Gumpy" McGumpford, and he and Joseph officially joined the largest ring of the booming Crawford County moonshine business. At first, being young of age, Buck and Joseph merely stood watch or were sent out to make small collections. No one would suspect a couple of kids making visits to shops and houses to pick up monies owed to the local shiners. As they aged and grew and learned more about the operation, greater responsibility was thrust upon the duo.

Now, as young men, Buck and Joseph had become thick in the mix of the underground business that supplied illegal booze to most of Kansas and parts of Missouri. They liked their job, and they were good at it.

Chapter 9

"What do you mean, you don't got it?" Buck said to the middle-aged man behind the counter of the general store.

"I mean I don't got it. Not yet, anyway."

"That's not an option. Is that an option, Joe?"

Joe shook his head. He was leaning on the wall beside the door, ensuring that no one else would enter the shop.

"You been sellin' our products outta your store for over a year, Cal. What's changed now?"

"Times are slow, Buck. People just ain't spendin' anymore. I can give you what I got left, but you'll have to come back in a week or two for the money."

Buck looked at Joe. Joe looked back at Buck. Joe turned and walked out of the general store.

"Do you know where he's goin'?" Buck asked.

The man just shook his head nervously.

"I suggest you open up your cash drawer there and find what I need."

"Like I said, Buck, I just don't got it. I wouldn't lie to you."

Joe reentered the store, cocked his rifle and pointed it at the man's head without saying a word.

"Okay, okay!" the man said. "Just hold up there!"

He raised his hands between himself and the gun.

"I been good up till now, Buck. You know that. I been good. Always paid on time…"

"Joe –"

"My kid's sick, Buck, okay? Don't shoot. My kid's sick. The store's been closed. I ain't got no money."

"Fuck, Cal. Why'd ya have to go and say that?"

"It's the truth, Buck. I ain't lyin'. Hang on now… Just let me think. Hang on now."

Cal began to walk around the counter, his hands still in front of him.

"Now where you goin'?"

"I maybe got somethin'… somethin' you can have, Buck."

Cal scampered across the creaking wooden floor.

"Hold up now," Buck said. "I'll lead the way."

Buck led Cal and Joe to the back of the store and up a flight of stairs. Cal unlocked a door and they entered a small apartment. He walked into a bedroom and reached for a drawer. Joe raised the gun.

"Slow down there, Cal," Buck said.

"It's okay, I'm just gettin' somethin' for you."

"Do it slow, where I can see."

"Here," Cal said.

He pulled something from a drawer.

"A watch?"

"It's gold. Check it. Worth more than what I owe ya."

"Give it here."

Cal tossed the watch to Buck.

"I ain't no jeweler, Cal."

"Trust me, Buck. I got no reason to swindle ya. It's worth a bundle more than what I owe. It was my Pa's. Take it."

Buck threw the watch to Joe. Joe looked it over.

"You tellin' me this thing is worth –"

"It is, Buck. It is. Like I said, I ain't got no reason to lie. Take it to Harry down the street. He'll give you a sum. Tell him I said so."

"I don't know Harry."

"He's got the pawn shop not a two minute walk north o' here."

Buck looked over at Joe. Joe had lowered the rifle and was looking the watch over.

"Cal…"

Buck approached the man.

"I like you, Cal. You know that, right?"

Buck put his hand on Cal's shoulder and the pair took a seat on the end of his bed. Buck took off his old, weathered hat and placed it on his knee. Cal seemed to calm down.

"We don't want to come in here with a rifle. Why would we want to do that? But I got people that depend on me, Cal, and that means I gotta depend on you, ya see?"

Cal nodded, ashamed.

"If all goes well with your friend Harry and this watch, we'll be square," Buck assured. "No hard feelings at all."

"No hard feelin's," Cal repeated.

"How many kids you got, anyway?"

"Four. I got four kids."

"Which one's sick?"

"My youngest, Michael. Got some sort of coughin' he can't get rid of."

"Where's he now?"

"He's with my wife at her mother's house. She was a nurse."

"You try Doc Malcahy? Out Sherbrook way?"

"I ain't got the money for a doctor like that."

"Uh-huh."

"Buck…" Joe said, nudging his head toward the door.

"Okay," Buck agreed. "Cal, we best be goin'. We'll see you again in a few weeks, okay?"

"Okay, Buck, Joe."

"Take care of that kid, okay?"

Buck and Joe left Cal sitting at the end of his bed. Cal let out a sigh and rubbed the back of his neck.

It wasn't thirty minutes later that the front door of Cal's store swung open again, and Buck and Joe entered once more.

"Everything's okay, boys, right?" Cal said nervously.

Joe approached the counter without saying a word. He put his hand in his pocket, withdrew it, and slapped down a wad of cash in front of Cal.

"What's this?"

"With regards from Harry," Joe said.

"We took out our share, Cal, and then some," Buck said. "Take that kid o' yours to see Doc Malcahy."

Cal looked up from the counter.

"Thank you, Joe. Both of you, thank you."

Joe nodded once.

Buck and Joe left the store, and this time they did not return.

Chapter 10

Buck drove the Ford Pickup. Joe sat in the seat beside him.

"Anything left on the list?" Buck asked.

"Nope. That's it for today."

"Then let's head on back. I'm a gonna have a talk with Gumpy."

"What about?"

"This nickel and dime shit. When was the last time we collected? Let him send someone else out to clean up Willy's mess."

"Like who?"

"That ain't my problem. We been puttin' together proper deals. Doin' smash 'n' grab runs for supplies when he asks us to. We been puttin' money in his pocket for long enough. It's time we got our fair share."

"You think now's the best time to be rufflin' feathers?"

"Why wouldn't it be?"

"What with the Colonel and all?"

"That's a bunch o' malarkey. The Colonel's got his business in his territory and we got ours."

"It wouldn't seem like that's the case anymore."

"Why? Because of what went down in Shylow Hills? That ain't gonna happen again. Gumpy'll see to that."

"That's what I'm afraid of."

"What's that?"

"You start making noise and we'll be the first to go up against the Colonel when the time comes. Best we just keep our mouths shut and do what we've been doing."

"Where's yer sense of adventure, Joe?"

"I got a better mind to stay out of trouble."

"You're already in it, Joe. You think your hands are clean?"

"I never hurt anyone."

"Not yet."

"That's what I'm saying. I don't want to start."

"What you worried about? You got the surest shot of anyone I ever seen."

"That's when I'm aimin' at cans or deer or targets pinned up on a tree. I never killed a man before."

"That day will come, Joe," Buck said, looking out the side window. "That day will come."

When Buck and Joe returned to the barn in the woods, Gumpy was waiting there to greet them. The name Gumpy suited the man quite well. He was tall and wide and very round. The way his gut protruded from his front made it look as though he was hiding a dog under his shirt. He was a soft-spoken man, much to the surprise of those who judged him by appearance, and of course to those who knew his line of employ. And there was one thing that was glaringly evident to all who conversed with the bulky man: Gumpy spoke exceptionally slowly. He always seemed to pause before it was his turn to speak, as if he was thinking excessively about each and every sentence he uttered. Those that knew him well knew to wait for his words; they knew that thoughts were rattling around in his head or on his tongue. The gaps in a conversation with Gumpy could be filled with a conversation all their own.

"It's the Bladwell boys," Gumpy said upon their arrival.

"There's somethin' I wanna talk to you 'bout, Gump," Buck said as the three sat down at an old wooden table.

"Buck…" Joe interjected.

"After we take care of business," Gumpy said, following a prescribed pause.

All the money they were sent to collect was accounted for, and all three shared in a drink from the latest batch of bathtub gin.

"We don't wanna clean up after Willy no more. No more collections," Buck said. "We been workin' for you for too long. I think we earned more than that."

Gumpy looked at Buck. He looked at Joe. He took a sip of the white liquid in his small glass.

"You think that's so?" he said.

"I know it is. We want somethin' bigger."

Gumpy took a deep breath. He looked around the room. He saw that no one else was near.

"You heard about the Colonel?" he finally asked.

"Yeah, 'course. We were just talkin' about that mess in Shylow today," Buck said.

"I was going to send someone else... but how would you like to pay a visit for me?" Gumpy said slowly.

"Pay a visit to who?"

"Pay a visit to a man named Arland Garry."

"I know that name," Buck said.

"And so you should. Where the Colonel goes, so does Arland Garry."

"And what's the meetin' for?"

Gumpy took the last swig of liquor from his glass.

"I want you to arrange a truce. Surely the Colonel would be familiar with that term. I want no more war over territory. No fighting, no blood."

"What will we be offering? Surely he'll want terms," Joe said.

Gumpy took another deep breath. His belly raised and lowered like a balloon.

"He keeps what's his now, and I keep what's mine. Tell him he can move to the south and to the west of the Oklahoma border. I move only north and to the east of Kansas. I think that is a fair deal, one that will see to it that we stay out of each other's way. There're plenty of towns for the both of us."

"You think he'll go for it?" Buck asked.

"From what I know of the man," Gumpy said after his mandatory linger, "I would say no."

"Then why offer?" Buck asked. "Why meet at all?"

"I want you to talk to Arland. Get a feel for the man, and for the mind of the Colonel. But you, Buck, you'll be there just to help."

"Help? Help who?"

Gumpy looked over to Joe.

"I see you reading all the time," he said, lifting his chin and looking down his nose.

"I read some," Joe said.

"When you sat watch outside the barn for me when you was just a kid, you would be reading all those books and such."

"Yes."

"Then you'd know much about the mind of a man, would you not?"

Gumpy paused.

"Short of going myself, which I will not do, you are the person I will send. Besides, you have an unthreatening look about you, something I'm sure you know."

"I suppose so," Joe said.

"Don't suppose, know. You've looked in a mirror, haven't you? You've seen your young, innocent looking face."

"Yes."

"Then Arland Garry will be surprised to see you."

"He might."

"He will. He will be surprised. Buck, I want you to speak to the man as well."

"I will."

"The Colonel sends one, I will send two."

Gumpy took out a piece of paper from his shirt. He scribbled something down and then slid the paper across the table to Buck. Buck took the paper, looked it over, and placed it into his pants pocket.

"Now," Gumpy said, "was there something else?"

"Just the matter of Calvin Billox."

"I don't know the man."

"He has a kid gotten ill and may not be able to sell for us no more."

"Then you find someone else who will."

"Already taken care of. Man named Harry Creedy, owns a pawn shop. Not a typical location but gets a fair number o' people comin' in."

"Then the job is done."

"I think that's it, then, for business," Buck said.

Buck and Joe got up to leave.

"One last thing," Gumpy said.

He did not get up from the table.

"You asked for this. So be aware of what I'm asking you to do and do it right. Have your wits about you with Arland. He's a dangerous man."

"Dangerous how?" Buck asked.

Gumpy smiled.

"Don't you find out."

Buck and Joe left the barn and returned to the truck in the dimming light. The day had come and gone and the road-weary pair were headed for home.

Buck pulled the piece of paper from his pocket as he drove. He handed it to Joe.

"This is outside Billingston," Joe said, reading the paper.

"You think it's a smart idea that you be the one to talk to this Alrand guy?"

"Arland. And why not?"

"You don't think –"

"I don't think what?" Joe interrupted.

Buck paused.

"When're we meetin'?"

"Says, tomorrow afternoon."

"Tomorrow? Outside Billingston?"

"Yeah, why?"

Buck slammed on the breaks and yanked the wheel. The tires skidded along the gravel road and the Ford pickup kicked up a cloud of dust as it swept forty-five degrees to the side. Buck put the truck in reverse, backed up, and then turned the wheel and headed down the road in the opposite direction.

"We headin' out now?" Joe asked, confounded.

"You got a better idea? If we're going to make it there by tomorrow, there's no time to be wastin'. We'll find somewhere to stay the night along the way."

Chapter 11

Joe didn't say anything else for the duration of the drive. By the time they pulled up to the small inn near Bristol Falls, Buck had grown tired of the silence. He pulled up to the white building and turned off the engine.

"You got somethin' on your mind?" he asked.

"Huh?" Joe said.

He was lost in thought, his eyes still peering out the window of the truck.

"You been quiet like someone cut yer tongue out since we left. You got somethin' on yer mind?"

"It's nothing. Just the first time I been back is all."

"Back? Back where?"

"Oklahoma. Haven't been back."

"Since that copper brought you to the house?"

"Alfred, yeah."

Silence once again filled the vehicle.

"Let's get somethin' to eat," Joe said, finally taking his eyes from the window. "You think they got a diner in this town?"

Buck turned off the truck.

"Let's go see about a room. I'm sure the innkeeper will know of somewheres to eat."

A short, rotund woman was the first thing the pair saw as they entered the front door of the converted manor.

"We're here about a room for the night," Buck said to the woman who was cleaning up some broken glass on the floor of the foyer.

"Rooms? We got plenty o' those," she said, looking up from the ground. "How many you be needin'?"

"Like I said. Just the one will do."

The lady looked the pair over.

"We don't put up with no funny business here. You two ain't no —"

"Ain't no what?" Buck interrupted.

The small lady relented and rested the broom against the wall, never taking her suspicious eyes off the men.

"This way," she said.

The woman waddled across the room. Joe and Buck followed behind.

"What do they call ya?" the woman asked.

"I'm Buck. This is Joe."

"Name's Bess. This here's my place. My husband is Jim. He's already asleep for the night."

"Good ta meetcha."

"You made it just in time, fellas. I was fixin' to close up for the night."

Bess walked around a wooden bar and pulled a key out from under it. She placed it on the table.

"This here's a fine room. Right at the top of the stairs and to the left."

Buck took the key from the counter.

"Anywhere to get a bite around here?" he asked.

"Diner across the way should still be open. Just turn right out the front door. You can't miss it. If Annie's there, be sure ta tell her I sent ya. And try the pie."

"Will do. Thank you, ma'am."

Buck and Joe exited the front of the inn.

"What do you think she was goin' on about?" Joe asked as the pair began to walk along the side of the empty street.

"Goin' on about?"

"When she said no funny business. Who did she think we were?"

"Beats me. Probably could tell we was from outta town or somethin'."

"Wouldn't everyone she meets be from out of town?"

"Don't be botherin' yourself with that stuff. She probably needs glasses or somethin'. Anyway, there's no accountin' for people's smarts down here."

Just as Bess had said, the diner could not be missed. It was the lone bright spot on the otherwise darkened road.

The door jingled as Joe and Buck walked in.

"Evenin'!" a woman called out.

"Still servin'?" Buck asked.

A pretty blond-haired woman approached the front. She was retying her blue and white waist apron as she walked.

"Gettin' ready to close up. Depends what you're lookin' for, I suppose. I got some meatloaf and beans, and I think I can rustle up some warm coffee, if that'll do ya," she said.

"That'll be fine," Joe said.

"Comin' right up. Have yerself a seat where ya like."

The young woman disappeared behind the counter and into the back of the diner. Joe and Buck took a seat at a table near the window at the far end of the narrow building.

"Ya'll from around these parts?" the woman asked as she placed two cups of coffee down on the table.

"Joe here grew up not far from here," Buck said.

"Is that right?"

"It's been a while since I been back," Joe said.

"What brings you back around?"

"Just a little business."

"You don't say. What sort of business you folks in?"

"The sales kind," Joe said.

"Well, name's Annie. If you need anything, just holler."

"Bess told us to try a piece of your pie," Buck said.

"Oh, she did, did she?"

"Yes, ma'am."

"Well, we're all out for today, but if you come back tomorrow, I'll be sure to save you a slice."

"We're just in for the night."

"Ain't that a pity," Annie said.

She smiled at Buck.

The door jingled and two men walked through. Annie turned and took a step back.

"Now I told ya, I don't want any more trouble from you two," she said.

"Trouble? Who said anythin' 'bout trouble?"

It was apparent from his walk and faltering speech that the first man was drunk.

"We're closed for the night," Annie said. "Why don't ya'll come back another time?"

"Closed? Well then who're these two peddlers?"

The drunken man began to approach Annie.

"Who's askin'?" Buck said.

The second man began to follow behind his drunken friend as he changed direction and headed for Buck. He looked much more in control of his faculties.

Annie retreated. She hurried over and stood behind Buck's chair, if only to get away from the others.

"I'm askin', stranger."

"And who might you be?"

"Name's Billy," the man said in a jovial way. "This here's Henry."

Both men were plenty older than Buck and Joe. They were dressed in suits and each had on a preened fedora. Henry had a stoic look about him. He barely moved. He just stood a few paces behind the drunken man with his hands in his pockets.

"Like the lady said, why don't ya'll come back another time?" Buck said.

"Oh! Another time. Why don't we come back another time?" Billy replied, mockingly.

He came right up to the table and stood over Buck.

"Billy, is it?" Buck said.

"That's right."

"You seem like a decent fella, but you're drunk. So why don't you go on home and sleep it off?"

"Do we look like we got a home in this tar pit town?"

"Then why don't you just keep goin' on through, then?"

The look on Billy's face grew stern. He leaned over, bringing his face closer to Buck.

"Why don't you just –"

Billy didn't manage to get out the next word before Buck lunged upward and landed his fist on the man's chin. Billy tumbled back and fell like a bag of sand. Before his body could make a thump on the floor, Buck had yanked a pistol from his boot and pointed it straight at Henry's head. Henry just smiled.

"What the hell?" Billy whined from the floor.

He patted at his lower lip, looking for blood.

"You came too close. I don't like it when people come too close. Now like I said, why don't ya'll just keep on goin' through?"

Billy found his way to his feet, using a chair for support.

Annie looked at Joe, perhaps waiting for him to get involved too. Joe just stared at Henry.

Billy glared at Buck. If not for the pistol, now pointed at his own head, he might have done something. But instead Billy backed his way to the door. He passed by Henry, still standing motionless with a grin on his face.

"We'll come back another time," Billy said. "Try some o' that coffee."

Billy walked out the door of the diner and didn't look back.

Henry soon turned to follow.

"Say," he said, his hand on the knob of the door, "what did you say your name was?"

"I didn't."

Henry gave Buck a good hard look over before turning and walking out.

Buck watched as the two men disappeared into the darkness. He threw his pistol down on the table and took his seat.

"Thank you," Annie said.

"Not at all," Buck said.

"They were here earlier. Smelled like booze from the start."

"He was just runnin' his mouth. Wouldn't have done you no harm."

"Even so, your suppers are on me."

"Thank you, Annie."

"Speakin' o' which, I better go check on 'em."

Annie disappeared into the back of the diner.

"I left my rifle in the truck," Joe said.

"I know ya did."

"Who woulda thought?"

"Who woulda?"

Annie returned with two hot plates of meatloaf and baked beans. She carried one in each cloth-covered hand.

"Sorry," she said, placing the plates down in front of Buck and Joe. "It's overdone. I'm still a little shaken. We don't see things like that around here too often."

"Not at all," Buck said.

"Why don't you join us?" Joe offered.

"Oh no, I couldn't," Annie said. "I should finish cleanin' up."

"I don't think you'll be gettin' any more customers tonight. Go on, have a seat," Buck said.

"Well, all right," Annie said.

She pulled out a chair and took a seat.

"Do you mind?" she shyly pointed at the pistol still sitting on the tabletop.

Buck smiled and returned the pistol to his boot. He lifted his fork and dug into the meatloaf, shoveling a slab into his mouth with a nod of approval.

"So," Annie said, still shaken, "where'd ya'll say you were from again?"

Chapter 12

Joe returned to the inn after his supper. Buck indulged in another cup of coffee, but more so in the company of Annie.

The room at the inn was small, but it was generally clean. The white lace window coverings and yellow embroidered bed sheets had a female's touch, and by the looks of the dust on top of the dresser, no man or woman had stayed there for quite some time.

It was late. Everyone in the house was asleep. Joe retired into the bathroom, locked the door, and drew himself a hot bath. He returned to the empty room as soon as his bathing was done. Perhaps it was an effect of the balmy water or the silence or the darkness of the warm room lit by a single lamp, but Joe fell asleep the moment he put his head on the pillow.

"Woah!" Buck said. "Cover yourself up, would ya?"

It was morning. The sun was beaming through the holes in the delicate drapes. Joe got up from the bed and began to dress.

"You just getting in now?" he asked, sliding his shirt over his head.

"Slept on the couch downstairs. Couldn't remember which room it was."

"You seem to have found it okay this morning."

"Wasn't my first try."

"You stay at the diner long?"

"Walked Annie home to be safe. Nearly got turned around on the way back."

Buck sat down on the end of the bed. Joe finished dressing.

"Only about a hundred miles to go," Joe said.

Buck nodded.

"That all?" he said.

"Thinkin' maybe we can take a detour," said Joe.

"Where to?"

"Not far. 'Bout an hour or so out of the way."

"Don't see why not."

Buck didn't press for more detail. Joe had a feeling he knew why.

"You ready to head out?" Joe asked.

"After breakfast," said Buck. "Any idea where to get a bite around here?"

Joe smiled and didn't wait for an answer. He headed out to the hall and down toward the bathroom. Buck took a good look around the room before taking leave of it himself.

Buck was making his way down the creaky steps when the front door of the inn opened. He saw the legs of a woman entering. As he neared the bottom, the figure appeared in full. Annie was holding a pie in her hand.

"Mornin'," Buck said, surprised to see her.

"Wanted to thank you for last night."

"That for me?"

"Sure is."

Buck took the pie from Annie's hands and gave it a whiff.

"Pumpkin," he said.

Annie smiled.

"Heya, honey," Bess said from the other room.

"Excuse me a second," Annie said to Buck.

She turned to meet Bess in the room in which Buck had spent the night. Buck walked in the opposite direction, pie in hand.

"Mornin'," Buck said, finding his way into the kitchen nearby.

"Mornin' to you," an old man said.

The man came around a baker's table in the middle of the room. Buck took quick notice that the man had a wooden leg from the knee down on his left side. He used a single wooden crutch to help him get around. Buck did his best not to stare.

"I was hopin' for a spoon, maybe even a plate if it's not too much trouble," Buck said.

"I can help you with that," the man said. "Why doncha have a seat?"

Buck sat down at the wooden table and watched as the man with one good leg ambled about the kitchen.

"You one o' them boys came in late last night?"

"Yes, sir."

"Where ya'll comin' from, if ya don't mind me askin'?"

"Just up in Kansas. Passin' through is all."

"Name's John," the man said, placing a plate and cutlery down in front of Buck.

"Come to think of it, John, how about a few more plates for this pie? One for yourself too."

"Alrighty," John said with a smile. "Can't pass that up."

"I'm Buck."

"Glad to meetcha, Buck."

John returned to the table with a handful of small plates and spoons, and took a seat across from Buck. Buck dug the knife into the pie and cut out two big slabs. He slid one across the table to John and kept the other for himself.

"Already had my breakfast, but this smells good," John said.

He dug his spoon into the pie and took a mouthful. Buck did the same.

Annie and Joe came into the kitchen together, both no doubt looking for Buck.

"Hiya, Annie," John said.

Annie walked over and kissed John on the forehead.

"I see you wasted no time," she said to Buck.

"I got you a plate," Buck said.

"None for me, thanks."

"Why don't you at least join us?"

Annie smiled and took a seat at the table.

"Joe?"

Joe sat down beside John and was promptly served a piece of pie. Joe nodded in approval as he tasted the first bite, though Joe was not partial to pumpkin pie.

"You folks headin' out this mornin'?" John asked, cleaning what was left of the pie from his plate with his spoon.

"Yes, sir," Buck said. "Soon as we finish our breakfast here and settle up."

"Be back around, will ya?"

"Don't know just yet."

"Well, you be sure to think of us if you're ever back in Bristol Falls."

John picked up his plate and wobbled to the sink. Buck and Joe finished off what was left of their pie servings.

"I have to head over to the diner," Annie said.

"I'll walk you out," Buck offered.

He picked up the remainder of the pie and followed Annie from the kitchen.

"It's goodbye for now," Joe said to John, delivering the plates to the sink.

"Take care now," John replied.

Joe made his way to the front of the inn, where he had received the key from Bess. The small woman was sitting atop a stool scribbling something in a book.

"Thank you, ma'am," Joe said, placing the room key on the counter. "I'd like to settle the bill."

The woman looked up at Joe. She got down off her stool, reached her arms up and put her pudgy hands on Joe's shoulders, tugging him down toward her. She planted a kiss on his cheek.

"Ma'am?" Joe said.

"Your room is on us."

"Why's that?"

"You did a fine thing for my daughter. Helpin' her an' all."

"Your daughter?"

"How big you think this town is, son?"

The sullen woman cracked a smile.

"I insist," Joe said.

"Take your hand outta that pocket."

"Let me at least pay Annie for the pie."

Joe took a five-dollar bill from his pocket and placed it on top of the bar. Bess reached up and yanked Joe down for another kiss.

"Okay," Joe said, mid-kiss. "Thank you."

Buck was leaning against the side of the truck. Joe walked out the front door just in time to see Annie prop up on her toes and kiss Buck on the cheek before walking away down the road.

"Friendly family," Joe said, reaching the car.

"Indeed."

"Why didn't you tell me they were her folks?"

"Never really came up."

Buck watched Annie walk into the distance.

"You coulda told me."

Buck slapped Joe on the shoulder and walked around to the driver's side. He opened the door and threw the rest of the pie on top of the dash before leaping in.

Joe joined Buck in the car. He reached under the seat and put his hand on the rifle, just like he always did. He wasn't planning on using it, but he liked to know it was still there. Buck started the truck and shifted into gear. In just a few quiet moments on the road, Bristol Falls was behind them.

Chapter 13

A few hours later the truck came to a stop outside an old white building. Joe stared ahead out the windshield. Buck gave him a moment before he spoke up.

"So?" he said. "You gonna go in or what?"

Joe didn't respond.

"Looks like no one's been here in years," Buck said.

"Let's get outta here," Joe said.

"You sure?"

"This was a bad idea."

"We can wait a while."

"Just drive."

Buck did as he was told. He turned the truck around and drove away from the Tilley farm.

Though they had planned on an early arrival in Billingston to meet with Arland Garry, a flat tire stayed their progress and forced Buck and Joe to a service station along the way. It was Joe's idea to get there before the man they were to meet and take up a position of power in the neutral location. Joe felt like they would have the upper hand with Arland arriving to meet them, rather than the other way around. As it happened, they arrived in Billingston right on time and quickly found the small, secluded house they were after.

The house was old. It was a single-level, gray wooden house that looked almost as run-down as the Tilley farm. The front of the roof that covered the long porch drooped in the middle, and the screen that was meant to cover the front door was torn and hanging.

There was a black car waiting at the side of the house. Arland had beaten them there.

Buck turned off the engine. He tucked his pistol into the waist of his pants. Joe reached under the seat.

"Leave it," Buck said.

Joe looked at his cousin sharply, but he didn't argue.

"You remember the plan?" Buck asked.

Joe nodded.

"South and west of the border," he said.

"South and west."

Buck got out. Joe soon followed. The two men walked up to the front of the house. They did not knock. They walked right in.

The inside of the house was as disheveled as the outside. A few pieces of old furniture remained, but it was clear that the place had not been recently inhabited. There was a room to the right where Buck and Joe found a gathering of chairs strewn about. One of the chairs was upright, and against it leaned a pristine hunting rifle, but no person was nearby. Buck lifted two chairs from the pile and set them upright. Neither he nor Joe sat down.

They heard the sound of a door. It was the back door of the house. A man appeared in the room. He stopped in his tracks at the precipice, folded his arms, and took a good hard look at the two newcomers.

The man was tall. He looked to be well into his forties, and his age showed heavily on his face. His arms seemed as big as tree trunks, and his chest was as round as a barrel. He wore a suit, though it was not new, and he wore a hat that was tilted to the side just a bit. The hat covered his brow, dropping down nearly to the tops of his eyes. His longish dark hair spilled out on all sides, in all directions, from under the hat.

"Where's McGumpford?" the man asked.

"You Arland?" Joe asked.

The man unfolded his arms and took a slow, leisurely stroll to his chair. He sat down, paying no attention to the gun resting by his side. Buck and Joe sat down across from him. Joe eyed the rifle.

"You like it?" the man asked.

"You Arland?" Joe asked again, taking his eyes from the rifle.

The man picked up the gun in both hands.

"Bolt action Winchester 54," he said.

He looked the gun over. The man then turned the gun on Joe and looked down the sight. Joe tried his best to look unconcerned about it.

"Where's McGumpford?" the man said again, pointing the gun at Joe's chest.

"Sent us to talk to you instead. I can assure you, we speak directly for him. You're Arland, right?"

"You like this gun, don't you?"

Joe didn't answer.

"I said, you like this gun?"

"I like the gun," Joe said.

In a swift motion, the man flipped the gun around and held out the butt to Joe. After a moment's pause Joe reached out and took the rifle.

Joe indeed liked the gun. He liked the gun a lot. It was a noticeable upgrade from the model he currently carried.

"I am Arland," the man said.

Joe finally took his eyes off the hardware in his hands.

"I'm Joe. This here's Buck."

"I guess McGumpford's smarter than I thought," Arland said.

"What's that mean?" Buck interrupted.

"Well, usually you backwoods types aren't all that clever."

Arland took out a cigarette and lit it with a silver lighter.

"I'm assuming McGumpford sent you two pipsqueaks to see how I would react... see what kind of man he's dealing with."

Arland took a big pull from his cigarette and blew out a waft of white smoke.

"Gump sent us with terms," Joe said.

He placed the gun on his lap instead of returning it to its owner.

"Terms, huh? What makes him think he's in a position to set terms?"

"Terms for a peaceful resolution."

"You don't say?"

"There will be no more problems if we can agree on territory."

"Territory for what?"

Joe and Buck exchanged a glance.

Arland smiled. He took another heavy pull on his cigarette and blew out the smoke.

"This a twenty-six inch barrel?" Joe asked, looking down at the gun.

"Twenty-four."

"What sort of range you get with it?"

"Can't say. I only shoot things close up."

Joe and Arland stared at one another.

"Why you figure he sent you, of all people?" Arland asked.

"He trusts us."

"Doesn't seem right that a man sends someone else to do his business, though, does it?"

"Why's that?"

"You wanna talk terms or what?" Buck interjected.

"I want it back," Arland said.

"What?"

"I want it back. The gun. Give it to me."

Joe sat silently for a moment, motionless. He watched Arland do the same before he finally handed him back the rifle.

"Have we met before?" Joe asked, holding his gaze on the man across from him.

"I'd remember you," Arland said, yanking the gun from Joe's hands as his expression grew stern.

A loud noise came from the back of the house.

"What was that?" Buck asked, apprehensively.

"Those are my men," Arland said, unaffected.

"Gump said it would be just you."

"He also said it would be just him."

"Buck…" Joe said.

"You wanna talk terms or what?" Buck said, abruptly.

"Buck…" Joe repeated, only this time louder.

"What?" Buck said.

"Buck and I are gonna go talk outside," Joe said to Arland.

Arland didn't respond.

Joe got up from his seat and stood over Buck. Buck stared at Arland, who only smiled in return. Buck finally got up and the pair exited the front of the house. Joe was making his way back to the truck, parked thirty or so yards away.

"What is it?" Buck asked.

Joe opened the passenger side door. He reached under the seat and pulled out his rifle.

"He's not here to talk. Never was. He was here to kill Gumpy."

"How do you know that?"

"See the way he looked at us when he walked in? We threw him off. He wanted Gump. And Gump knew it."

"You're crazy."

"Maybe I am. But he ain't interested in talking about who gets what. Not in the least. He wasn't expecting to, either. Man like that would tell us what he and the Colonel are taking, not gab about what works out best for everyone, anyhow."

Joe came face to face with Buck.

"Gumpy knew it, Buck. We ain't here to talk about nothin'. He's testing us."

Buck placed his hand on the pistol in his waistband.

"So now what?" he said.

"We get outta here alive."

Joe turned and began to walk back to the house. Buck fixed his shirt and followed his cousin.

Arland was still sitting in his chair when they arrived back in the room. He had lit another cigarette.

"Why you here?" Joe asked.

"What's with the guns?" Arland said calmly.

"You got yours, we got ours. Why you here?"

"Same reason you are."

"I'm not so sure."

Arland threw his cigarette to the ground and left it there to burn. He grabbed the barrel of his rifle and lifted the gun a foot off the ground. Joe clenched his rifle; Buck put his hand on the pistol in his waistband and held it there. Arland didn't lift the rifle to his hand but instead hammered the butt against the floor two times.

The back door opened and footsteps approached. Joe raised his gun to his shoulder. Buck yanked the pistol from his waistband and pointed it at Arland. Two men appeared from the back of the room.

"You gotta be fuckin' kiddin' me," Buck said.

He quickly turned his gun, pointing it at the newcomers. A man with a fat lower lip had a gun pointed at Buck's head; the other pointed his at Joe.

Arland remained in his seat, his hand still resting comfortably on the barrel of his gun. He leaned on it as if it were a crutch.

"You," one of the men said.

"You know 'em?" Arland asked one of his men.

"This asshole's the one socked me in the face last night in the diner."

"Look," Buck said, clearly rattled. "We're just gonna turn around and walk outta here."

"You are?" Arland said.

"We're gonna turn around, walk outta here, and drive away."

Arland stood.

"What're you doing?" Buck said, taking a step backward.

"Ain't we all leaving?" Arland said.

"You gonna just let 'em go?" Billy asked.

"The way I see it," said Arland, "there's three of us and two o' them. We all start shooting and most of us end up dead."

"Yeah, but boss…"

Arland took off his hat, brushed his long hair back off his brow, and returned the hat to its resting place atop his head. He looked over at Henry. Henry gave him a short and simple nod.

Joe flinched. He lifted the rifle to his eye and pointed it at Arland's head.

"What you lookin' at?" Arland said.

Joe remained silent and held his aim.

"Joe…" Buck said.

Joe swallowed what tiny amount of saliva remained in his mouth.

"Joe, it's time to go. Come on."

Buck put his hand on Joe's shoulder. Buck started to back out of the room toward the front door of the house, pulling Joe along with him. Joe never took his gun off Arland.

They backed out the front door and headed quickly back to the truck. Joe walked around to the back, leaned over behind it and began to throw up, leaving a wet pile of orange and brown on the sandy ground.

"It's over," Buck said. "Let's just get outta here."

Joe put his hand on the tailgate and held his balance. He looked up at Buck. Buck could see something in his cousin's eyes.

"What is it?" he asked.

Joe looked up at Buck.

Back in the house Billy stood by the front window. He watched as Buck and Joe talked behind the truck. Buck turned his head and saw Billy peering at them through the dirty glass.

Joe tried his best to regain his composure. Buck gave Joe a pat on the back and the pair made their way into the truck. Buck turned on the engine, whirled the truck around, and began driving away down the long dirt road.

After a few minutes of calm, Billy, Henry, and Arland walked out the back door of the house. They approached the black car parked at the side. Henry got in on the driver's side. Billy, holding Arland's rifle, opened the trunk to stow all the firearms for the ride. Arland put his hand on the passenger side handle but paused before he opened it. His head turned toward the road.

"What is it?" Billy asked.

Arland said nothing. He was peering curiously into the distance, as if trying to focus on something.

Like a bumblebee traveling at immense speed, a whizzing sound flew by Arland's ear.

"My gun!" Arland yelled.

Arland lunged toward Billy. He yanked the rifle from Billy's hands just as a bullet pierced the back of Billy's neck, sending splatters of blood onto Arland's face and chest. Arland raised the rifle to his eye and scanned the distance.

Henry turned the ignition and peeled out toward the road, leaving a cloud of sand and dust in the air. Another shot whizzed through the air. The black car tore down the road away from the house. Arland fired back from where the car had stood. Henry rolled down the window and stuck his gun out into the open.

Buck, standing a ways down the road beside the parked truck, saw him coming and fired at the car. The first shot missed the car entirely; the second entered through the windshield but missed the driver. Henry, getting even closer, opened fire. Bullets passed one another in the air like cars on the highway.

Henry let go another shot. He hit Buck. A bullet entered Buck's thigh, just below his right hip. He let out a scream and fell to the ground.

Joe, standing on the back of the truck, the barrel of his gun resting on the top of the cab, turned the rifle quickly. He took aim at the speeding black car barreling down upon them. Joe took his shot. He hit the front right tire, exploding it and sending the black car swerving. Henry tried to correct the skid but couldn't regain control. The black car veered off the road and smacked headlong into a tree with utter violence.

Joe quickly turned his attention back toward the house. Arland was walking toward him, gun to his eye. A bullet hit the grill of the truck. Joe did not waver.

Joe shut one eye and took aim. He took in a deep breath and held it in his lungs. He pulled the trigger and the sound of the gunshot rang through the air.

Joe opened his eye and peered out across the field. In the distance he saw Arland fall down to his knees. The man dropped his gun and grabbed at his chest with both hands. He soon fell forward, smacking his face on the ground.

"Buck!" Joe yelled, jumping down from the bed of the truck.

Buck yelled out in pain. He was clenching his leg.

Joe knelt beside his cousin and pressed his hand against the wound, trying to stop the bleeding. Buck screamed out again. Joe ran to the truck and grabbed a cloth from under the seat. He pressed it against the wound and placed Buck's own hand atop it.

"Hold it there," Joe said. "Tight. It'll be all right. We'll get you out of here."

Joe took the pistol that lay on the ground beside Buck. He got up and began to walk toward the house.

"Where you goin'?" Buck yelled from the ground.

Joe didn't answer; he just continued to walk down the road. He turned into the field and headed down the slight slope that led to the house.

Joe reached Arland's limp body. A pool of blood had dyed the dusty ground red around him. He stood over the man and stared. Joe could see the man's back rising and falling with short, deep heaves. Arland was still alive.

Using his foot, Joe rolled Arland onto his back. He stared down at the man's pain-filled face. Arland coughed, and bloody mucus came spurting out of his mouth.

Shaking, Joe reached down and grabbed the hat that was still affixed tightly to the top of the man's head. He held the hat in his hand before throwing it out into the field. His eyes remained fixed on Arland's face. With his foot pressed to his cheek, Joe turned Arland's head to the side.

He had caught a glimpse in the house when Arland had taken off his hat to fix his hair, but Joe's inclination was now a certainty. Arland Garry, lying on the ground before him, was missing his left ear.

Joe pointed the pistol at Arland's head.

"You don't remember me, do you?" he said.

Arland sputtered and coughed again.

"Well, I remember you," Joe said softly.

He pulled the trigger and put a bullet into Arland's forehead. Arland's head jolted to the side. He ceased to sputter. Ceased struggling. Ceased breathing. Arland Garry was dead.

Chapter 14

"He found the man who killed his parents," Madeline said, her eyes agape.

"He did," Liza confirmed.

"And he killed him," Nathaniel added.

"He did."

"That's some story," Nathaniel said.

"Indeed."

"But…"

"But what?"

"Well, you mentioned Dillinger and Baby Face Nelson and all of those people. What does this story have to do with them?"

"I imagine those men had interesting lives before they became notorious thieves and outlaws."

"I'm sure they did."

"Well, this is Joe's life… before he followed a similar path."

"So he turned to a life of crime after he killed the man with one ear?"

"Many things changed for Joe that day, and for all the days that followed. He was never the same, really. At least not for a long time."

"Did he ever find out if he was set up?" Madeline asked.

"What do you mean?"

"Were Joe and Buck sent to meet the man with one ear as bait, to see if he meant to kill whoever came to the meeting, like Joe assumed?"

"Oh, I don't know that. I'm not sure anyone would. What I do know is that Joe and Buck realized that day that they could never return to Kansas."

"Why's that?" Nathaniel asked.

"Well, they had just killed Arland Garry, hadn't they? He was someone very powerful and close to the Colonel, an even more powerful and nasty man. Had they returned to Kansas and to Gump, only bad things could have resulted. The Colonel would not sit idly by and do nothing in reprisal for this act against him. He would come after them... and Gump too, don't you think? And, whether they were set up by McGumpford or not, they had just made an enemy out of that man too."

"How so?"

"Well, whether or not they'd been deliberately sent to the slaughter by the man, they had now set McGumpford up to be slaughtered in retaliation for their actions. The Colonel would surely know who was responsible for the killing of Mr. Garry. There was nothing that McGumpford would, or could, do for

Buck and Joe anymore, and neither of them wanted to return with their tail between their legs to find that out. To them it was clear: even if McGumpford hadn't sent them to be killed in the first place, he would certainly have their heads now to save his own. Why, they had just started a war, hadn't they?"

"I suppose they had," Nathaniel said.

"What would you have done, Mr. Bishop?" asked Liza.

"What would I have done?"

"Yes, what would you have done?"

"I really can't say. But given how you just explained it, I suppose I would have run."

"And you?" Liza asked Madeline.

"I'd have run."

"So would I," Liza offered.

"Is that what they did?" Madeline asked. "Did they run?"

"First they had to tend to Buck's wound. He had a bullet lodged in his leg. He was bleeding badly, and it looked like he might be dying."

"So what happened?" Nathaniel asked.

Liza hesitated. She turned her head and looked out the window.

"It's late," she said. "Let's save that part until tomorrow."

"Are you sure?" Nathaniel asked.

"I'm sure," Liza said.

"It's getting late," Madeline agreed. "Can I walk you out?"

Nathaniel reached over to his voice recorder and switched it off.

"Until tomorrow, then," he said.

Madeline walked Nathaniel to the front door.

"Some story," he said.

"I know. I can hardly believe it."

Nathaniel looked at his watch.

"Hey, it's not really all that late. Can I buy you dinner?"

"I should really stay here in case Grandma needs anything."

"Right. Of course."

Nathaniel reached for the door handle.

"Another time, perhaps," Madeline said.

"Another time," Nathaniel said, smiling.

"See you tomorrow?" she asked.

"It's a date."

Madeline smiled and let Nathaniel out.

Chapter 15

1924

Joe drove the truck like a man possessed.

"We need to get to a hospital," Buck said, his face pale and anxious.

"We go to a hospital and the laws will be all over us."

"Where the hell we goin', then?"

"Just hang on."

Joe looked down to Buck's wound. The small rag he was using to curtail the leaking blood was soaked in red.

In less than one hour he pulled the truck to a skidding stop. This time he did not hesitate. Joe got out of the vehicle with haste and helped Buck limp into the old, abandoned Tilley farmhouse.

The house was a mess. Someone had by to take anything of value and left the remainder in disarray. There was a layer of dust atop everything in sight.

Joe tugged an old cot mattress from the upstairs to a room at the front of the house. He threw it down onto the bleak, gray wooden floor. Buck dropped down onto it with a visceral grunt of pain.

Joe knelt down, pulled away the rag, and inspected the gunshot. Buck's wound was at the very top of his right leg, almost dead in the center.

"Missed your hip by just a little," Joe said. "Don't know about the thigh bone, though. Can't really tell."

Joe unbuckled his cousin's belt and yanked it from the loops. He wrapped the belt around the top of Buck's leg, only an inch or so above the entry point. And then – though Buck screamed out in pain – Joe tightened that belt as far as it would go.

Joe ran to the bathroom. He turned the tap but no water came out. He ran to the bedroom upstairs and managed to find some old clothing still in the closet. Joe grabbed what shirts remained. The significance of the garments flashed quickly though Joe's head; they were his father's shirts. He pictured his father wearing them, standing out in the field waving to Joe as he ran into the woods. Joe quickly banished the thought from his mind and returned to his cousin.

"Here, press this onto the wound and hold it there."

Joe knelt down and handed Buck one of the garments. He threw the rest down beside the cot. After helping Buck get pressure on the wound, Joe hurried to the front door.

"Where're you goin' now?" Buck cried out.

"We gotta get that bullet outta you."

Joe jumped back into the truck and tore out from the farm. He sped toward the nearest town. Wyla, Oklahoma, was a town that Joe had once known well. He pictured its streets in his mind as he drove, wondering how it might have changed, whether any of the same people were still there, and even more, if any of them would recognize him.

With the tank nearly empty of fuel, Joe pulled into a service station at the edge of town. He ran into the building as an attendant began filling the car.

"Any alcohol?" Joe said quietly to the old, fat man behind the counter.

"Nothin' here, friend," the man said. "We abide by the law."

Joe approached the counter.

"Look…" he said abruptly, but he quickly stopped.

The demeanor on the man's face was one of trepidation. Perhaps he had a bottle or two of his own stashed behind the counter, but what was Joe going to say that would make him give it up, and to a complete stranger, no less? He couldn't tell him of the situation back at the farm, and he wasn't about to stir up any more trouble than he already had that day.

"You okay, friend?" the man asked.

"Sure. Yes, fine."

"Seems you got some… What is that there? On your clothes."

Joe looked down. He had fresh blood all over himself.

"Dinner," Joe said in a calm voice.

He smiled at the man.

"Just comin' back from hunting. Just need some rubbing alcohol to clean some scrapes and such."

"Pharmacy in town will do ya," the man offered, still looking inquisitively at Joe.

"Yes, of course. Thank you."

"You sure you okay?"

"What do I owe you for the gas?"

The attendant entered and Joe paid the man. He got back in the truck and continued on into town.

Joe needed a better plan. He was arousing the wrong kind of attention by his appearance, and contrary to his initial idea, he soon resigned himself to the fact that he had neither the knowledge nor the skill to remove a bullet from a man's body safely.

Back at the farm Buck was not doing well. When Joe finally returned he saw that Buck's face had gone from a frightened pale to a stark, dreary white. Though his eyes were open and he saw Joe come in, Buck didn't so much as mumble a word.

A man carrying a small black bag walked into the house behind Joe.

"What is this?" the man said.

"Look, Doc –"

"There's no pregnant woman here, is there? You've lied."

The man turned to walk out.

"Doc, please," Joe pleaded, grabbing the man by the arm. "Look at his face. He's lost too much blood. He'll die if you don't help him."

"This man needs a hospital. He needs a surgeon."

"It's too late for a hospital, Doc. You're the surgeon."

"I'm sorry, fella, I can't. I just can't."

"What will it take, Doc? Just tell me what it will take."

"Who are you people?" the doctor said after a moment's pause.

He looked around the disheveled house.

"Please, Doc, what will it take for you to help him?"

The doctor stared at Joe. Joe was sure he was about to leave and head right to the police.

"Two hundred," the doctor said.

"Two hundred?"

"Two hundred, cash. I help your friend, and I was never here."

"I don't have two hundred."

"Then the nearest hospital is –"

"Okay," Joe said. "Okay, I'll get you the money. You have my word."

"And how am I to know what your word is worth?"

"I'll still need you to keep this quiet, Doc. Believe me, I'll get you the money."

The doctor held Joe's gaze.

"Help me get him onto that table," he finally said.

Joe ran and yanked the long wooden eating table from the other room to the side room of the house where Buck lay. With one man at either end, they lifted the thin mattress with Buck still on it and placed it down on the dusty top.

"Now get me a pot of boiling water," the doctor said, opening his bag.

"There's no water here."

"Well, you better find some, and right quick, or this man will be dead before the sun goes down."

Joe ran out the front door and around to the back of the house. There he found a familiar tin pail among other garden debris. He grabbed the dented bucket and kept on running into the forest. Joe reached the stream. He scooped up some water and headed back toward the house. He walked as fast as he could, trying not to spill the contents.

Joe reached the back of the house. He placed the bucket on the back stoop and headed to the small shed at the side of the yard. Inside the once orderly toolshed were rusted odds and ends and more spider webs than Joe enjoyed wading through. He threw bits of this and pieces of that around the tiny room, looking for things that would be of use. He found a small kerosene lamp and shook it. If there was any oil left in it, it wasn't making a sound.

"Matches," Joe said to himself.

Joe left the shed. He tossed the lamp toward the bucket of water and went running to the truck. He reached under the seat and pulled out a box of matches.

On his way back to the house, Joe stopped every few steps to gather whatever sticks and kindling he could find. He even tore off a piece of wood jutting from the side of the house itself. Joe threw the small sticks and dried leaves into a pile in the back yard. He opened up the lamp and shook it over the pile. A piddly stream of oil trickled out. It would have to do. Joe struck a match and lit the kindling. It went up in an instant. He began adding larger pieces of wood to the flame and fanned the fire with his arms to get it going.

Joe halted and thought. He ran back to the shed and grabbed an old, rusted leaf rake he had tossed aside before.

Placing the metal end on the ground, Joe stomped down as hard as he could where the metal met the wood, severing the rake into two pieces. Joe returned to the fire. After throwing the dried out handle onto the now sizable flame, Joe looked about once again. He headed to the breach of the trees and collected more wood, along with as many fist-sized rocks as he could muster.

Throwing more fuel onto the now roaring fire, Joe began to place the rocks around it in three piles. When the piles were sufficiently high, Joe carefully balanced the metal rake atop them. He took a step back and examined the contraption. Joe fetched the bucket of water and gingerly laid it atop the rake head. The rusted metal dipped in the center but held the weight of the bucket.

It seemed to take forever for the water to boil. Joe kept sneaking more wood onto the fire and even took off his shirt to fan the flame. Eventually the water did bubble.

Joe wrapped his shirt around his hand, grabbed the bucket's thin handle and walked briskly back to the front of the house.

"Where do you want it?" Joe asked.

The doctor was wearing his glasses and was nose deep in Buck's leg. He didn't even notice the nearly naked man making the delivery.

"Right down here beside me," he said.

Joe did as was instructed.

He thought about staying in the room and watching the procedure, but instead Joe left the doctor and his cousin and escaped to the front porch of the house. He sat down on the step and stared straight ahead.

Sweat dripped from his brow. Joe didn't bother to wipe it away. Perhaps he was too exhausted, or perhaps he just didn't care. Or maybe it was because the sweat that trickled down his face and tickled his chin helped to mask the tears that had begun falling from his eyes.

Chapter 16

"He lost a lot of blood," the doctor said.

Joe turned around and looked up at the man standing over him.

"Will he live?" he asked.

"Hard to say."

Joe got up and stood face to face with the doctor.

"Is there anything I can do?"

"Yes, you can take him to the hospital."

"I can't do that."

The doctor looked at Joe and opened his mouth as if he had something more to say, but he remained silent.

"I will get you the money," Joe said, disrupting the silence.

"Yes. That…"

"I just need a few days."

"I have to protect myself, you see."

"I'll get you the money."

The doctor looked at Joe with compassion.

"Come on," he said, "I'll help you take him down from the table. He'll be more comfortable on the floor."

The doctor placed his bag on the porch and followed Joe back into the house. Together they lifted Buck and the mattress, and placed both back on the ground in the corner of the room. Buck looked pallid and worn.

Joe walked the doctor back outside.

"I never did get your name," the doctor said, picking up his bag.

"It's Joe."

"Joe…"

"Tilley."

"Dr. Clark."

The doctor held out his hand and Joe shook it.

"I'll keep your secret, Joe Tilley," he continued. "But if anything out of the ordinary should happen –"

"I assure you, Doc, I'll bring you the money, and then you'll never see or hear from us again."

The doctor let go of Joe's hand and nodded his head.

"Make sure he eats something. He'll need his strength."

The doctor tipped his hat and made his way to his car.

"It's getting dark," Joe said. "Should I wait until the morning to bring him food?"

The doctor turned.

"I wouldn't," he said. "He may not live that long."

The doctor got in his car and drove away down the dirt road. Joe watched as the car drove off the farm and turned toward town. He went back inside.

"Buck?" he said, hovering over his cousin.

There was no answer. Buck didn't move a muscle.

Joe looked around the room. He walked over and stood in the foyer of the house. He turned and looked down the hallway. There in front of him was the kitchen, the room Joe had purposefully avoided.

Joe went out to the truck and reached under the seat. He pulled out the brand new Winchester Model 54, the one he had so admired and recently seized from Arland Garry. He looked the gun over.

The sun had nearly hit the horizon, so Joe knew he had little time. He circled the house and walked into the woods. He stood by the stream behind the house. The trees and bushes had grown and changed and altered the landscape enough to make the surroundings look somewhat foreign. Joe began to walk along the stream, gun in hand.

He knew from his childhood spent there that those woods were flush with wildlife. Plenty of rabbits, wild turkeys, squirrels, foxes, and more could be found on better days. Even the occasional deer would saunter by from time to time. Joe leapt onto a rock in the middle of the stream and bounded to the other side. He slowly began to walk up and along the hillside.

He thought about the last time he'd been in the woods behind the farmhouse. He thought about his parents and what had happened in the kitchen. He thought about the man with one ear, the man he now knew as Arland Garry – the man he had shot and killed only hours earlier.

It was almost getting too dark to see when Joe heard a rustling in the trees. Two squirrels scurried along a branch, one chasing the other. And then they were gone, but the rustling remained. Joe lifted the gun and pointed it in the direction of the sound. He walked slowly, trying not to make much noise. Out of the corner of his eye Joe spotted movement. He turned to his left and caught sight of not one but three black-tailed jackrabbits not far from his position. Joe moved to the side just enough to get a clear shot. He sucked in a breath and fired.

The gun felt like it was made for his hands. As he pulled back the bolt and the shell was ejected, Joe felt a warm rush in his gut.

Approaching the kill spot about fifty yards away, Joe came upon two dead rabbits. The bullet had entered and exited the first and lodged itself in the second, killing both. Joe threw the gun strap across his shoulder and picked up his dinner.

He leapt over a narrow part of the stream and headed back toward the farmhouse. Joe was remembering the woods even more now. A certain tree or rock or stand of wildflowers that remained the same would stoke his memory. The smell also thrust him back in time. And then along his walk Joe caught sight of the small cave. He'd returned at last to Fort Joseph.

Joe laid the rabbits down on the ground and, taking the gun from his shoulder, placed it down beside them. He approached the opening of the cave.

It seemed so small. He wondered if it could have always been that small. Joe barely fit through the opening, but fit through he did.

Inside, on one knee Joe looked around. He picked up a handful of dirt from the ground and let it slide out between his fingers. There wasn't much to see, but a welcome sight it was nonetheless. Joe noticed something small at the back of the cave. He got up and, with back arched so as not to hit his head on the rock above, he approached the item. The light was all but gone. Joe picked up the object and brought it closer to his eyes. It was a black rabbit's foot. It was *his* black rabbit's foot. Joe closed his eyes and remembered back to the day he had last sat in that cave, the day he had last held that rabbit's foot.

Putting the memento in his pocket, Joe shimmied out of the cave. He lifted the rabbits and his gun and made it back to the house just as the sun had nearly vanished altogether from the sky. He grabbed the box of matches from the back porch and walked around to the front of the house.

Joe checked on Buck. He was in the same shape as when he'd left him not an hour prior. It was quickly getting too dark to see. Joe placed the rabbits and his gun on the wooden table and returned to the foyer. He took a deep breath and let it out.

He walked down the hall and entered the kitchen. From what little he could see, most of the cupboards had already been looted and left bare. The stove was gone, as was the sink.

Joe lit a match. He looked down onto the ground. A small brown stain remained on the wood beneath his feet. Joe tried his best to ignore it.

Joe scurried around, searching through whatever remained in the kitchen drawers and cupboards. He knew what he was looking for and where to look. But the cupboards were even emptier than he'd imagined.

Then, as if through some spiritual intervention, an image appeared in Joe's head. He headed into the basement, a place mostly off limits to him a child. It was his father's basement, for his father's things.

Joe thought back to a time when his father had taken him down there. Joe had been just a boy, but he remembered that it was dark and wet and smelled like something Joe had never smelled before, like a dirty sock or a muddy dog. It tickled his nose to breathe it in.

Mr. Tilley had kept many things in the basement: canned food, extra tools, boxes of his wife's old clothing. (He never could get rid of the clothes she'd sewn, even when they grew tattered and shabby.) But it was something else Joe was after.

As with the kitchen, the basement had been ransacked. Joe lit another match and searched the homemade shelving. Broken glass crackled under his feet.

The canned food was gone, and so were all the shovels, sickles, and seeders. But Joe wasn't looking for any of those things. Under a small pile of burlap Joe found what he was looking for.

Overturned, on the floor, Joe found an old, dirty, brown wooden box. To the uninformed it would have looked like an ordinary crate or stepping box, but Joe knew better. He knelt down and flipped the box over. The small metal latch was blackened and covered in a sticky kind of paste. Joe lit another match and held it close to the box. The goop on the latch burst into flame. Joe grabbed a patch of burlap and smothered the fire. He threw aside the fabric and picked up a thick piece of glass from a broken mason jar. He used the glass to swipe away the remainder of the gooey substance and then to pry open the weathered box.

Inside the box were just the things Joe was looking for. He lifted the old thing and carried it upstairs to the main room where Buck was lying, still unconscious.

Joe placed the box on the ground, lit another match, and lifted the lid once more. He reached in and pulled out a handful of beeswax candles. He took one from the pile and lit it. He used that one to light three others. If balanced with a little care, the candles were thick enough to stand on their own. Joe placed three candles around himself to light the area. With a candle still in hand, Joe continued to look through the box. He reached his hand to the bottom. He pulled his empty hand out only to have it covered with the same sort of black goop that had been all over the latch and the top of the box. Something had spilled or gone rotten or died in there. He brought his fingers to his nose.

Joe looked around the room and saw the bucket of water he had brought for Dr. Clark. He shimmied along the floor toward it. Inside the bucket was water, but it was anything but clear. The water was so red it looked purple in the dim light. Looking away, Joe reached into the bucket and used one of the cloths therein to clean off his hand.

Joe took one of the unused shirts still on the floor in the room and wrapped his hand within it. He sank his hand back into the box and pulled out a roll of twine and then a fishing knife. He then retrieved a bag of tobacco and half a can of lamp oil. The small lamp at the bottom had broken into several pieces; its once oily contents perhaps accounted for what had transformed into a thick goop after years of rot and neglect.

The last item Joe pulled from the box was an old black Colt revolver. The gun was sullied and worn and had gone unused for what looked like decades. The Colt insignia just above the handle was almost indecipherable. Joe inspected the gun further. He had never seen it before, in his father's hands or otherwise. Joe set the gun aside along with the knife, the rope, and the can of oil.

Buck groaned and moved his head.

"Buck?" Joe said.

He shuffled over to his cousin.

"Buck? You awake?"

Buck did not move again or make another sound.

Joe pushed the box to the side. He picked up an unused shirt from the ground and used it to wrap the knife, the gun, the rope, and the lamp oil. All the items that needed to be washed clean of the old, sticky oil. Joe took the bucket of bloody water and rags and headed out to the back of the house.

The old lantern he'd found in the shed was still sitting beside the now paltry fire. The rocks he used to secure the rake had kept the fire contained. Only white, gray, and blackened ash remained, with a few glowing orange embers in the center. Joe opened the lamp oil and filled the small lantern. It took some cajoling, but the old piece finally lit up with the aid of the beeswax candle. Once the lantern was lit, he blew out the candle to save it for another time.

Joe dumped the contents of the bucket onto the grass. The bloody rags plopped down and looked like a dead animal on the ground. Carrying the lantern in front of him, he headed back to the stream.

On the shore Joe reached down to the water's bottom and came up with a handful of sand and tiny stones. He used the concoction as a scrubbing agent, along with the shirt, and washed the various items. The bucket was easy to clean. After a few good rinses it looked as good as knew, or at least as good as Joe had found it. The thick, oily residue wouldn't easily come off the other items, though he tried his best. Joe was satisfied for the time being to leave the oilcan and gun somewhat unclean, but he was in need of the knife and wanted it as unsoiled as possible.

Joe looked around and soon found a fair-sized rock, one that would fit easily into the palm of his hand. The rock had just the jagged edge he was looking for. Joe used the rock's edge to scrape the residue from the knife. The rock scuffed the handle quite a bit, but the process did get the blade clean enough to use and perhaps even sharpened it, if only a little.

Joe wrapped the gun and the lamp oil in the wet shirt, and with the clean knife and a bucket of clean water, he returned to the back of the house to start preparing supper.

Chapter 17

Having spent much time alone in the woods, Joe had become expert at preparing meals outdoors. He unraveled the roll of twine until a fresh, clean layer was revealed. Assembling a four-legged teepee with thick branches and twine, he removed the rake head and hung the bucket from the wood structure above a newly built fire. The bucket hung in the air over the flame, its weight keeping it centered and stable.

Joe skinned and cleaned the rabbits by lantern light and buried the leftovers along with the bloody rags in the ground.

Joe chopped up the first rabbit and dropped the meat into the bucket of water to make soup. Once it was cooked, he removed the soup to let it cool and fashioned a spit from another piece of wood. He placed the second rabbit on the spit and secured it on the teepee above the fire.

Joe went inside the house to check on Buck, who remained asleep and motionless. Returning to the fire with his father's bag of tobacco, Joe rolled a cigarette and lit it. It hung from his lips as he sat on the grass whittling a piece of wood, every so often looking up to check on the second rabbit as it cooked above the fire.

Joe smoked three cigarettes. He drank in the sounds of the cracking and hissing fire that broke the silence of the darkened night.

After some time the second rabbit was cooked and the fire began to die down. Joe rose to his feet and removed a fair chunk of tree bark from a nearby oak to use as a plate. He removed the rabbit from the fire and placed it atop the bark. He went inside with the food and two spoons he had whittled.

Joe tried feeding Buck first, lifting spoonfuls of soup to his mouth and forcing it through his lips. Most of the liquid just ran down Buck's chin, and whatever drops did make it past his tongue were promptly coughed back up.

Joe tried for what seemed like half an hour to feed Buck, but his efforts were fruitless. Buck didn't have the strength or the wherewithal to eat.

Joe was famished. He ate more than half of the other rabbit right off the spit. He might have eaten more if not for Buck's sudden movement. Perhaps it was the warm soup, or just the poor state in which he found himself, but Buck began to writhe on the mattress. Joe put down the food and sat up against the wall beside Buck. Buck's entire face had become covered in beads of sweat. His hair had darkened with moisture, and his teeth chattered together. Joe put his hand on Buck's damp brow. His forehead was sweltering.

Joe returned to the kitchen, this time with the lantern, which served as a better aid than a single match had. He returned to the cupboard wherein he remembered seeing a single ceramic serving bowl and a small cup. Though chipped in several places near the rim, the bowl would still serve its intended purpose well.

Joe returned to the stream once more and filled the bowl with cool water.

Joe set the bowl beside Buck's cot and went to retrieve more clothing from the rooms upstairs. He tore a pair of men's pants into rags and threw them down beside the mattress. He dunked one of the rags into the bowl of water and placed it on Buck's forehead. Buck let out a muted groan as the coolness dripped across his temples. Joe dipped another rag in the water and placed it behind Buck's neck. He removed Buck's shoes and socks. He took off what remained of Buck's pants and with the knife cut his shirt from his chest. Joe dipped the small cup into the bowl and lifted it to Buck's mouth, urging him to drink. Buck was unresponsive.

Every ten or twenty minutes Joe would replace the rags, each time dipping them in the water. Every hour Joe would head back down to the stream to fetch fresh, cool water.

Joe did this throughout the night. He sat up and watched his cousin suffer. He wondered whether Buck would make it to the morning alive. He wondered what he would do if he didn't. He needn't wonder, however, who was to blame for the predicament. Joe placed that burden upon himself. Had he not sought revenge on the man with one ear, he and his cousin could have been halfway to California or Mexico or Canada by then.

He didn't remember falling asleep, but when Joe awoke on the floor hours later, all the candles had burned out and Buck's body was shaking like a frightened dog. His sweating had turned profuse and the wetness had soaked his body and the mattress below. Joe put his hand on his cousin's arm. The sweat was cold and slimy. Joe rushed upstairs and scoured all the bedrooms yet again. He gathered all the remaining clothing he could find, and even came upon a still-folded bed sheet underneath one of the piles of discarded garments.

Joe returned to Buck's side, his arms filled with the bounty. He removed the wet rags from Buck's head and used a red sundress to wipe the remaining sweat from his body. He covered his cousin with the bed sheet and laid out several garments atop his body, tucking them under Buck's legs and arms and torso. He wrapped him up in a clothing cocoon.

Exhausted, Joe sat back down on the floor and leaned his back against the wall. From where he sat, he could see out the window and far off into the distance. Just above the horizon began to appear a hint of blue. The sun had not yet come up, but it was announcing its impending arrival.

Though he tried his best to fight it off, Joe was soon overtaken by sleep once more.

Chapter 18

Joe's eyes opened. The sunlight was flooding through the window. Buck had stopped shaking but his face was still colorless and bleak. Joe placed his hand on Buck's forehead. It was warm but not as warm as it had been only hours before.

The pharmacy in town would now be open. Joe rose to his feet and rifled through the pile of clothing on top of Buck. He found a few articles not wet or spattered with blood in which to change into. The fit was not perfect, but they would have to do.

Joe drove into town and entered the bustling pharmacy. He began collecting a basket of goods from the shelves: soap, toothbrush and paste, a shaving kit, two water bags, some gauze wrap, and a bottle of aspirin. Joe pulled out what money he had left and was just able to cover the cost. He was left with a few coins and nothing more. The remainder was just enough to stop at the market and purchase a few pieces of fruit.

Joe was on his way back to the farm when something made him stop. Still in town he pulled up along the side of the road and turned off the engine. Joe stared out the window at the front of the town bank. He watched, thought, waited.

Buck's eyes were open when Joe returned to the house.

"You're awake," Joe said.

Buck grunted in response.

"How do you feel?"

"Like I got shot," Buck mumbled.

He rubbed his dry lips together. Joe shook three aspirin into his hand. He lifted the bowl of water to Buck's mouth. Buck took a sip. Joe placed the aspirin in his mouth and returned the bowl to his lips.

"It's for the fever," he said.

Buck swallowed the pills down.

"I can't feel my leg," Buck said.

"The feeling will come back."

"Am I dying?"

"You're not dying. Just take it easy. It's probably something the doc did."

"The doc?"

"I brought a doctor to take the bullet out."

Buck lifted his head as best he could to get a glimpse of his body. Joe leaned over, removed the clothing and the sheet, and revealed the white bandages that covered the wound.

"I'm not dying," Buck said with relief as he put his head back down.

"Can you eat?" Joe asked. "You need to eat."

"Sure, yeah. Eat."

Buck closed his weary eyes and was asleep in seconds.

"Buck," Joe said. "Buck."

Buck grunted but did not wake.

Joe went down to the stream to fill the water bags. He made another stop at the cave to see it in the light of day. He did not go in but instead only peeked through the opening.

Back at the farmhouse, beside Buck's mattress Joe left one bowl of cold rabbit soup, a cup with pieces of apple and banana, a water bag, and three more aspirin. Joe searched through Buck's bloody clothing and found his small wad of cash. Joe once again left the house. He did not return for several hours.

Buck was awake again when Joe returned.

"This is your farm, isn't it?" he said.

"You eat anything?"

"Where were you?"

"In town," Joe said. "Did you eat?"

Buck shook his head. "So tired."

"You need to eat."

Joe sat down beside the mattress. He took a piece of apple and put it to Buck's mouth. Buck took a bite and chewed slowly.

"What were you doing in town?" Buck asked.

"We need to find a way to get some money, and fast."

Buck gave his cousin an inquisitive look. Joe put the apple back to Buck's mouth. Buck reached up and took the apple from Joe's hands.

"I'm no invalid," he said.

Buck tried to prop himself up on his elbows. Joe helped him lean up against the wall. Buck cringed as he moved.

"We have to pay off the doc," Joe said.

"How much?"

"Two hundred."

"We don't got two hundred."

"Not yet, we don't."

"How you gonna get it?"

Joe shook out three aspirin and handed them to Buck. Buck put them in his mouth and took another bite of the apple.

"There's a bank in town," Joe said.

"A bank?"

Joe nodded.

"Don't suppose you're gonna ask for a loan…"

Joe smiled.

"You're no bank robber," Buck said.

"Maybe not. But I have an idea."

"Yeah, what's that?"

"I'll tell you about it later. Right now you need to rest."

Joe put his hand on Buck's forehead.

"You're still warm."

"I have to piss," Buck said.

Joe looked around the room. Then he went outside and emptied one of the water bags and brought it back for Buck to do his business. Joe then emptied the bag and placed it beside the mattress again.

Buck squirmed his way back down flat and shut his eyes. Joe sat beside him against the wall and ate the remainder of the roasted rabbit. He stayed beside Buck for the rest of the day.

When the sunlight had vanished, Joe built a fire behind the house. He had no water to boil or rabbits to cook, but the warmth of the flames and sound of crackling wood made him feel calm.

Every once in awhile Joe would go back into the house to see Buck. When he did, he forced him to eat and fed him more aspirin.

Chapter 19

In the morning Joe woke up to the sight of Buck looking down at his own wiggling toes.

"I can feel my leg," Buck said.

"We have to change your bandage," Joe said, rubbing his eyes open.

"I'll do it myself."

"Don't be a fool," Joe said, retrieving the gauze he purchased at the pharmacy.

Joe knelt down beside the mattress and uncovered the leg. Blood had seeped to the surface of the bandage. He used the knife to remove the fabric, exposing the wound. The stitches that closed the opening were few in number. The purple and black bruising that surrounded the area was more severe than the day before. Joe lightly tapped the tips of his fingers around the stitches.

"Feel that?" he asked.

Buck's painful flinch revealed the answer.

"Doc said nothing about broken bones, so you should mend just fine in a while. How you feeling otherwise?"

"Tired. And I gotta piss again."

Joe wrapped the gauze around Buck's leg. He handed him the water bottle to urinate.

Joe left Buck to rest. He emptied the water bag on the ground in the back yard and then continued on into the forest, carrying only the roll of twine and his knife.

He returned to the cave on the bank of the stream and searched around for rocks. He found the jagged rock he had used to clean the knife, but it was too small for his needs. Joe took care to gather several rocks and made a pile outside the cave.

One by one Joe then threw the rocks against the outside of the rocky cave wall. Most of the rocks simply bounced right off in varying directions. A few of the rocks, however, chipped or broke into multiple pieces after a few heavy impacts.

Joe inspected the broken rocks and found a nice-sized piece to use. Joe placed the rock on a log. He began to hammer away at it with one of the sturdier pieces. Joe took the rock to the stream. He entered the water and approached a large river rock protruding near the center. In water up to his shins, Joe began to scrape the sharp end of the rock against the one in the river. He scraped hard and long. Eventually he had a smooth, sharp edge.

Joe searched about the woods for a suitable piece of wood. As with the rocks, he found multiple candidates. He chose one good forearm's length to use. Joe bore a hole near the top of the wood handle with the knife, and using the twine, affixed the jagged rock to it tightly and securely. He swung the creation through the air. It looked good. It felt good. Joe's homemade hatchet was ready for use.

Joe once again searched out branches. This time he was looking for live pieces still attached to trees. Using the hatchet, Joe downed three similar sized oak branches and dragged them back to the yard. He removed the leaves and smaller twigs that obtruded. He cut down one of the branches to about five feet in length.

In the tool shed Joe found a broken broom handle. He used the hatchet to hack at a piece of wood from the side of the shed. He tugged away the plank, sure to bring the protruding nails along with it.

Joe used the branches, the broom handle, and the nails to fashion a worthy crutch. He tucked it under his arm and leaned on it to test the strength. He brought the piece into the house, where he weaved an old cloth around the top to soften the wood.

Buck was asleep. He would have little time to learn to use the crutch. If Joe's plan worked, it meant they would be leaving the Tilley farm much earlier than expected, and in a right hurry.

Chapter 20

"There's something I gotta do," Joe said, standing over Buck as his eyes opened.

"When will you be back?"

"Not long."

Joe began to leave.

"While I'm gone, see if you can get up," Joe said, standing at the door. "Try using that."

He pointed to the crutch leaning against the wall beside the mattress.

Joe got in the truck and drove into Dermott, a fair-sized town nearby. The drive only took him twenty or so miles west of the house, but it had been a while since he had navigated the roads of Oklahoma, so he took extra time and care in getting there.

Joe pulled up to a building on the main stretch of the road. He walked through the door and sidled up to the long, bar-like counter.

"I'd like to report a criminal in the area," he said.

"A criminal?"

A young man approached the wooden partition separating the two men.

"Yes, but I would like to talk to that man over there," Joe said.

He pointed over the man's shoulder to another sitting at a desk in his office. The man was looking down, concerned with the papers in front of him and not with Joe.

"One second," the young man said, giving Joe a curious look.

The man walked over to the office, leaned in, and whispered something in the older man's ear. The older man got up and approached the partition.

"Can I help you?" he asked.

"I hope so."

"Something about a criminal –"

The older man paused.

"No," the man said.

"Hello, Alfred," Joe said with a smile.

Alfred Winter came out from behind the partition and embraced Joe.

"What are you doing here, Joseph?"

"Just passing through."

Alfred held Joe at arm's length.

"You've grown," he said. "I was expecting a letter, but this is certainly better."

"It's good to see you, Alfred."

"Come on, let's go have a chat. Dale," Alfred said to the other man, "I'm across the street. Don't come get me."

Alfred and Joe crossed the road to a shop across from the police station. The shop had a small bar and a flattop grill along with three booths for patrons, and the two men sat in one.

"Margery, cuppa coffee for me and my friend," Alfred called out to the woman at the counter.

"Sure thing," the woman called back.

"How are you, Alfred?"

"I'm keeping well. Governor's got me running around like crazy, truth to tell. Just got back to town today, actually. But forget about that. How 'bout you? How are you liking those books I been sending?"

"I read them all."

"Don't suppose you got the last one I sent, you bein' here and all?"

"Which one was that?"

"Some new one. Haven't had the chance to read it yet myself. What was the name of that author? Gerald something, I think."

"I'll look forward to it."

"And you're doing okay an' all, otherwise? It's been a while since I heard from you."

Margery put two cups of coffee on the table and left with a smile.

"I been meaning to write more," Joe said.

"You said you were just passing through? Can you stay for a spell?"

"Heading out soon. Just found myself in the area and thought I'd drop by and say hello."

"I'm glad you did."

"Say, what's that badge there?" Joe asked.

"This, you mean?"

Alfred pulled back his coat to reveal a silver medal on his breast pocket.

"Like I said, Governor's got me running around like crazy. Part of this new outfit he's put together."

"State Bureau of…"

Joe tried to make out the words.

"State Bureau of Identification and Investigation. Mouthful, ain't it?"

"What's it mean?"

"Been a rash of gangs runnin' amok in towns around these parts."

"What kind of gangs?"

"You don't wanna hear about it."

"Sure I do. It's a good promotion you got."

"Scofflaws mostly, bank robbers some of 'em. They been around for some time now, selling liquor and such. Been runnin' county lines to get away from the cops, so the Governor created this. Statewide jurisdiction and orders to bring 'em in or shoot 'em dead. Couple o' fellas found themselves on the wrong end of a gun just a few days ago upstate."

"Upstate?"

"Billingston way. Curious scene. Like I said, just got back today. It's good luck, doncha think? You being in town?"

"Good luck," Joe agreed.

"You gotta come by the house and see Marie. She'd love you to visit."

1995

"Grandma?" Madeline said, getting up from her chair and crawling onto the bed.

Liza's story had been interrupted by a fit of coughing. The coughing continued and shook the old woman to the core. Madeline sat her up and held her in an upright position. Nathaniel left the room and returned moments later with a glass of water. He handed it to Madeline, who put the glass to Liza's mouth. She took a sip.

"My apologies," Liza said, catching her breath.

"You okay?" Madeline asked.

"I'm fine, dear. I'm fine."

"I think that's enough for today," Madeline said.

"Nonsense. I'm fine."

"It's getting late anyway," Nathaniel said. "Why don't we pick it up again tomorrow?"

"If you insist," Liza said.

"I can show myself out."

Nathaniel packed up his things.

"Until tomorrow," he said. "Get some rest, Mrs. Meacham. Maddy, see you tomorrow."

"See you tomorrow," Madeline said.

Nathaniel left the room and could be heard departing the house through the front door. Liza lay back against the headboard of her bed and held the glass of water on top of the blanket on her lap.

"Maddy?" Liza said.

"He told me to call him Nate. What was I supposed to say?"

Liza smiled at her granddaughter, giving one more cough.

"It's late," Madeline continued. "I'll go fix us something to eat."

"Oh, I'm not hungry," Liza said, waving Madeline off.

"Some tea, then."

"Okay. Some tea would be fine."

Madeline set the chairs to the side of the room and left to make tea. Liza watched her leave and muffled a quiet cough in her hand.

Liza fell asleep right after her cup of tea.

When the phone rang early the next morning, Madeline was preparing breakfast in the kitchen. She answered right away.

"Listen to this, from a newspaper in 1924," Nathaniel said over the sound of rustling papers. " 'Today Oklahoma Governor M.E. Trapp created a special agency to curtail the state's growing crime problem…' It says a gang was terrorizing towns, robbing banks, holding up gas stations…"

"Yeah?"

"Apparently it started out as a small group, just a handful of men, but the agency was created to stop outlaws from escaping across county lines. Here's the name: 'the Oklahoma State Bureau of Identification and Investigation.' "

Madeline felt chills run up her arms.

"It's still around, Maddy. Only now it's called the Oklahoma State Bureau of Investigation."

"Wow!" Madeline said.

"I know. The first thing in the story I can actually corroborate."

"Wait... You still doubt the story?"

"I didn't say that."

"You didn't have to."

"I want to believe it, Maddy. Trust me, I do."

"I know."

"How is she, anyway?"

"She seems okay today, though I don't know... She's awfully tired."

"Do you think maybe we should give her a break?"

"Are you kidding? She looks forward to your visits, Nate, more than you know. Besides, if she wanted to stop, you know she'd tell us."

"I'm sure she would," Nathaniel said, laughing. "How about I come by around lunchtime then? Get started a little earlier."

"I'll let Grandma know."

"I look forward to seeing you... seeing both of you," Nathaniel said, stumbling.

Madeline chuckled.

"Me too," she said.

Chapter 21

Joe pulled the truck over at a spot with a clear view of the front of the Wyla First Township Bank. He sat there. He waited.

He bought a cup of coffee in a shop nearby and returned to the truck. He waited.

He bought a newspaper and brought it back to the truck. He waited some more.

It was about six o'clock that evening that a man in a brown suit came out through the bank's front doors. At first he seemed like any other man who had come and gone that day. But when he pulled out a ring of keys and put one into the front door lock, Joe straightened his lazy posture and paid careful attention. The man had black hair and a brown hat to match his clothing. Unfortunately that was about all Joe could see from his vantage point.

The man in the brown suit walked along the sidewalk. Joe turned on the truck's engine. The man went into a shop. Joe turned off the engine. The man came out carrying a bag. Joe started the truck once more. The man walked a little farther before again pulling out his large ring of keys and unlocking the door of a car. The man got into his car and drove off.

Joe followed as the man in the brown suit drove through the streets of Wyla. The man traveled to the west until he pulled his car into the driveway of a house on a friendly, tree-lined street. Joe passed by the man's house without stopping. He smacked the steering wheel with the palm of his hand in frustration. He had not gotten a good look at the man's face.

Buck had the crutch under one arm and was holding onto the wall with the other when Joe walked into the house.

"You're up," Joe said.

"Barely."

"Can you walk?"

Buck took a step with his good leg, but when he tried to follow along with the other leg, he winced in pain and stopped.

"Hang on," he said.

Buck hopped on his good foot and regained his balance. He tried to move again, this time swinging his right leg out wide instead of trying to step forward normally. He took a successful step.

"That's better," he said. "Now where's the bathroom?"

"Outside," Joe said.

"Right."

Buck slowly but surely made his way out to the back of the house. Joe followed behind him in case he required assistance.

"What the hell you been doing back here?" Buck said, reaching the yard.

"Made a fire."

"I can see that."

Holding on to a porch post, Buck hopped down the two back steps on his good leg. He took a few hampered steps and looked down at the homemade hatchet on the ground by the fire pit.

"Let me see that," he said.

Joe picked it up and handed it to Buck.

"Where'd you learn to do this?" Buck asked.

"Spent some time alone in the woods when I was younger."

Buck inspected the hatchet's integrity.

"Impressive," he said, swinging it through the air.

Buck dropped the hatchet back down to the ground. He made his way to the side of the shed, slowly, where he dropped his pants and squatted down as far as his injured leg would allow.

"Been needin' to do this for a while," he said.

Joe turned away.

"I'll get the soap so you can wash," he said.

Buck finished his business and made his way down to the stream, once again with Joe following behind him all the way. Buck stripped down and got into the water. At its deepest the stream only reached to Buck's waist, but that was deep enough for him to wash his body.

"Feels good," he said, cupping water in his hands and splashing it onto his face.

He rubbed himself down with the bar of soap. A white lather covered his skin all the way up to his brow. Joe was busy looking down into his lap, hard at work cutting pieces of twine and tying them together in some sort of design.

"We gotta get moving," he said to Buck.

"Say what?" Buck said, using his finger to pull white foam from his ear.

"I say we gotta get going."

"I'll be done in a minute. What's the hurry?"

"No, I mean from the farm. We gotta leave."

"When?"

"Soon. So be ready."

"You gonna tell me about this plan of yours?"

"When I figure it all out, I will."

"Why don't you wait a few more days? I can help."

"Don't think we can wait."

"Tell me again why we don't just skip town and leave it all behind?"

"For one thing, the doc has my name."

"What the hell you tell him that for?"

"It was part of the bargain. Besides, he knows the house. It wouldn't take much thought for someone looking to put the pieces together."

"Well, who's lookin'?"

"Laws are looking for the killer of Arland Garry. A guy shows up in town with a gunshot wound, and he might be someone they'd be interested in talking to."

"How you know the laws are lookin'?"

"More than the local cops, state outfit is looking. And either way, you know the Colonel will be coming after whoever shot his man. We can't stay here, or anywhere, for long. Not for a while, anyway. And if we can leave town knowing the doc will keep quiet, that there's no one else to know we were here, that's what we should be doing."

"It's the bank, then?"

"Unless you got two hundred hidden somewhere."

"We could put it together back home easier."

Buck got out of the water. He used his shirt to dry himself off and then put his pants back on.

"We can't go back. That's the first place the Colonel will look. That is, if Gumpy wouldn't put a bullet in us first."

"Why don't you go talk to that doctor and tell him you need more time? Hell, tell him you're *takin'* more time. I'll be better by then and we –"

"You think you'll be better in a few days?"

"Look, can't hurt to go tell the doc it's gonna be more time. We can skip town, find the money, then circle back and pay 'im."

"We could…"

"You know where to find him, the doctor?"

"I know his house, yeah."

"Well, then…?"

Back in the yard Joe built a small fire and hung what remained of the bucket of soup up over it to boil. Buck sat on the porch with his back against a porch post.

"I feel as weak as a girl," he said. "I'm serious. I mean my leg hurts, sure, but hell, it's like I was hit by a truck or somethin'."

Buck rested his head against the post and put his hand up to his forehead.

"You need to eat. Doc said."

"Got a bit of a hunger, actually. Got a hankerin' for some chocolate."

Joe stoked the fire. Buck watched his cousin and rubbed at his hip. He looked around the yard.

"So what happened?" Buck said after a few minutes of silence.

"What do you mean?"

"I mean what happened… here? How'd they die?"

"I told you not to ask me about that."

"Joe…"

Joe looked up from the fire and could see that his frequently jovial cousin was serious and asking out of more than mere curiosity. Just brushing off the inquiry wouldn't be satisfactory this time.

As if they hadn't reached it before, the pair knew they had come to a point where there was no room for secrets. They had just gunned down two men and helped a third go headlong into a tree. They were on the run from everyone they knew, and Joe had just saved Buck's life. They needed one another, and more than that, they had only each other left to trust.

"You're not going to believe it when I tell you," Joe said.

"Try me."

Chapter 22

It was late at night. The town was quiet. Joe passed by only one other car heading in the other direction on the main road. He turned down a side street. He drove slowly, trying to remember his directions. He slowed the truck to a crawl. The vehicle soon eased to a stop as Joe guided it to the side of the road. Joe looked at the gauges on the dash. He got out of the car and opened the hood. He peered inside, though in the darkness it was too difficult to see. Joe looked around. He saw no one about.

The closest house was a few hundred yards away. Joe began to walk.

He came upon a long driveway and turned up it toward the house. All the lights in the house were off. Joe stood and stared at it for a moment. He decided to go up to the door. Joe held his fist in front of the wooden door for a spell and then knocked. After a brief pause and no reception, Joe knocked again. A light in the house came on. Joe heard the sound of the door unlocking.

"Yes?" a man said, poking one eye out of the crack.

"Hi. I'm so sorry to bother you at this hour, really I am, but my car broke down just up the street. I think I'm out of gas…"

"Out of gas?" the man said, opening the door a little wider.

"I woke you," Joe said. "I'm sorry, I'll try someone else."

Joe took a step to leave.

"No, no, it's okay. I wasn't asleep yet."

The man opened the door. He was wearing blue pajamas and a red robe.

"I can walk to a service station," Joe said. "Really, I don't want to bother you."

"You're not from around here, are you?"

"No sir."

"The nearest station is four miles away. Wouldn't advise a walk all that way at this hour."

"Can I use your telephone?"

"You're not likely to get a tow this late."

The man looked back into his house.

"I'll tell you what, let me get some clothes on and I'll drive you to the station."

"Would you mind?"

"Just one moment."

The man closed the door. Joe walked out onto the driveway.

The man came out a few minutes later. He was wearing a long coat.

"I'm Hank," the man said.

"Joe."

"The car is just over here."

"I really appreciate this. Is your wife okay with you driving me?"

"I live alone."

The man opened the passenger side for Joe and then walked around and got in himself. He looked at his watch.

"You'll be lucky to get fuel at this hour, but I've known Merl to be there this late from time to time."

"You know the man at the station?"

Hank turned on the car.

"It's not a very big town," he said. "Most folks around here know one another."

He drove down the driveway and pulled out onto the street.

"Where'd you say you were from?"

"Arkansas. Just here visiting my aunt."

"You don't say? Who's your aunt?"

Joe wiped his brow with his sleeve.

"You're going the wrong way," he said.

"No, no, this is the way to the station."

"Hank," Joe said, turning his head to look at the man. "Turn the car around."

Hank took his eyes off the road. He looked down into Joe's lap to see that Joe had a pistol pointing to his head.

"What is this? What's going on?"

"Turn the car around, Hank."

"Who are you? What do you want?"

"Less questions. I'll tell you where we're going as soon as you turn the car around. You do everything I say and you go back home and sleep in your bed tonight. You don't, and I'll put a bullet in you before you get a second chance."

With Joe's gun pointed at him, Hank was eager to follow instructions. He made a U-turn and headed in the opposite direction.

"I don't have any money, you know."

"Yes you do, Hank. Just drive."

Hank's hands were shaking on the wheel. Joe was strangely calm. Perhaps it was because he had gone over the scenario so many times in his head.

"Turn here," Joe said, pointing out the windshield.

Hank did as he was told. A little bit down the road Joe had Hank turn once more.

"Now pull over and stop the car."

Hank did just that.

"Now," Joe said, turning to face the man, "we're going to get out of the car together. I'm going to put this gun in my pocket and you're going to walk with me calmly, like we're two old friends out for a stroll. If you make a noise or draw attention, I'll shoot you. If you try to run, I'll shoot you. If you walk beside me like nothing was amiss, you'll live. It's that simple. Got it?"

Hank nodded.

"Now put those keys into your coat pocket."

Hank did so.

"Open your door, then place both hands back on the steering wheel."

Hank did that too.

Joe got out of the car and walked around to the driver's side.

"Come on, get out."

Hank got out of the car and the two men walked along the sidewalk together.

"How long you worked here?" Joe asked.

Hank didn't respond. He kept his eyes forward and walked along the sidewalk.

"It's okay, Hank. Like I said, you do what I say and you'll be home within the hour. I'm not here for your life. I'm here for the money. You get me the money and you'll never see me again. That's a promise. Now, how long you worked at the bank?"

"Twelve years," Hanks said.

"You like it?"

"I like it fine."

The two men reached the front door of the bank. There was not a soul around. Joe needed only to nod and Hank pulled out the keys and unlocked the door.

"See," Joe said. "Easy. A few more minutes of this and we're done."

They entered the bank.

"Leave the lights off," Joe said.

Joe reached into his pocket and pulled out a wad of twine. He unraveled the ball.

"Show me your hands."

Hank put his hands out in front of his body. Joe slid loops of layered twine around each of Hank's wrists. He pulled at the middle and the loops tightened snugly together.

"Like little rabbit traps," Joe said. "We have to be sure you don't set off an alarm or something."

Hank squeaked out a nervous smile.

"Now, Hank," Joe said, "there is a car outside with two men in it. Both have a clear view of this place. There's a rifle pointed right at the door. If I don't walk out first, they shoot. Got it?"

Hank nodded.

"You'll also notice I didn't bring any bag to fill up. I only need what I need. So you take me to where I can get myself the cash I'm after, and we're as good as gone."

"Well…" Hank said hesitantly, "how much is it you need?"

"Take me to the cash, Hank."

Hank took a few steps toward the back of the bank. When he saw that Joe was following behind, he walked with a quicker pace. Hank came to a large safe behind the main bank counter. With his hands still tied he wiggled in a key and turned it. He began to twist a dial on the face of the safe. He pulled at the lever. The safe did not open.

"Sorry," Hank said.

"It's okay. Try it again."

Hank put his shaky hands on the dial and began to turn it once more.

"So how come you're not married, Hank?"

"Never did meet the right woman, I guess."

"There's still time. There's always time. You seem like a nice fella."

Hank pulled at the lever and the weighty safe door creaked open.

"Well done, Hank." Joe said. "Now have a seat on the ground. Fold your legs and put your hands in your lap."

Once again Hank did as he was told.

Joe took a good look at the stacks of cash in the safe. There wasn't an abundance of bills, but there was certainly enough to suit his needs. Joe began to line his waistband with the short piles of bills. He counted out two hundred dollars first and then kept on stuffing. For the first time Joe's blood began to course and he could feel his heartbeat race.

"Okay," Joe said, "it's time to go."

Joe reached down and helped Hank to his feet. As directed, Hank closed the safe and took back his ring of keys. Joe took the keys from him.

At the front door Joe removed the twine cuffs and placed them back in his pocket.

"You ready, Hank? Just like before. We're going to walk back to the car and you're going to get in first. I'll give you the keys and we go home. That simple. Got it?"

Hank nodded.

Joe was first outside. Hank soon followed. After Hank locked the front door, Joe made sure to nod out into the distance as if he was signaling someone. He made certain that Hank saw him do it.

Hank was first to get back into the car. Joe took the seat beside him and handed him the keys.

"Let's go," he said.

Hank wasn't shaking anymore. Joe wasn't certain how he felt about that, but he was sure to keep a close watch on the man and the pistol always pointed at him.

They pulled up the driveway and stopped in front of Hank's house.

"Okay, Hank. You're going to stay in this car for twenty minutes. If you think it's only been fifteen, stay longer. Those men in the car, they'll be watching. You come out too early... well, you just don't want to do that. You understand?"

Hank nodded.

"Tell me you understand."

"I understand."

"What're you gonna do?"

"Stay in the car for twenty minutes, no less."

"Hank," Joe said, putting his gun away, "this is goodbye."

Joe got out of the car and walked down the drive, turning back to look at Hank several times. He turned the corner and was out of sight. Joe began to run back to his car, holding tight to his waistband and the contents therein. With a rush of adrenaline coursing through his body, Joe slammed down the hood of the truck and leapt into the seat. He started it right up. And, with an audible, window-rattling scream of delight, Joe hit the pedal and peeled away.

Buck was doing circles around the room, practicing walking with his crutch.

"You bring me chocolate?" he asked when Joe walked in.

"Better," Joe lifted the bottom part of his shirt to reveal his belt of cash. Buck's eyes lit up.

"Holy shit. How much you get?"

Joe started pulling out stacks of bills and laying them on the wooden table. Joe took the two hundred and put it aside. What remained was just over two thousand dollars in both large and small bills.

"Not bad for a night's work," Buck said. "Did you have any trouble?"

"None," Joe said with a smile.

"Looks like you enjoyed yourself."

"First thing tomorrow, we pay off the doc and get out of town."

"Where we goin'?"

"Anywhere but here."

Joe lifted a handful of cash and put it to his nose.

"You think it's wise to be sauntering back ta town tomorrow?" Buck asked.

"No, that wouldn't be wise at all. I'm sure the place will be crawling with laws."

"Then how you gonna pay the doc?"

"I'm not. You are."

"I'm gonna do it?"

"In the morning. You'll drive into town and hand him the cash, then come back and get me and we'll leave this place behind."

"I'm in no shape to drive."

"Your foot broken?"

"Well, no, but —"

"Then this is the way it's gotta be. Drive into town, pay the man, and come back and get me."

Buck picked up a wad of cash and like Joe took a sniff.

"We're outta food, you know."

"Too late to do anything about that now. Let's just try to get a few hours' sleep."

Chapter 23

When the sun came up the next morning, Joe had already been awake for some time. He'd managed to get a bit of sleep, though he was still too excited for a proper rest as his mind raced with thoughts of the day ahead. He reached over and nudged Buck, who was sleeping like a bear in winter.

"Get up," Joe said. "It's time to go."

Buck took a few extra minutes to rouse himself. Sleep had come easily to him the past few nights, and his exhausted body welcomed it. When Buck got to his feet, Joe noticed that more color had returned to Buck's face, and that his eyes had become less glassy.

"You know where you're going?" Joe asked.

"It ain't hard, you know. You told me five times."

Joe wrapped the two hundred dollars in a cloth and handed it to Buck. Buck wedged it into his pocket, though part of the bulky mass still protruded.

Joe helped Buck into the truck. The step up caused him issue, but once he was inside, his leg seemed not to bother him much.

"I'll be waiting," Joe said.

Buck nodded and closed the truck door. Joe watched as he drove off.

Back inside the farmhouse Joe began to tidy the room. He wanted it to seem as though no one had been there. He put the mattress back upstairs along with the remainder of the clothing. He pulled the wooden table back into the center of the room and turned it upside down. He figured that should anyone venture through and see a dustless top, it might arouse suspicion. Once he had the inside of the house back in a state of neglect, he began to do the same for the back yard, dispersing the various pieces of human evidence. He threw the rocks and wood back into the forest. He covered the fire pit with dirt.

With his father's knife tucked in his waistband and Arland's rifle over his shoulder, Joe carried the remainder of the articles into the woods. He reached the cave and dug a small hole with his hand just inside the opening. Into the hole he placed the rope, the can of oil, and his hatchet. He buried them all.

Emerging from the cave, Joe paused to breathe in the air and take in his surroundings. He listened as the water softly lapped against the rocks. Out of the corner of his eye he caught a flicker of movement that turned out to be just a stone-colored starling pecking at the ground.

He began to make his way back to the farmhouse. When he'd reached the edge of the woods, he heard the sound of a car door closing. He peered at the side of the house in the distance. Then the sound of a second door opening and closing came from the same direction. Now suspicious and concerned, he stopped in his tracks. He returned swiftly to the woods and ducked behind the trunk of a large tree.

It did seem too quick for Buck to be back so soon, but that was still a possibility. Joe peeked out from behind the tree but saw nothing. He took a few hurried steps deeper into the woods and made his way sideways, hoping to get a better look at the front of the house. He scuttled along the tree line, taking care not to expose himself for long moments.

Joe took the rifle from his shoulder and got down on his stomach. The vehicle that stood empty in front of the house was not the Ford truck in which Buck had left on his errand. It was a car Joe had never seen before. He grew nervous.

Through the window of the house Joe saw movement, though he could not make out a form. He took the black rabbit's foot from his pocket and held it in his hand. He rubbed it with his thumb.

The back door of the house opened and a man appeared. Joe lowered his head. The man stood on the porch and looked out into the yard. He wore a black suit and a black hat. He looked like a lawman. The man walked down the steps and approached the mound of dirt where the fire pit had recently been covered. He squatted down beside it. A second man came out from the back door.

"Well?" he said.

"Don't know," the man in the black suit said.

The second man came down the steps, wearing a similar black suit. The second man didn't stop at the fire pit but instead made his way past it to the back of the yard. Joe got down even lower.

As the man got closer to Joe, his face became clearer. It was red and purple and banged up badly. The man also walked with a limp. Joe tilted his head to the side just a bit to get a better look.

At the foot of the yard, looking out into the woods, was Henry, evidently not dead from the crash into the tree in Billingston.

As quietly as he could, Joe turned the rifle toward the yard. He took aim at Henry. His heart beat down onto the soft ground below, and he could feel the thumps through his whole body. Henry stood fifty yards away, looking, listening.

"Anything out there?" the first man asked.

"They were here," Henry said.

Henry held his gaze on the woods. Joe put his finger on the trigger. He had a shot. It wasn't a clean shot but one he could take if he had to.

Joe took his eyes off Henry for just a split second, enough to see a car whiz by on the road in front of the house. Luckily it wasn't Buck.

"Let's head into town," the first man said. "If they was here, someone would have seen 'em."

Henry stood motionless at the edge of the forest. Joe closed one eye and took careful aim. His finger curled tightly around the trigger.

"You're right," Henry said, finally turning away from the trees.

He began to backtrack and joined his cohort now standing beside the fire pit. The two men walked around the side of the house and approached their car. Joe tried his best to get a look at the automobile. Any distinguishing features would do: the plates, the color, anything that might help him identify it later.

The two men sat in the car for what seemed like an eternity. Joe prayed that Buck would not return. The car's engine turned and the two men pulled out and headed in the direction of Wyla.

Once the sound of the engine was long gone, Joe sprung from the forest and ran to the front of the house. He got down on one knee and peered around the bushes at the roadside. He watched the back of the black car as it drove away into the distance. The road was straight for some length, but soon enough the car was out of sight behind a cloud of dust and the lowering horizon.

Joe took to his feet and walked out into the middle of the road. He held the rifle despondently in one hand, down by his waist. If Buck was heading back at that moment, he was sure to be discovered.

The sound of another car engine approached. Joe got off the road. He turned around but saw no car coming. Then, like a lion at its prey, a truck sprung from the tall wheat grass across from the farmhouse. Buck skidded to a stop on the road.

"Get in," he snapped.

Shaking with surprise, Joe flung open the door of the truck and jumped in. Buck took off in the opposite direction.

"How did you –"

"Saw the car out front. Who was it? What'd they want?"

"It was Henry, and some other guy."

"Henry? The Colonel's man? He ain't dead?"

"Apparently not."

"And they didn't see you?"

"I was in the woods. I almost came running out when they pulled up. Thought it was you. What took you so long, anyway?"

Buck reached down into his lap and pulled out a half-eaten block of chocolate.

"Told you I had a hankerin'," he said.

"You get the money to the doc?"

"Taken care of."

"Good."

"Now where?" Buck asked, taking a healthy bite of chocolate.

"First things first. Get me to a telephone. There's someone we need to talk to."

Chapter 24

There was a public phone at the service station fifty miles out. Buck and Joe made sure no one was near before placing a call.

"Hello," a voice at the other end said.

"Get me Gumpy," Joe said.

"Ain't no one here by that name."

"Willy, put Gump on. I know he's there."

"Who is this?"

"It's Joe."

There was a pause on the other end.

"Hold," Willy said.

Joe tried his best to keep his voice down, it being a public phone and all. He held out the earpiece for Buck to listen in.

"Where are you?" Gump asked.

"How did they find us, Gump?"

"How did who find you?"

"You know damn well who."

"You need to settle down and mind your manners, boy."

"You ratted us out."

"I did no such thing."

"Like hell."

Gump paused his usual pause.

"You shoulda called me, Joe. I coulda helped you."

"I couldn't call."

"And why's that?"

"We had other business."

"Why don't you come back here and we'll take care of this?"

"How's that?"

"We'll work something out."

"You saying you'll protect us?"

"That's what I'm sayin'."

Joe looked at Buck. Buck shrugged his shoulders.

"Okay," Joe said, "we'll come back."

"Good. When will you be here?"

"Two days. We'll be there in two days."

"Shouldn't take more than a day. Why the holdup?"

"We have to make a stop on the way back… in Billingston."

"Two days, then."

Joe hung up the phone and placed it back on the wooden ledge. He and Buck just looked at one another.

"Somethin' still ain't right," Buck said.

"You hear what he said at the end there?"

"Which part?"

"The part about it taking us only a day to get back. How could he know it would only take us a day to get back?"

"'Less he was assumin' we were in Wyla."

"Which is where the Colonel's men came looking. They've been talking."

"You were right."

"They want us dead, Buck."

"That why you told 'im we'd be stoppin' back in Billingston?"

"Let 'em think we're heading in their direction. Buy us some time at least."

"You think Gump'll have someone waiting in Billingston?"

"We're not going to be there to find out."

Joe looked around. He eyed the service man still filling up the car with gas.

"All right," Joe said. "We need to get going west. We need new clothes, and we need a new car."

"What we gonna do about Gump?"

"Don't know yet. That's something we gotta figure out."

Buck paid the attendant for the gas and an Oklahoma road map, and the pair was soon back on the road, heading in the opposite direction of Billingston.

In only an hour's time Joe and Buck reached Granite Falls. The town would be as good as any to get what they needed before making a run.

Joe parked the car behind a building, out of the way of prying eyes. The Colonel had people all over the state. Joe and Buck knew they couldn't take unnecessary chances.

A clothing store was their first stop. Buck decided on a gray pinstriped suit, one just like he'd always wanted. Joe went with something more casual, hoping to attract less attention. They each purchased a few days' worth of additional clothing. Buck bought a new hat: a dark burgundy fedora with a black ribbon wrapped around it. And though they considered just stealing a car to replace the truck, Joe thought it better to purchase one with the cash they had remaining from the bank job.

"We already got enough people after us, what with Gumpy and the Colonel joining up," he explained to Buck back in the truck.

"Don't forget about the laws, too," Buck added.

"For the shootings in Billingston *and* the bank in Wyla."

"We really got ourselves into it this time, huh?"

"Strange how it all happened. Just a few days ago and we were nobodies with nothing."

"We still got nothin'."

"Nothing but the entire state after us."

"Don't seem right, does it?"

"No, it doesn't."

It was the first time Buck and Joe had taken stock of their current predicament. Neither was left with a happy feeling.

"Pull out that map," Joe said.

Buck unfurled the paper and located Granite Falls. "Closest spot is..." – his finger traced the road west out of town – "...Buford."

Joe leaned over and took a closer look at the map.

"Okay. Take the truck and head there now," he said, pointing to the map. "We'll meet at the end of this road, beside this creek. I'll get us a new set of wheels and meet you there in a few hours."

"You think it's a good idea to split up like that?"

"Henry made it out of Billingston alive, which means he knows you got a bullet in you. You get out of town and out of sight. I'll meet you in a few hours at the end of that road."

Buck nodded.

Joe got out of the truck and smacked on the hood as he walked by. Buck started the engine to do as planned. He pulled out from behind the building and drove off through the streets. He was out of Granite Falls just after noontime.

Joe walked down the street. It looked like a nice town, one not unlike Wyla. The main street was mostly quiet, but people were out, going about their business on an otherwise ordinary day. Joe strolled along, looking in shop windows and nodding to passersby.

A car began to approach from behind. It was going slow enough to make Joe uncomfortable, so he quietly ducked into a diner he was passing. The car drove past without a second look. Joe looked up to see the man behind the counter smiling at him. He walked over casually and took a seat at the counter.

"What can I get for ya?" the man in white asked.

"What's good?" Joe asked.

"Made up a batch of buttermilk hotcakes this mornin'…"

"Sounds good."

"Side o' corn beef hash?"

"And a coffee."

"Comin' right up."

Joe reached down the counter and picked up a newspaper that an earlier patron had left behind. He looked through the pages hoping not to see anything too familiar. He read a few articles about local happenings and, happily, saw nothing about a few dead gangsters upstate.

"Shame what happened," a man a few seats away from Joe said.

"Come again?"

The man shuffled down a seat to get closer to Joe.

"I say shame about the fire, doncha think?"

Joe flipped back to the front page of the paper.

"Oh, yeah, shame."

"Them bastards are just running wild, I tell ya."

The man looked to be in his thirties. He was well dressed in a suit and tie, and his hair was greased back with what looked like an entire bottle of cream.

"That fire wasn't no accident, if you ask me, thank you very much," the man said.

"Is that right?"

"You don't think?"

"Couldn't say."

"Course they did it. Think they run this town, they do."

The server came back with Joe's coffee. He placed it down in front of him and looked around the restaurant.

"I may have something stronger, if that sort of thing interests ya," he said softly.

Joe looked to the man on the stool two down from him. He gave Joe a wink.

"I might be interested, sure," Joe said.

"And how do you like your coffee? Dark or light?"

"Dark would be fine."

"Dark it is."

The server disappeared into the back.

"You ain't from around here, are ya?" the man on the stool said.

"Just here visiting, on my way back home today."

"Carl Ballard," the man said, holding out his hand.

"I'm… Jim."

"Fine ta meet ya, Jim."

Carl gave Joe a good look-over.

"Say, mind if I ask you something?"

Joe didn't answer, but that didn't stop Carl.

"How would you like to get your hands on some of the latest and most desirable stationery items you can find? I got some of the finest goods you'd ever want to see. Paper, ball-point pens, envelopes of all shapes…"

The man tugged a big brown case from the floor up to his lap.

"Thanks, but no," Joe said. "Like I said, I'm just visiting."

"Are you sure? Why don't you just let me show you –"

"Maybe after lunch, Mr. Ballard?" Joe interrupted.

The server had arrived with Joe's lunch and a teacup half filled with a dark brown liquid.

"Call me Carl."

"Okay, Carl. Perhaps after my lunch."

"Well… Cheers, then," Carl said, raising his own teacup with a smile.

Joe nodded and took a sip of the drink. The liquid burned his throat going down. He did all he could not to cough.

"Not bad, huh?" Carl said.

Joe smiled.

"So what do you do?" Carl asked.

"I work a farm."

Joe dug his fork into the pile of hotcakes.

"You?" Carl laughed. "You work a farm?"

"Yeah, I do. Why do you find that funny?"

"Just the look of you, that's all. What with your fancy new clothes an' all. Kinda small for farmwork too, doncha think?"

Joe took his eyes off his plate and glared at Carl.

"Okay, okay," Carl said. "I didn't mean ta insult ya. Just runnin' my mouth is all. Say, I grew up on a farm myself. Not too far from here. But now it's the salesman's life for me."

Joe took another bite of his lunch.

"I find the life suits me," Carl went on. "People tend to trust me, tell me I got a good face. I can't say I see it, but who am I to argue? Why, I could sell just about anything to anyone, any day. Just yesterday –"

"I don't suppose you know where I could find a car for sale?" Joe asked.

"Hmm," Carl said. "Let me think. You know, I don't know that I do."

"There'd be a fee in it for you."

"A fee, you say?"

Carl moved over one more stool so that he was sitting directly beside Joe.

"Now let me think about it again. I don't know anyone off the top of my head…"

"Sure ya do," the man in white said.

"I do?" Carl asked.

"Ol' man Tawbry is always looking to unload a car or two."

"Hell, that's true," Carl said. "I can take ya to see ol' man Tawbry."

"Who's that?" Joe asked.

"Local man," said Carl. "Bit of a strange one, if you ask me. Used to own the service station till his son ran him out. Now he buys and sells all kinds of things. If he doesn't have somethin' to suit your needs, he sure would know who does."

"If you wouldn't mind…"

"Always happy to help… for a fee."

Carl winked and smiled and poked his elbow at Joe.

"Okay, then. Let me finish up and we'll go see your friend."

After Joe paid the bill and thanked the man in white, he got into Carl's car and the salesman drove across town, talking all the way.

Old man Tawbry's house looked like a library from the outside: a tall, square, white-bricked building that stood out from the rest in the area. It also looked like a swap meet, with all sorts of things, apparently for sale, packed onto the front porch and strewn out across the front lawn. The goods ranged from vases and tea sets to car parts and appliances.

"Mr. Tawbry!" Carl called out from the front yard. "Mr. Tawbry, it's Carl Ballard here!"

An old man came out from the front of the house.

"I ain't buyin'!" Mr. Tawbry shouted back. "Be on yer way."

He turned to go back inside.

"No, no, Mr. Tawbry," said Carl, laughing in Joe's direction to shrug off the embarrassment. "I brung you a feller lookin' to buy."

"Oh, why didn't you say so?" the old man said. "Come on up."

Joe followed Carl up to the house to meet the old man.

"Winston Tawbry," the man said, holding out his hand.

"This here's Jim," Carl answered before Joe could speak.

"Nice to meet you," Joe added.

"We got all sorts o' things here," Mr. Tawbry said. "Got this here knife and fork set just today. I can let it go for only –"

"I was hoping to find a reliable automobile," Joe interrupted. "You have anything that would suit me?"

"Have I got anything that would suit you?" Mr. Tawbry said. "Follow me, son."

Joe and Carl followed the old man to the back of the house. He walked slowly, hunched over and dragging one bad foot behind the other. He had a spring in his step, but it was one that hadn't been oiled for a long while.

Mr. Tawbry swung open the old white door of a wooden building. Inside were two horrible looking pieces of mangled metal.

"So," Mr. Tawbry said. "Whaddaya think?"

"Well," Joe said, "I was hoping for something... in better shape."

"How much better?"

"A lot better. Like I said, I need something reliable, something sturdy. I have money, you know, and plenty of it. You show me something good and I'll pay."

"How much money?"

"More than these are worth put together."

Joe pulled out a thick wad of cash and fanned it in the air.

"Well, why didn't you just say so?" Mr. Tawbry said with a blistering smile. "Follow me this way."

The three men walked back to the front of the house. Mr. Tawbry led them to the street.

"Whaddaya think?" the old man said, proudly displaying a car in pristine condition.

"Is this… your car?" Joe asked.

"Heavens, no," Mr. Tawbry said, unconvincingly. "It's for sale, it is, sure as the sun come up."

"How much?" Joe asked.

"Well, see here," the man said, wobbling right up to the car. "This here is a 1924 Buick Master. It's a fine automobile, in fine condition. Barely ever been ridin'."

"Fine indeed," Joe said. "What's that color? Black?"

"No, no, it must be hard to see in the sunlight. That's a dark blue. Only a couple hundred miles on 'er."

"How much?" Joe asked again.

"Well, let me just see," said Mr. Tawbry, looking up to the sky. "I say you can have it for four hundred."

"Four hundred?"

"Plus my finder's fee," Carl added with a wink.

Joe wasn't concerned about the money. He had more than enough to pay for it twice over with the cash in his pocket, even if the price was more than the car was worth brand new. But there was something about being taken for a fool that didn't sit well with him.

"Thank you for your time, Mr. Tawbry. I'll be on my way now."

"Okay, okay, hold on there, boy. That was just my opening offer."

"I can let you drive away for, say, three hundred seventy-five."

"Three hundred," Joe said.

"Three sixty."

"Three fifty, and you pay Carl here a finder's fee out of your end."

"Deal."

Mr. Tawbry threw out his hand. Joe shook it.

"Let me get you the key."

Mr. Tawbry waddled up to the house. Joe reached into his pocket and pulled out a stack of cash. Carl's eyes lit up like Christmas lights.

"You sure you won't be needing any envelopes or –"

"Not now, Carl, I'm counting."

Joe thumbed out three hundred and fifty dollars and stuck the rest of the hefty wad back in his pocket.

"Here you go, friend," Mr. Tawbry said, handing Joe the keys to the car.

"Thank you, sir."

Joe didn't dally. He had no business left or any other reason to stay in Granite Falls. He handed the old man his money and made for the driver's seat. He started up the car and with a nod of his head squealed away down the road.

Looking in the rearview mirror, Joe saw Mr. Tawbry waving his arm through the air as he drove away in the old man's car.

Chapter 25

Joe pulled to the end of a short dirt road and stopped near the shore of the creek. He got out of the car.

"Buck?" he called out.

Buck emerged from behind a tree.

"Where's the truck?" Joe asked.

"In the bushes, just there."

Buck pointed off to the side but was too busy looking over the new car to offer more details.

"Buick," Buck said.

"Yeah."

"She's real nice, Joe."

Joe headed to the shore and knelt down beside the creek. He cupped water into his hands and took a drink.

"We need to do something with the truck," he said to Buck, though he was addressing the great wide emptiness beyond the water.

Joe got up from his knee, and he and Buck made for the old Ford.

After they had taken all their belongings out, Buck put the truck in neutral, and Joe got behind and began to push. Buck helped as best he could with the pushing from the driver's side but only made it one heavy step before giving up and wincing in pain.

The few shoves were enough to get the heavy mass moving. Soon the truck began to roll on its own as it caught the top of a decline. Buck and Joe stood watching as their old, trusty hunk of metal and rubber glided backwards down the hill before hitting a tree and coming to a violent halt, the front wheels lifting off the ground as the rear made impact.

"You think that'll do it?" Joe asked.

The cousins looked at one another. They each smiled and headed toward the truck.

The old Ford was ablaze when the two got into the Buick together. Joe hid his rifle under the seat and took position behind the wheel.

"Got anywhere special in mind?" he asked.

"Tell me about the bank job again."

Joe looked out the front windshield.

"Hey, Buck," he said, "you see that?"

Buck leaned forward and looked in the direction of Joe's gaze.

"What? What am I looking at?"

"Over there? At the end of the road?"

"I don't see nothin'."

"There, beside that willow, the white thing. Is that a car?"

"Can't really tell."

Joe leaned forward as far as he could go.

"You didn't stop anywhere on your way here, did you?"

"Stopped for lunch."

"You did?"

"I was hungry."

"Did you talk to anyone?"

"I dunno, maybe."

"Colonel's got people all over the place, in every town. You show up in a diner with a bullet wound and leave in the truck that Gump probably told them to look out for…"

"How can we be sure that's the Colonel's men, if that's even a car at all?"

"We can't."

"So what do you suggest we do, then?"

"I don't know."

"Start drivin', slowly," Buck said. "Let's see if they move."

Joe turned on the car. He put it into first gear and let up on the brake. The short dirt path that led to the creek only allowed for a little leeway before they would be back to the main road. Joe stopped the car before the intersection.

"That's a car," he said. "And there's someone in it."

"Yeah, I see 'em now," Buck said. "Hit it, Joe, let's get outta here."

Joe turned the wheel and shot out. The car hit the main road with a skid and took off westerly. Buck turned around quickly.

"Nothin'. They ain't movin'."

Joe felt a moment of relief.

"Hang on," Buck said. "Here they come, Joe."

Buck turned to face his cousin.

"They're followin'."

Joe shifted gears, lunging the car forward.

Buck reached under the seat and pulled out Joe's Winchester. He laid it on Joe's lap as he drove. He reached into his waistband and pulled out his pistol.

"We either gotta lose 'em or shoot 'em," Buck said, "and they're catchin' up."

The sound of a gunshot rang out.

"They're shootin'!" Buck yelled.

"Hang on."

Joe yanked the wheel and turned the car down a side road at the very last second. He turned the wheel again and pulled into an open field.

"Take it easy!" Buck yelled, holding his leg.

"How close are they?"

"That bought us a little bit of room, but they're still comin'."

The car rumbled through the field. Somewhere near the middle Joe slammed on the brakes and the car came to a stop atop a small mound. Not bothering to turn off the engine, he leapt from the driver's seat and out into the open. He got down on one knee. Buck stepped out of the car as quickly as he could but stumbled on his bad leg. He got up and began to fire.

Joe closed one eye, took a breath, and shot at the car barreling down upon them. The first shot entered the windshield and hit the driver square in the forehead.

"I think you got 'im!" Buck yelled.

"Only one," Joe said.

The white car slowed but maintained its line. It was still headed straight for them. Joe could see the second man reaching for the wheel. He closed his eyes and took a second shot. He hit the man in the shoulder, knocking him back into his seat. He pulled back the bolt and closed his eye again. The car was only thirty yards away and gaining quickly. Joe took a third shot, this time hitting the second man in the side of the head. The white car rolled up the small hill. It hit the back of the Buick with minimal force. Joe held the gun up to his shoulder, waiting for even the slightest movement from inside.

Nothing moved. The white car was still, the windshield painted with spatters of blood.

Buck limped to the side of the car, his pistol out in front of him.

"They're dead," he said.

Looking in the window, Joe dropped his gun from his eye.

"Turn off the car," Buck instructed.

Joe approached the white vehicle, reached in, and turned off the engine. The car sputtered and died.

"Colonel's men?" Joe asked, looking at the limp bodies inside.

"What else?" Buck said. "Let's get 'em off the hill. Don't need anyone else seein' us."

"Joe opened the door, put the car in reverse, and like the truck only minutes before, the white car began to roll away down the slight decline. It came to a stop near the edge of the field.

Buck sat down on the side of the hill. He needed to rest his still-aching leg. He and Joe stared down at the white car amid the yellow and green grass.

"Colonel ain't never gonna stop chasin' us, Joe," Buck said.

Joe looked over at his cousin.

"They're gonna find us, and they're gonna kill us," said Buck.

Weary himself, Joe took a seat on the hill.

"We gotta do what we gotta do to look out for ourselves," said Buck, rubbing his leg below the wound. "And you know it."

Buck took his eyes off the white car and looked Joe dead in the eyes.

"We gotta kill 'em first," he said.

Chapter 26

It wasn't unusual for Joe to spend the night in the woods. After a visit to the store for a small tent, some sleeping bags, and many other supplies they would need, he and Buck found a quiet clearing deep in the Oklahoma forest where they set up camp.

Both Buck and Joe were wary of staying out in the open, so the confines of the woods suited them well. The Colonel had men working for him throughout the state, and it would be near impossible to identify who exactly those men were. Even if certain members of the community didn't directly report to him, an innkeeper or shop owner might find opportunity in aiding the man of growing power and influence.

They had decided to stay in Oklahoma, at least for the time being, and that meant staying out of sight if they meant to get a good night's sleep. Going back to Kansas was not an option, and while running to a faraway corner of the country seemed like a viable alternative, the cousins knew that if they did, they'd be looking over their shoulders for the rest of their years.

Buck stoked the fire. Joe sat on a log and held a wad of minced meat secured to the end of a stick over the flame. Even though they were there to live like vagabonds, they meant to use their newly acquired funds not to eat like ones.

"And what about Gump?" Buck asked.

"If the Colonel goes away, Gump will go away too."

"You mean to say that he'd forget everything if we got rid of the Colonel?"

"I don't know if he'd forget it all, but his problems would be all but gone. He wouldn't have to worry about retaliation anymore, and all the territory the Colonel carried would be free for the taking. Killing the Colonel would be the best thing we could do for Gump."

"I'm sure there's someone just waiting for the Colonel to bite it, someone working for him, ready to take over."

"Yeah, there *was*. His name was Arland Garry."

"There'll be others."

"Could be," Joe said, testing the temperature of the meat with his fingers. "Even if that's so, we'll have done them a favor too."

Buck handed a blue metal pot to Joe. Joe dropped the ball of meat into it and placed it on the log beside him. Buck struggled to maneuver but eventually managed to take a seat on the log.

Lit only by the moon and the glow of the fire, Joe opened a can of black beans and a can of tomatoes and emptied them both into the bowl. He used a hunting knife to break up the meat and mix all the ingredients together. Joe placed the bowl atop the fire to warm up.

"Where do we even begin?" Buck asked, pulling a cigarette from a fresh pack.

"Beats me."

"We can't simply go after 'im. He'll see us comin' a mile away."

"More than a mile, I suspect."

Joe got up and stood over the fire.

"It's not like we even know what he looks like, or where he lives," Buck said.

"We know he's in Oklahoma."

"You sure 'bout that?"

"No."

Joe took the bowl off the fire. He portioned out half its contents into a second bowl and handed it to Buck.

"I think we lay low for a bit," Joe said, poking at the food with a metal fork. "Give you time to heal. There are a lot of people looking for us right now. The more we move around, the easier it will be for them to get hot on us."

"You think the laws'll catch on?"

"Can't say."

"Maybe we should just turn ourselves in, may be better than what would happen if the Colonel gets us."

"I'm not going to the pen, Buck. I won't do it."

"I was just makin' a joke."

Buck and Joe ate their supper. When he was done, Buck took a seat on the ground, leaned his back against the log and looked up. The sky was clear and dark and peaceful. Their surroundings were quiet, the kind of quiet you only get when no one else is around for miles. There was nothing to keep them company but the sounds of the wind in the trees and the birds all around.

"Lotta stars up there," Buck said.

"Yup," Joe said, not bothering to look up.

After a while Joe set up the small tent and readied the rest of the provisions. He placed all the food in a sack and tied the sack to a rope. He threw one end of the rope over a tree branch and lifted the bag of food a good twenty feet in the air. It was well out of the reach of anyone, or anything, that couldn't undo the knot that Joe used to secure the rope to the base of the tree.

"Might as well get some sleep," Buck said, struggling to his feet.

Buck was still making use of the crutch Joe had made for him, though his steps were getting stronger by the day.

"I'm gonna stay awake a little longer."

"Suit yourself."

Buck crawled into the tent and rustled about. Soon enough, the sounds ceased and Joe was left alone with his thoughts.

Joe sat awake, staring at the fire. The stillness the forest afforded was time well spent as far as he was concerned. When he began to get tired, Joe reached into his pack and pulled out a brand new book, one he had bought at the store in town. He looked at the cover in the light of the campfire. It read, "*The Great Gatsby* by F. Scott Fitzgerald."

Joe opened the book to the first page and began to read. He wondered if Alfred was doing the same.

Chapter 27

Joe didn't make it into the tent that night. He did, however, make it most of the way through the book, the fire providing enough light to read into the early hours of the morning. He woke up on the ground at first light, the book resting on his stomach.

Buck was still asleep when Joe went down to the pond nearby. He took with him a bar of soap and made a bath of the large pool of water. It was a cloudy day, not ideal for wallowing outdoors. The sky threatened rain.

Getting dressed on the shore, Joe heard a loud rustling in the trees. He froze, not wanting to tempt whatever it was, though he knew if it was an animal large enough to be looking for blood, it would surely pick up his scent with no trouble. Nothing materialized from the bushes, and Joe soon continued to dress and headed back to camp.

Buck was still asleep. Joe took a seat on the log and stirred the embers of the fire. There were clusters of bright reds and oranges still hot from the night before. Another sound emanated from the bushes. Joe rose to his feet and grabbed his rifle. Again nothing emerged.

Joe didn't want to wait to be surprised by an animal. Black bears were known to wander those parts and he wasn't looking to make any new friends.

Joe recalled a trick he'd been taught by a wandering, one-eyed Indian many years before in the woods. He gathered the empty tin cans from the previous night's dinner. He emptied two more cans of beans into the pot and hung it above the still-dying fire. Joe took the four cans down to the river. He washed the insides until they were shining silver. He walked up the bank, collecting small rocks and pebbles and filling each tin to the midpoint. He was making his way back to camp when the cloud cover broke, opening a big blue spot in the sky. Joe looked up. The sun felt good on his face.

Buck crawled from the tent upon Joe's return.

"I thought I heard you," Buck said, only his head and shoulders poking out from the opening.

"I was at the water."

"What you got there?"

"Pebbles."

"What you gonna do with those pebbles?"

Buck wriggled free of the tent and rose to his feet without assistance.

"Hey," Joe said, "no crutch!"

Buck took a few steps and sat down on the log.

"What's fer breakfast?" he asked.

"Beans… and coffee. You grow the fire, the beans are in the pot."

"What're you gonna do?"

"Make sure we don't get snuck up on."

Joe took a can of pebbles and the roll of twine and stuck the hunting knife in his pocket. He walked about twenty paces out into the forest on the southern side of the camp.

"Need help out there?" Buck yelled.

"Not yet."

Joe tied a length of twine around the base of a small tree. He did the same to another tree about thirty yards away. He pulled both ropes until they met each other in the middle. He picked up a fallen branch, one about the length and width of a man's arm. With some difficulty he managed to snap the thick branch into pieces, using a rock as a fulcrum. With the knife and a flat rock, Joe scraped and flattened the tops and bottoms of the branch parts as flush as he could get them.

Joe then shoved the almost-severed lid of the can back inside to its original position. He used a small piece of twine to secure it back in place. He shook the can in his hand. The sound of the pebbles on the metal was tinny and high-pitched like a Mexican maraca.

Joe tied each of the two long pieces of twine around the tin can so that it made one solid unit, the can as near to the middle as Joe's eyes could measure. Joe pulled the ropes taut around the base of the trees; the can hovered about half a foot in the air, rattling in the air as it wobbled. He placed one of the branch pieces under the can. The weight of the can lowered the wood just enough so that it rested lightly on the ground. Joe removed his hand carefully. The can sat well atop the wood. Joe stood by for a few moments, waiting to see if the can would fall of its own weight or if it would be pushed over by a gust of wind.

The can held strong.

Joe flicked the can with the back of his finger. The can wobbled but did not fall.

He reached out and plucked at one of the rigid strings with his hand. As he had hoped, the can of rocks fell from its perch, making a discernable rattling sound as it bounced. The piece of wood even acted as a drumstick of sorts, giving the can something to rap up against until it was eventually knocked over. Joe was pleased with this result and with himself.

Joe was surprising himself with what he could fashion with simple tools when the need arose. It was a skill he had inherited from his father and honed as a youngster, left alone in the forest to prosper or die. On that day Joe's need was for a simple warning system, should man or beast approach the camp. The deep satisfaction he got from building something with his own two hands was never lost. It was a feeling many a man missed out on if he was not inclined to see something through to completion.

"Breakfast is on!" Buck shouted from not too far away.

Joe returned to camp.

"What you smilin' about?" Buck asked.

"Come on, I'll show ya."

"After we eat."

Joe sat down and was handed a bowl of beans. He happily partook of the warm food. His stomach had been rumbling.

"What's this all about?" Buck asked, lifting Joe's book.

"Read it. You'd like it."

"Not much of a reader," Buck said. "Never was."

"If you practice at it, you'll get better."

Buck flipped the book to the middle with one hand and shoveled a spoonful of beans into his mouth with the other.

The pair finished their breakfast and went down to the river to clean their bowls. On the way back Joe had Buck take a longer route.

The low-hanging rope tripped up an already hobbled Buck, sending him to the ground, and sending the can of rocks from its perch and shaking in the air.

"What the fuck!" Buck shouted, wincing.

He tried his best to mute his cry of pain. Joe couldn't help but laugh.

"Now that you know how it works, you can help me with the other sides," Joe said.

"Son of a…" Buck mumbled through his teeth, still on the ground.

"Come on now, you can do it."

Chapter 28

Buck and Joe spent five days and nights in the woods. Buck's leg was healing well. Though the crutch might still have helped, Buck insisted that he no longer needed it. In a ceremony to mark the occasion, Buck chopped the homemade utility into pieces, threw it on the fire, and watched as it heated their supper.

It was only when supplies began to run low that they decided to venture into the nearby town of Jackson Hill. They walked over to where they'd stashed the Buick in the brush, removed its coverings, and drove into town.

Food supplies, a fishing rod, some soap, and fresh clothing were on the shopping list. Joe made a point to purchase another burgundy hat as a gift for Buck.

After a hearty meal at the local diner, the cousins sat in the parked car on the side of the road. They both looked ahead at the Jackson Hill Savings and Loan. They lingered a while before Joe turned on the car and the pair set off back to camp.

In the afternoon Joe caught a fair-sized northern pike with the new fishing rod. When the sun went down, he cooked it up on the fire.

"You think it'll work?" Buck asked, pulling a fishbone from his teeth.

"No one gets hurt," Joe reiterated. "No bankers, no citizens, no laws."

"I got it."

"I'm serious, Buck."

"I said I got it."

"If it comes to it and we shoot back, we aim to miss."

"I suppose it'll hurt 'em enough when we take their money."

"No one is going to lose his living. Banks are insured."

"Whaddaya mean, 'insured'?"

"Banks have insurance. Means if they get taken, the money gets replaced. The government sees to it."

"You don't say?"

Buck tossed his empty plate to the ground.

"I could go for a cold beer right about now."

Through the darkness and over the crackling of the fire, the sound of pebbles against tin struck Joe's ear. Buck must have heard it too. He was the first to pull out his gun. Joe reached for his rifle and the pair stood motionless at the center of camp.

A rustling came from the dark woods.

"Get outta the light," Buck whispered.

Joe followed Buck backwards into the shadows. Both men stood ready, their firearms cocked and pointed. The rustling grew nearer. Buck tilted his head left and right, hoping to catch sight of what approached.

"There," Joe said, pointing in the direction of the tent.

"Is that...?"

Buck took steps back toward the camp. Joe, a little more hesitant, soon followed.

Out from behind the tent a reddish-brown fox scampered toward the light. It stopped and stared at the fire. The fox was the size of a full-grown shepherd dog, healthy and thick all the way through. Its eyes, illuminated by the fire, were dark and piercing, its ears jutting upward like two sprouting leaves. Its tail was dense and round and caressed the surface of the ground as it walked. It had a look of curiosity on its face, intrigued by the sight of fire in the night.

The fox turned its head and stared at the two men now standing only paces in front of it.

"He's not afraid," Buck said quietly.

The fox held its gaze. Buck took a step toward it. The fox dropped its head down nearer the ground. Buck took another step. The fox lifted its front paw. Buck flinched aggressively and the fox scurried backwards a few feet, never taking its eyes off the men.

"Buck," Joe sneered, "take it easy."

Joe decided to take the lead with the animal. He got down low and placed his rifle on the ground. He came eye-to-eye with the fox, on its level. The fox stayed steady. Joe began to crawl closer; the fox still did not move.

"Don't get too close," Buck said.

"He doesn't want to hurt us. You can tell. He's just curious at the light."

"He's a wild animal, Joe."

Joe reached out slowly and took the fish carcass from his supper plate, a few scraps of meat still clinging to the ivory-white bones. He tossed the carcass at the feet of the fox. At the first sight of Joe's movement, the animal flinched its head and straightened his front legs. Joe returned to his unthreatening position and remained still. Buck moved to the side, slowly, and took a seat on the log. The fox's eyes were fixed on Joe, and Buck's movement seemed of no concern.

Joe and the fox stared each other down. Joe leaned back and sat down with his legs crossed in front of himself.

The fox slowly relaxed its front legs. Its white-haired chin bent down toward the fish carcass. Its black nose tickled the air as it took in the scent.

"Go on," Joe said. "Take it."

The fox held its eyes on Joe's.

Quiet moments passed.

The fox then took its eyes off Joe for just a second, long enough to take the fish into its teeth. The fox then looked back at Joe, the bones hanging from its jaw like a freshly killed trophy.

Joe and the fox shared another few moments in silent staring. And then, like a guest taking his leave of a dinner party, the fox turned its back on Buck and Joe and casually scampered back into the darkness.

Chapter 29

Buck and Joe sat in front of a large wooden desk, both dressed in their fine new clothes. Buck wore his new burgundy hat.

The office was small and comfortable, like a sitting room in a lakeside cottage. On the brown walls hung framed pictures of maps and one largemouth bass mounted for display. The desk was adorned with a silver cup of pens atop a green felt desk pad. A pile of unopened letters rested in the center. At the front of the desk a nameplate read "Marshall Bridgewater, Bank Manager." The windows of the room were covered with slender blinds, with the slats on just one side left open so the manager could see out onto the bank floor.

"Sorry to keep you waiting," Mr. Bridgewater said as he entered the room.

He took a seat behind the desk.

"Thank you for seeing us," Joe said.

"It's my pleasure. And what can I do for you today?"

"We'd like to make a withdrawal," Joe said plainly.

"That would be fine, but one of our tellers could gladly help you with that."

"It's a sizable withdrawal, I fear."

"Be that as it may, I -"

Buck leaned back in his chair and pulled out his pistol from his suit jacket. He held it in his lap, pointed at Mr. Bridgewater.

"What is this?" the frightened bank manager said.

"I believe they call it a stickup," Buck said with a smile.

"You can't be serious."

Buck wagged the gun in his hand.

"What part of this looks like we're playin'?"

Mr. Bridgewater raised his hands up.

"Put your arms down," Buck said. "I can see you ain't got no gun."

Joe lifted a brown leather bag and placed it on the table.

"Open that safe behind you and fill the bag."

"There's no cash in there," Mr. Bridgewater said.

"Open the safe," Joe instructed.

Buck got up from his chair and walked around to the other side of the desk, leaning against the corner.

"Go on, open it," he said.

Mr. Bridgewater turned his chair around and reached for the safe's dial. With a few swift motions he spun the wheel and pulled the lever, and the safe door opened.

"You were right," Buck said, peering over the man's shoulder. "Now fill the bag, and place it on the desk."

Mr. Bridgewater emptied the contents of the safe into the brown bag. The second that the bag was full, Joe snatched it from the desk and turned toward the door. He didn't look back.

Buck followed closely behind, backing his way out of the room. Before leaving, Buck winked at the bank manager.

"The Colonel says thanks," he said, putting his gun into his pocket and following Joe out.

Once free of the bank doors, Buck and Joe leapt into the awaiting car and sped off. The bank's alarm bell rang out, but the cousins were already well on their way. Buck let out a scream of joy as the car's engine roared. Joe, too, had an unmistakable smile on his face.

At high speed it took only a minute or so to reach the outskirts of Jackson Hill. Twenty more minutes down the dirt road and they were back at the secluded spot where they had previously stashed the car. Buck and Joe threw the branches and leaves back over the Buick that was nestled comfortably at the bottom of a hill and between two trees. The two men walked briskly, one behind the other, through the woods and back to their isolated camp.

"Oh, man!" Buck said. "That was wild!"

Joe dropped the bag and received his jubilant cousin's energetic embrace.

"I feel like I just won the World Series!"

Buck took off his hat and flung it through the air.

"That ought to get the Colonel's attention," Joe said.

Buck ran over and snapped up the brown bag. He took a seat on the log.

"Open it," Joe said, eager to see the contents.

Buck opened the bag and pulled out a portion of its contents. Like a proud artist displaying his latest masterpiece, Buck held up a thick stack of hundred-dollar 1918 U.S. war bonds.

"Holy shit!" Joe said. "How many are in there?"

"Bag's full."

"Lemme see."

Joe rushed over and grabbed a stack of bonds from the bag. He wanted to feel the paper in his hands.

"There must be... dozens of stacks in there," Joe said.

Buck took off his jacket and threw it down on the log beside him. He used his sleeve to wipe his brow.

"You think this'll make him show his face?"

"It may take some time," Joe said. "Besides, him showing his face is only the first step."

"Whaddaya mean, 'first step'? He pops up and, bam, he's dead."

"We're trying to get the Colonel to come out in the open to find us, sure, but he's already lookin' for us. If we make enough noise and shake him out, maybe someone else finds him first."

"Someone else?"

"The State Bureau of Criminal Identification and Investigation. They already want him about as much as he wants us."

"And if they find him first?"

"They get rid of him for us, one way or another."

"That means..."

Buck thought for a moment.

"That means somewhere along the line we gotta let the Colonel catch up to us."

"We gotta let the Colonel and the laws get close."

"Not yet," Buck insisted.

"Not yet," Joe agreed. "We gotta get the laws absolutely starving to catch him, and get him so sour that he'll stick his neck out."

"And if the laws don't get 'im, we will."

"That's the idea."

Buck changed out of his warm clothes and put on something more befitting the weather – pants alone. The Oklahoma summer was reaching its peak, and often the only respite was to wear as little clothing as possible. Buck and Joe sat on the bank of the river the rest of that day and talked more about their plan, often wading into the water just to cool off.

It was fish again for dinner that night. Joe and Buck laughed and joked under the stars and rehashed the story of the day's triumph. After dinner Buck rolled a cigarette. He lay on his back on the ground and blew the smoke up into the darkened sky, watching the grayness waft and then fade away into the air. After his cigarette he closed his eyes, and it wasn't long until he fell asleep beside the fire.

Joe welcomed the quiet. Often, he found, being alone in the woods was the elixir that soothed his mind the most. And even though his cousin was asleep beside him, Joe could feel that it was just him and the trees. Joe, too, fell asleep beside the fire that night.

It was sometime later that night that something caused Joe to open his eyes at a dark and unknown hour. Joe needed only to look down his nose to see what had woken him. As he peered through the diminished light of the dwindling fire, Joe saw a reddish-brown fox sniffing at his feet.

Chapter 30

In the morning Joe went out to check on the cans of pebbles, expecting to find one on the ground. Instead all four cans were still intact, sitting atop the wood where Joe had left them. It had only taken the fox one misstep to figure out how to avoid the alarm.

Buck returned from the river with two freshly caught fish in his hand. He had risen early and made good use of his time. Buck cleaned and cooked the fish, and he and Joe shared in a hearty breakfast.

"You'll be back by tonight?" Buck asked, sucking the last piece of meat from a bone.

"Should be."

"And then we move on."

"I think we should stay a while longer."

"I know you do. But I think stayin' in one place is a mistake."

"We can talk about it tonight," Joe said, putting his plate aside.

Joe gathered his things and took the walk to the car alone. He removed the branches and leaves, turned on the engine, and pulled up onto the road.

It was nice to drive through the country in no particular hurry. The breeze from the window felt good on Joe's face and across the side of his head.

Joe reached the Tilley farm. He didn't go inside but instead walked around back and to the creek just to hear the sounds and smell the air. He'd never had a chance to say goodbye and only a few days prior thought he might never see the old place again.

Joe stood in the back yard and looked at the house. The once-white structure looked tired. Where bits of white did remain, the paint was off-colored and peeled away from the house, as if it were trying to escape.

Returning to the car, Joe made his way back to the road and arrived at his destination soon thereafter. He got out of the car and walked the rest of the way, about half a mile. He made his way up a sandy path toward a green house that stood alone. Joe walked up the steps and took a breath before rapping on the screen door.

"Joe!" Alfred said, opening the inner door. "Come in, come in!"

Alfred reached out and opened the screen door wide for Joe.

"I told you I'd come," Joe said, taking a step inside.

Alfred put his hands on Joe's shoulders, and even though he had seen him a few weeks prior, he gave Joe a look-over as if he still hadn't done so since he was a boy.

"Marie is just out back," Alfred said. "Come on, she'll want to see you."

He led Joe through the house.

"Can I get you anything? Some lemonade?"

"No, thank you."

They walked out the back door.

"Marie!" Alfred said. "You remember Joseph?"

Marie was hanging a white sheet on the laundry line.

"Well, I'll be!" Marie said, taking a clothespin from between her teeth.

Marie embraced Joe with a warm, welcoming hug.

"Look at you," she said. "My, you've grown. You look… you look just terrific, you do."

Joe smiled and felt bashful. It had been a long time since a woman near to the age of his mother had paid him a compliment or showed him any affection. It was something to which he was unaccustomed.

"Can I get you anything?" Marie asked. "Some lemonade, perhaps?"

"No, thank you, ma'am."

A golden dog came running up to Joe and barked and bounded about at his feet.

"Settle down, Duke. Leave the boy alone," Marie said, swatting at the dog. "Now get!"

"It's okay. I don't mind," Joe said.

He knelt down and the dog came right to his face for a sniff. Joe rubbed the dog's head and ears with both hands.

"He's just excited is all," Alfred said. "Hasn't seen many strangers in a while."

"How old is he?" Joe asked.

"We've had him for five years now," Alfred said. "Tell you what. He seems to like you. Why don't you and I take him for a walk and we can visit?"

"Sounds good," Joe said.

"Be back in time for Sunday lunch," Marie said. "I know how you like to take your time out there."

"We will."

Alfred leaned over and kissed Marie's cheek.

"And you'll be joining us, Joe, won't you?" Marie offered.

"I don't want to impose."

"Nonsense. I won't take no for an answer. I'll set you a plate."

"Okay, then. Thank you."

"Come on," Alfred said, waving him forward.

Joe and Duke followed Alfred around the side of the house, Duke far more enthusiastically. By the time the trio reached the road, the rambunctious dog had settled his pace and strode obediently beside his master.

"I know it's just an animal, but you'd be surprised how much Marie loves him," Alfred said, looking down proudly at the retriever. "She plays modest and might never say, but short of having kids of our own... well, Duke here keeps her company, at any rate."

"You've been gone a lot for work?" Joe asked.

"What's that?"

"You said Duke is good company for Marie."

"I go away from time to time. I been gone more lately, what with the new job and all. Only go for a few days at a time, really. Duke here helps me feel better about it, I s'pose. But enough about that, what about you, Joe? You were supposed to be heading out. I thought I wouldn't see you again."

"I thought I'd stay a while longer."

"You have business in town?"

"No, no business."

"Just here for a visit, then?"

"I'll be heading back to Kansas first thing tomorrow morning."

"Headin' out tomorrow morning myself," Alfred said, leaning over and picking up a stick from the ground.

Alfred led Joe and Duke into a wide-open field of grass. Patches of wildflowers mingled with the unkempt green blades that reached almost to their knees. Alfred hurled the stick into the air ahead. Duke took off like a bullet from a gun.

"Where you headed?" Joe asked.

"Across state, only a few hours from here."

"For work?"

"For work."

Duke came back with the slobbery stick in his mouth. Alfred yanked it from his teeth and sent it flying once more.

"Is there trouble?" Joe asked.

"There's always trouble," Alfred said, smiling.

"I hope nothing too dangerous."

"Just some boys out causing a ruckus."

"If it were just a ruckus, they'd be able to handle it without you, wouldn't they? Must be more than that."

Alfred looked at Joe.

"You really want to hear about it, doncha?" he said with a coy grin.

"I once spent some time in a jailhouse when I was younger. Been interested ever since."

"Is that right?"

"We can change the subject if you'd prefer."

Alfred yanked the stick from Duke's mouth and tossed it once more. Duke brought it back again, a little wetter than the time before. The game continued.

"There are men out there that cause all sorts of trouble, Joseph," Alfred said. "They've been around for a while, but ever since the Volstead they've been causing more and more harm around these parts."

"You're talking about the Colonel," Joe said.

Alfred turned to look at Joe.

"So you've heard of him, have you?" he said. "Of course, it's much more than just one man alone. But he seems to be the one that's calling a lot of the shots. Has been for some time now. Sure, he's got all sorts of hoodlums and thieves running around for him. But this one... well, he's a hard man to get a handle on."

"Do you know his name?"

"His name? Now why would you want to know his name?"

"I just been hearing a lot about him the past few days, that's all."

"Ah, you're talking about the bank in Wyla?"

"Yes, sir."

"Well, I'm headed out tomorrow, first thing. It seems they think he's robbed another one not too far from here, just yesterday."

"How do you know it's him?"

"Didn't say I did," Alfred said. "It seems a bit out of the ordinary for him, truth to tell."

"Why's that?"

"I like to think I know the man, at least a little. Know about his ways and such. These past few bank heists… Well, they seem strange," he said, shaking his head.

"Why do they call him the Colonel, anyway?"

"Story goes," Alfred said, his voice perking, "he was in the war. Was on the front lines, almost from the start. As war goes, all sorts of men were gettin' shot, stabbed, and blown up all around 'im. Whole company was killed down in a foxhole one night, and only the Colonel walked away, just a few scrapes to show for it. After a while other folks started to take notice. Man would walk into battle, man would walk out. Walked in on another day, walked right out again. After a while it became something of a folk tale. Man like that shows up during wartime, well…

"Rumor started that he simply couldn't be killed. Of course that's not the case, but others started following him around like it was. Started calling him the Colonel. Guess they figured if he wasn't gonna die, maybe they might make it home too. Sometimes people will hold on to just about any hope, I guess."

"How do you know that's not the case?"

"What's that?"

"You said folks started thinking he couldn't be killed, but that's not the case."

"Every man dies, Joe," Alfred said, looking somberly at his companion. "So that means every man can be killed. I can't say exactly how he survived the war, or all the troubles he's found since he came back. But he is just a man."

Joe had been listening intently, and he now realized he hadn't paid much mind to where they had walked. If challenged, he'd have a difficult time finding his way back without Alfred.

"One day," Alfred continued, "I'll come face to face with the man, that I can guarantee. And when that day comes, it might just come down to his life or mine."

Alfred's eyes were staid and serious, pointing straight out to the horizon. The tenor of his voice too had changed, becoming more somber. Joe had never heard Alfred speak that way.

"Perhaps we should talk about something else," Joe said.

Alfred's stern demeanor was broken and he smiled at Joe.

"We best be getting back," he said.

Alfred tugged the stick from Duke's mouth and hurled it toward the sky once more.

Marie served up a bountiful lunch consisting of a perfectly cooked roast, mashed potatoes and gravy, and warm peas and carrots. It was an occasion upon which Joe wished he had skipped breakfast altogether. With nearly an entire fish still in his belly, Joe was hardly able to finish half of what he was served.

"Everything okay?" Marie asked.

"More than okay," Joe said. "I just wasn't expecting such a welcome."

"You'll take some with you," Marie said.

"Oh, I couldn't."

"I insist," Marie said from over Joe's shoulder.

She lifted the plate off the table from in front of him. Duke bounced to his feet and followed Marie into the kitchen.

"I started the last book you sent," Joe said.

"Did you?"

"I like it a lot. It's a terrific story."

"I haven't been able to start it myself yet. Don't you spoil it for me."

"I wouldn't dare."

The telephone rang. Marie came through the dining room.

"I'll get it," she said. "No need to get up."

"I wonder who that could be?" Alfred said.

Marie called out for Alfred, who got up from his chair and patted Joe on the shoulder as he passed behind him.

Joe could hear Alfred from the other room, mumbling into the receiver. He got up and took a few plates into the kitchen for Marie. He couldn't hear any better from there.

"I'm afraid I have to go," Alfred said as he joined them in the kitchen.

"It's Sunday, Al," Marie reminded.

"I know it's Sunday, dear. I'm sorry, but I have to go. Joe, can I give you a ride into town?"

"That's okay," Joe said. "I'd like to help clean up here, if that's all right with you, Marie."

"You really don't have to," Marie said, "but I'd enjoy the company all the same."

"Joe," Alfred said, approaching with his arm out in front. "If I don't see you before you go…"

They shook hands graciously.

"It was great to see you, Alfred."

"It was great to see you, Joe. I'll look forward to your letters."

"I'll be traveling some more, but I'll be sure to stay in touch."

"You do that."

And like Duke after the stick, Alfred advanced hastily and disappeared from sight.

Chapter 31

Nathaniel was sitting at his desk in the middle of a bustling newspaper room. His telephone rang.

"Grandma isn't feeling well today," Madeline said.

"That's too bad," Nathaniel said. "Is there anything I can do?"

"No, thank you. I think she just needs to rest."

"So you're calling to cancel, then."

"I think so. I think it would be best. I hope it's not too short notice."

Nathaniel looked at his watch. "I was about to leave in a bit, actually."

"Oh, you were?"

"But if she's not well... Can I ask what's wrong?"

"She barely slept last night. She's coming down with something, I think. She's fallen asleep now and I would hate to wake her."

"Of course, don't wake her. We'll do it again when she feels up to it."

"You know…" Madeline started.

"Yes?"

"Well, I was going to say, if you were about to leave… you could come by for a coffee or something and perhaps she'll wake up."

"I could do that," Nathaniel said.

"I can't promise anything, though. I don't want to push her."

"I wouldn't want that either."

"So, you'll be by, then?"

"I'll see you in about an hour."

"I'll see you then."

Nathaniel was about to hang up the phone when Madeline spoke up.

"Oh, and Nate…?" she said.

"Yes?"

"I almost forgot. I found something I think you'll find very interesting."

"Did you? Okay, now I'll really look forward to it."

The two said their goodbyes and hung up the phone. Nathaniel looked over the various stacks of paper on his desk. After a moment of hesitation he dragged one of the piles into a drawer, grabbed his voice recorder and his bag, and made for the elevator.

Madeline opened the door with her finger to her lips, sure to keep Nathaniel from making any noise.

"I thought she could sleep through a hurricane," he whispered, entering the house.

Madeline smiled and motioned Nathaniel to follow. He did just that. She led him to the kitchen, where she closed the door behind them.

"Tea?" she asked.

"I'm okay."

"Have you had lunch?"

"Yes, thank you."

Nathaniel took a seat at the kitchen table.

"So? What is it you wanted to show me?"

Madeline sat down and placed her hand atop a small, brown wooden box sitting in the middle of the round table.

"This is it?" Nathaniel asked.

"I was down in the basement this morning, and... what can I say? My curiosity got the better of me. I was looking through some of Grandpa's old boxes. Nothing too exciting at first. An old suit, some letters, things like that."

"I don't suppose you found any old photographs?"

"We have plenty of photographs, but they were all taken in Charleston."

"I wouldn't mind seeing those, if that would be okay."

"Of course," Madeline said. "But I think you'll like this more."

"Sorry, go on."

"So, I had never paid much attention to the boxes in the past. You can imagine... But who knew there was so much I didn't know about my grandfather? Well, this morning, I found this with his things."

Madeline slid the brown box across the table.

"Should I open it?" Nathaniel asked, his hands eager to lift the lid.

"Go ahead."

Nathaniel opened the top of the hinged box. Inside was an old white handkerchief, clearly covering something underneath – of that he was sure. Nathaniel reached in and lifted the contents out. As soon as he held the item in the palms of his hands, he knew what it was.

He peeled back the handkerchief. In his hands Nathaniel held an old, black Colt revolver. His eyes lifted and met Madeline's.

"Look at the handle," Madeline said.

Nathaniel looked closely at the grip of the gun. He touched it with his fingers. There were patches of a dark, greasy film on it.

"Oh, wow!" Nathaniel said. "And the Colt insignia is nearly worn… you can barely make it out."

"I don't think we should mention this to Grandma," Madeline said.

"Oh, no. I agree."

"If she wanted us to find it –"

"Yeah."

"At least for now."

"Did you find anything else down there?" Nathaniel asked, finally laying the gun back down in the box.

"Just some old clothes and things. Nothing like this."

Joe pulled back the handkerchief and took one more look at the gun.

"Stay here," Madeline said.

She got up from the table and left the room. When she returned, she did so with a large black photo album. She took a seat at the table, this time opting for the one beside Nathaniel. Madeline opened the book.

"This is Grandpa," she said, pointing to a middle-aged man.

"He looks nothing like I pictured," Nathaniel said.

"What where you picturing?"

"I don't know, really."

Nathaniel smiled. He turned the page.

"This is him and Grandma."

"Wow, she looks so different!"

"This was…" Madeline looked up to the sky, "about forty years ago?"

"They look so happy."

"They were."

Nathaniel turned the page again.

"That must be your mother," he said, pointing to a young girl.

"You keep looking," Madeline said. "I'm going to go check on Grandma."

Madeline got up and left the room in a hurry. Nathaniel made a point to recall that reaction the next time he thought to raise the topic of her mother.

Nathaniel turned the pages. He took a close look at the man in the pictures. He wasn't a big man. He was slim, and even in his older age, rather fair looking, which fit Liza's description well. In most of the pictures he smiled. But it was one picture in particular that caught Nathaniel's attention. There was Madeline's grandfather, caught unaware in the background of a photo. He was looking straight into the camera. In this photo he was not smiling. Nathaniel dipped his head and looked closely. To him there seemed to be a lot more behind those eyes that peered back.

"She's awake," Madeline said, poking her head into the kitchen.

Nathaniel closed the photo album.

"And she's asking for you."

Chapter 32

1924

Joe returned to the campsite and offered Buck Mrs. Winter's leftovers. Buck devoured the food.

"I think it's time to move," Joe said.

"Like I been sayin'," Buck agreed, his mouth full of potatoes.

"We'll spend the night and then be on our way."

"Any place in particular you got in mind?"

"Any town with a bank. We'll head west for now."

Clouds rolled in and threatened rain. The sky turned gray, the temperature dropped, and the wind began to blow. Joe retreated to the tent to read as Buck went down to the river for a swim.

The summer storm that rolled through was not enough to pull Buck from the river. He splashed about through the water, opening his mouth wide to catch the falling rain on his tongue. When he finally did return to the tent site, late in the afternoon, the storm was beginning to move on.

When the last of the rain finally let up, it took with it the daytime sun. The sky opened up just enough to cast a few last shadows and then the night arrived.

Joe had managed to finish his book by then, alone in the tent. He'd closed the book's back cover and immediately thought of Alfred. He wondered where Alfred had been called off to in such a hurry.

It took a while, but Buck was able to get the fire going again with some dry branches he found under a thicket of bushes. He had many a scrape on his hands and arms for the trouble of retrieving them.

Neither Buck nor Joe had much to say that night. Each sat still, watching the flames dance in the humid air. Joe was first to turn in. He left his cousin by the fire and took refuge from the moist ground inside the tent.

Joe awoke sometime later in the night and found that Buck had still not joined him. Joe closed his eyes and fell back to sleep.

Outside the tent the heat had dried the ground, and as on previous nights, Buck had fallen asleep up against the log. There was no telling what time it was when his eyes opened with a start. He looked to the side, out into the darkness. Though the sound did not linger, Buck could have sworn he'd heard the rattling of pebbles against a tin can coming from somewhere in the trees. Buck kept his eyes locked on the darkness in the distance. Though the fire was a mere pittance of what it once was, its light still painted a dark black canvas behind it.

There was a quiet rustling in the bushes. Buck sat up and reached for his pistol. He thought to call Joe but didn't dare make a sound.

A figure began to appear. Out from the shadows the head of the neighborly fox poked. Buck eased and laid his gun to the side.

"It's just you," he said.

The fox was apprehensive but made its way toward the fire one small step at a time. Sniffing at the ground, it approached the metal plate lying beside the fire. It stuck out its tongue and licked at the remnants of gravy that had hardened around the edges.

Buck reached for his plate and lifted from it a piece of fat from the meat Joe had brought back. He dangled it in the air like a worm. The fox's eyes fixed on it. Moments passed and the fox did not move. No matter what Buck tried, the animal was steadfast. Buck got to his knees and wiggled the white, jellylike substance in the air again.

"Come on, you stupid thing, take it," he said.

Buck moved forward. The fox took a step back. Buck and the fox stared at one another. The animal's mouth was wide open as it panted at the air. It lowered its head and looked up at Buck with the sad eyes of a young dog. Buck moved forward again.

"Come on, you stupid –"

Without warning the fox lunged at Buck with a growl. It hit him square in the chest with its front legs, knocking Buck backward and onto the ground. The animal mounted Buck's chest for only a second before Buck was able to roll over, throwing the fox off. The animal lunged at Buck once more and nabbed his shoe in its angry mouth. Buck kicked at the fox with his bad leg, releasing himself from the grasp of his jaw but feeling a sharp pain run through his thigh and hip. The fox shook off the blow and bared his teeth. He growled fiercely. Buck let go of his leg and tried to get to his feet. The animal lunged and made for Buck's legs as he rose. The fox jumped through the air, its mouth agape. Buck turned his head and saw white teeth coming straight for him. He lunged back, hitting the log and falling backwards over it, landing hard on his side.

The fox jumped on top of the log and looked down at Buck with a mean, snarling rumble. It coiled its legs as it prepared to jump onto Buck yet again. And then out of nowhere a gunshot rang through the air. The sound of the blast reverberated through the woods and then left it silent once more. Buck lifted his head. He did not see a fox clamped onto his body. He saw the animal lying motionless on the ground beside him. Buck lifted himself to his elbows. Standing outside the tent with rifle in hand was Joe.

"I don't know what happened," Buck said. "I was tryin' to give him some food."

Joe looked at the fox, dead on the ground. He turned his gaze to his cousin, still on his back, his feet up on the log.

"Get some sleep," he said. "We'll leave at first light."

Joe crouched down and got back into the tent.

Chapter 33

The sun hadn't fully breached the horizon when Joe and Buck got back on the road. Neither mentioned the events of the night prior. Neither had anything to say about it, really. Buck's leg was sore, so Joe was at the wheel. Buck sat beside him with the map stretched out on his lap.

"Next town over is… Bethel," Buck said. "About fifty miles."

"Bethel it is, then."

"Not much but farmland after that. We'll have to keep drivin' a while to find a place to stay."

"That's fine. We should stay on the move."

Buck and Joe reached Bethel and stopped for breakfast there. It was a nice enough town but not one they planned on staying in for very long.

After breakfast Joe and Buck walked right into the bank next door. They followed the same formula they'd used for the previous heist. They met with the cordial bank manager in his office and made their intentions known. This time, however, there was no safe in the man's office. Instead Buck and Joe walked him out to the bank floor with their guns drawn. There were three citizens and two bank employees conducting business that day, and all were quickly made aware of the men with the guns. As instructed, they got down on the ground and covered their heads. Joe stood guard with the rifle as Buck oversaw the withdrawal from the safe.

"There are guns pointed at the front door," Buck told the people on the floor. "If you walk out, you will be shot. If you hit the alarm, you will also be shot. I suggest you stay on the ground, if you know what's good for ya."

He turned to leave.

"Oh," he said, tipping his burgundy hat, "and the Colonel says thank you."

Buck and Joe didn't run but walked from the bank. They reached the car parked in front of the diner and drove off as if nothing were amiss. It was as they were nearing the town limits that Joe thought he heard the sound of alarm bells in the air. He switched gears and the car took off.

All told, they made it out of the bank in Bethel with just over two thousand dollars in cash. Buck couldn't help but count the money as Joe drove on.

"You hear that?" Buck said, lifting his head from the cash.

Joe listened intently.

"Sounds like…"

"It's the laws," Buck said.

He stashed the money back in the bag and turned to look out the back window of the car.

"You see anything?" Joe asked.

"I think so. Dust coming up back there."

"Any cars?"

"I don't... Wait. Yup, it's the laws. Move it, Joe."

"I'm going as fast as I can."

"Then we gotta get off this road."

"What's on the map?"

Buck unfolded the paper with haste.

"Looks like... should be a road comin' up soon on the right. Then nothin' for a while."

"Where's it lead?"

"Capshaw County way."

"Don't know it. You know it?" Joe asked.

"I don't know it."

"It'll have to do."

Joe checked the rearview mirror. No car yet, but the sound of the siren was becoming more distinct.

"How far?" he asked.

"Should be coming up any time now."

Buck turned around and looked out the back window. Joe peered out into the distance ahead. They were coming up an incline.

"Look," Joe said. "If we hit the top of that hill, they'll see us for sure, if they haven't already."

"Looks like a whole fleet of 'em."

"Hang on."

Joe tugged at the wheel, veering the car left off the road and into a field of fescue and weeds. The car rumbled and bumped over the uneven ground. Joe could barely see atop the growth that surrounded the car, but he did not dare let up on the gas.

The car hit an unforeseen decline, and went downward like a bullet. Joe and Buck were both lifted off the seat.

Branches began to hit the windshield, smacking and cracking and breaking off against the metal and glass. Joe tried to regain control, but the wheels of the car were bounding up and off the ground too much for him to steer. With no other option, Joe hit the brakes. The car tried to slow, though the downward momentum paired with the bouncing wheels made it difficult for the wheels to gain any traction. The car heaved forward like an angry bull.

Soon they hit a small ditch in front of an embankment and Joe's side of the car dropped like a boulder, finally bringing the furious machine to a halt.

Buck gathered himself. To his surprise his leg was holding up quite well. As far as he could tell, he had made it through the ordeal unscathed. He perked up his ear. He listened.

"I don't hear 'em," he said. Then looking over at Joe, he said, "Hey! You okay?"

Joe looked back at his cousin.

"You're bleedin'," Buck said, nodding at Joe's forehead.

Dazed, Joe dabbed his brow with his fingers. He pulled them away and looked at a dark stain.

"There's blood," Buck said, pointing to Joe's window and the metal trim above it.

Joe winced and gnashed his teeth in pain. Buck was as far from a doctor as a man could be, but he knew that something was wrong with Joe right away. Joe's face looked blank, his eyes didn't look right, and of course the blood running down his temple was a clear indication.

Buck got out of the car. He walked around to Joe's side to help him out. He peered over the embankment as he passed behind the car, just to see if he could spot, or hear, anyone still behind them.

"Have a seat," Buck said, helping Joe from the car.

He lowered Joe to the ground. Joe lay back against the car in the thick grass. He held his head with both hands.

"What happened?" Joe asked.

"Whaddaya mean? Car hit a ditch."

"A ditch?"

Buck reached into the back seat and fetched a canteen of water. He opened the top and put it to Joe's lips. Joe took a sip.

"You hit your head somethin' good," Buck said, removing Joe's hand to get a better look at the wound.

The cut just below Joe's hairline wasn't long, but it was deep. It looked purple and blue, and the area around it was growing and puffing out like a golf ball.

"We should get you outta here," Buck said.

Buck wrapped Joe's head in a cloth and helped him back into the passenger side of the car.

"What happened?" Joe asked, as Buck got in on the driver's side.

Buck turned the engine. The car did not start. He tried it again. The engine struggled. On the third try the car sputtered to life.

It took several shifts from first gear to reverse to shimmy the car from its position, but eventually Buck was able to free the vehicle. He avoided the ditch and continued on down the hill. He drove slowly and carefully and held Joe in place with a hand on his shoulder.

Once on more even ground, Buck turned the car toward the nearest road on the map, which they eventually reached. The soft dirt was a welcome relief from the rutted ground of the unkempt fields.

Buck sped off.

"What happened?" Joe asked.

Buck looked over at his cousin but did not respond. He had a feeling his answer wouldn't have much effect.

It was nearing an hour later that Buck pulled into one of the farms just outside a small town. Joe had been asleep for half the ride. Buck drove down the winding path that led to the farmhouse. The house was tucked away, far from the road, surrounded by trees and tall corn. A man exited the home and stood on his front porch, looking down on Buck and Joe as the car came to a stop.

Buck emerged from the car.

"Looks like ya had some car trouble," the farmer said.

He pointed at the mangled front on the driver's side.

"Had an accident," Buck said. "Swerved away from a deer and went into a tree."

The farmer came down from his porch to get a closer look.

"He okay?" the man asked, seeing Joe up close.

"Not really, sir. Was hopin' you could offer some help."

The man came to meet Buck by the side of the car, where Buck was helping Joe out.

"He's bleedin'," the farmer said.

"Hit his head, I think."

"Let's get 'im inside."

Joe's legs were weak. He didn't fight the help offered by Buck and the farmer to get him into the house.

"This way," the farmer said. "Let's put him on the bed."

Buck followed the man's directions and helped lay Joe down on a bed in a room at the back of the house.

"What's his name?" the farmer asked.

"It's... Jim."

"Jim," the man said, leaning over the bed.

Joe looked at the man with a blank stare.

"Martha!" the man yelled out. "Martha, get on in here!"

A woman came in from the back of the house.

"Did you call –"

The woman stopped mid-sentence.

"Oh, my!" she said.

"Fellas here had an accident with their automobile. This one here hit his head."

"What can I do?" Martha asked.

"Cold cloths for his head would do."

Martha went to fetch them.

"Thank you," Buck said.

"Name's Randal."

"Eustace," Buck said.

"Your leg okay? Saw you was limpin'."

Martha returned with a wet rag. She handed it to Buck, who placed it on Joe's forehead after removing the cloth that was there to stem the blood flow.

"Looks like the bleeding's slowed," Buck said.

"Thank you," Joe said, looking up at Martha.

"What's going on in here?" a young woman said, entering the room.

"Millie, this here is Eustace and Jim. They've had an accident."

"What kind of accident?"

"One with their automobile," Martha said.

"On the road not far from here," Buck added.

Millie flashed a quick smile.

"We should let this one rest," Randal said. "Why don't we go on and leave him be for now. You boys will be all right to stay here the night, I reckon. Wouldn't want to send you out in the shape your friend's in."

"That would be awful kind of you, Randal."

"Come on, Eustace," Martha said. "I'll fix you something to drink. You must be weary from your ordeal."

"Thank you, ma'am."

"I'll come in and check on Jim in a bit. Change his bandage and such."

"Again, mighty kind of you."

Martha headed out of the room.

"You get some rest now," Buck said to Joe. "If you need anything, just holler."

Joe didn't say anything but managed to nod his head with his eyes already closed.

Buck tipped his hat to Millie as he passed her by on his way out the door. Millie again offered a quick and peculiar smile.

Chapter 34

Night came. Buck was sitting on a wicker rocking chair on the porch of the farmhouse. He rolled a cigarette and lit it up. He looked out into the darkness. If not for Joe's condition, Buck would have felt quite content. The Tucker farm was cozy. Randal and Martha were gracious hosts, and there was plenty of room for him and Joe to stay.

Joe was in Waylon Tucker's bedroom. Waylon was the eldest of the Tucker's three children. Jervis, his younger brother and the middle child of the three, hadn't made it back from the war. Waylon had made it back but had long since moved on for work. He had taken his wife and two small daughters down to Texas years earlier to make his way in the oil business. And make his way he had. Although his parents and baby sister would have managed without it, every three months they received a healthy injection of funds from down Texas way.

"Your cousin is asleep," Millie said, joining Buck on the porch.

"That's good. Thank you for checkin'."

"Pleasure."

Millie took a seat beside Buck. She watched him as he smoked his cigarette.

Millie reached her hand over and plucked the smoke from Buck's hand. She leaned back in her chair and put it between her lips.

"Help yerself," Buck said.

Millie took a deep drag.

"So where'd you say you were from again?" she asked. "I can't recall."

"Kansas. Douglas County."

"That's right."

"Ever been?"

"I been a few places, myself," Millie said, taking another puff. "Can't say I've ever been there, though."

"It's good country," Buck said. "You'd like it."

Millie crushed the cigarette out on the bottom of her shoe.

"What you do up there?" she asked. "If you don't mind my askin', of course."

"We do all sorts of things. A little o' this and a little o' that."

"You got a woman up there in Douglas County, Kansas?"

"I got what I got."

"Don't we all."

Buck turned his head and looked at Millie. She couldn't have been more than eighteen years old. But there was something different about the girl that sat beside him there on the porch. It seemed as though she was someone completely different from the girl he had met earlier in the day, the shy and obedient one he had sat next to at the dinner table.

"And what is it that you got?" Buck asked.

"I got what I got too," Millie said.

The two glared into each other's eyes. Millie grinned.

"Don't worry, *Eustace*," she said.

"Don't worry 'bout what, exactly?"

"I won't spill your beans to no one."

"I don't know what you're talkin' 'bout, girl."

Buck returned his gaze to the moonlit fields ahead.

"Why don't you tell me your real name, and how your friend in there got hurt, and I'll tell you what I'm talkin' about?"

"I told you my name," Buck said. "And he's my cousin."

He took out his pouch of tobacco and began to roll another cigarette.

"And if you turn your pretty little head thataway, you'll see the front of the car bashed in for yourself. That's how we got hurt. Him on the head and me in the leg."

Millie looked over at the car.

"Go on," Buck offered. "Go on and look."

Buck finished rolling the cigarette. He put it between his lips and struck a match. Millie leaned in closer to him.

"Tell me you ain't haulin' hooch," she said.

Buck smiled. He took the cigarette from his mouth, blew out a waft of white smoke, and handed it to Millie.

"What makes you think somethin' like that?" he asked.

"Probably running from the laws too," she said. "I know men like you."

"Like hell you do."

Millie took a puff, blew it out, and handed the cigarette back to Buck. She got up from her chair without another word and stomped inside the house. Buck snickered and rocked in his chair.

It wasn't a minute later that Millie returned with two jars of white liquid in her hands. She sat back down beside Buck.

"What you got there?" Buck asked.

"You tell me."

Buck took one of the jars, unscrewed the lid and took a swig.

"Where'd you get this?" he asked.

"Made it myself."

"You made this?" Buck asked, taking another sip.

Millie nodded.

"Not bad," he admitted.

"You speak a word of this to Pa and –"

"Don't worry, girl. I'm not gonna say a thing."

"All right. So now you gonna tell me your story?"

Buck took a good hard look at Millie.

"Already told ya my story, darlin'. Sorry it ain't more interestin' to ya."

Buck passed the jar back to Millie. She took a sip. Then she reached over and snatched Buck's cigarette yet again.

Buck liked the girl. She was young and eager and had enough smarts, it seemed, to keep things to herself. She reminded him of himself and Joe. But like her or not, Buck wasn't about to speak a word of the truth. Not to her. Not then.

"What about Jim?" Millie asked.

"What about him?"

"He got anyone waitin' for him back in Kansas?"

"You'll have to ask him that, woncha?"

"Maybe I will, when he's feelin' better."

Millie took a drink from the jar.

"So where to next for you?" she asked.

"Back to Kansas, no doubt."

"To do a little o' this and a little o' that?"

"You guessed it."

"Won't be for a while. Your cousin ain't seein' straight."

Millie got up from her chair. She screwed the lid back on the jar and walked toward the door.

"You forgot one," Buck said, lifting the other jar from the ground.

"No, I didn't," Millie said, not bothering to turn.

She disappeared into the house. Buck took another drink of the white liquid and wiped his lips with his sleeve. He waited a few minutes to be certain that Millie was gone. He got up from his chair and walked down to the car. He opened the door, pulled his pistol from under the seat, and tucked it into his waistband as he looked up at the house.

Chapter 35

Joe slept through most of the following day. Buck took the opportunity to help Randal with some work around the farm, work for which Randal was happy to have another man around. Martha and Millie were preparing dinner when Joe finally emerged from his room.

"Did we wake you?" Martha asked.

"Oh, no," Joe said. "I've been up for some time now."

"How do you feel?"

"I think I'm okay. My head hurts, but I feel all right."

"Can I get you anything?" Millie asked.

"Some water would do."

Joe looked the women over.

"I'm sorry," he said. "I can't recall your names."

"That's quite all right," Martha said. "You took quite a bump on the head. I'm Martha, and this is my daughter, Millie. Randal is my husband. He's out in the barn with your cousin, Eustace."

Joe was about to introduce himself but thought better of it after hearing Buck's pseudonym. Millie handed Joe a cup of water and urged him to sit down at the table.

"I can't thank you enough for offering your home."

"Nonsense," Martha said. "Any good Christian would do the same, given the circumstances. Besides, we don't get many visitors around here. It's nice to have the company."

Buck and Randal came into the house and entered the kitchen. Randal kissed Martha on the cheek.

"Jim," Buck said, "you're outta bed."

"I am."

"How are you feelin'?" Randal asked.

"Better, thank you."

"Dinner's almost ready," Martha said to Randal. "Why don't you and Eustace clean yourselves up? Millie will prepare the table."

"Yes, dear."

"We shouldn't impose any more than we have," Joe said. "We should be on our way."

"With the work Eustace did today, he's earned hisself a meal," Randal said. "Why don't you boys stay the night? You can head out in the mornin'."

"I am hungry," Buck said.

"You have to stay," Martha said. "I've made enough food to fill a trough."

"It's settled, then," Randal said. "Millie will prepare the table and we'll all enjoy Martha's supper."

Neither Buck nor Joe spoke up to argue with the decision.

Randal said grace over the food, and dinner was served. It had been some time since Buck and Joe had been treated to a proper supper in a welcoming home. For a moment they might have forgotten what had brought them there to begin with, that is, if it hadn't been for Joe's constant headache and Buck's aching leg. The conversation consisted mostly of discussion of farm duties and stories of younger days when Randal had two strong boys to aid with the chores. Millie stayed quiet for most of the meal.

Martha retired to bed soon after all the cleaning was done. As homemaker, she was happy to take on all the duties herself with her daughter by her side. Randal sat in his rocking chair on the porch and smoked his corncob pipe, and soon Buck went out to join him.

Joe, meanwhile, had settled down on Waylon's bed and was staring up at the ceiling.

"Want some company?" Millie asked, standing at the door of the bedroom.

"Come in," Joe said.

He sat up on the bed.

"I'm glad you're feeling better," Millie said, closing the door to the room behind her and sitting down on a dressing chair. "When you arrived, you were in poor shape."

"I don't really recall most of it, to tell you the truth. I remember the accident – bits and pieces of it, anyway – but I don't remember coming into this room."

"Eustace and Pa helped you to bed."

"Did they?"

Joe rubbed his head.

"I spoke with Eustace last night on the porch. He told me all about what you do up in Kansas."

"Did he?"

Millie got up off the chair and sat down on the edge of Joe's bed.

"Well, he wouldn't admit it all to me, but I know people. I think I know you too."

"What did he tell you?"

"He didn't have to say much. But I know you two weren't just out for a drive when that deer came out in front of your car. My bet is you were runnin'."

"Running from what?"

"Laws, probably."

"Eustace said that?"

"Didn't have to. Like I said, I know people."

"I'm afraid you got it wrong, dear. My cousin and I abide the law."

Millie moved closer to Joe. She put her hand on his arm.

"You can tell me, Jim," she said. "We're alike, me and you."

"You have a headache too?"

Millie smiled. She drew in even closer.

"I was watchin' you," she said. "At dinner. I saw you look at me."

"I looked at everyone, Millie."

"Not the way you looked at me."

Millie leaned in and kissed Joe on the mouth. She held her lips there until Joe finally pulled away.

"You're far too young to be doing things like that," Joe said.

"Take me with you."

"What?"

"Take me with you when you go. I can help you."

"Help us what?"

"I make my own hooch, I swear it. Ask Eustace. He'll tell you so."

"Millie –"

"Don't tell me no. I know what you are, I just know it."

Joe took Millie by the shoulders.

"Millie," he said calmly. "You've got it all wrong."

Mille grew irritated. She got up from the bed and scowled at Joe.

"You're no-good liars, you are, the both o' ya."

"Millie, just calm down now."

"I have a right mind to go out there and tell Pa you all tried to have your way with me."

"Millie –"

"What's your name?"

"You're letting your imagination get the better of you."

"Tell me your real name."

Joe looked at Millie. He could see a tear forming in her eye. He took a deep breath.

"Jim," he said. "My name is Jim."

Millie stormed from the room and slammed the door.

Moments later Buck arrived with a look of concern on his face.

"What did you say to her?" he asked.

"Nothing. That girl has some crazy ideas. She begged me to take her with us when we leave."

"You told her no, of course."

"Of course."

"And that's what set her off?"

"That, and, well…"

"Well, what?"

"Well that, and she kissed me."

"She kissed you?"

Joe nodded.

"She's an interestin' one, I'll say that," Buck said.

"We have to get out of here tonight."

"She's just a kid, Joe. She'll have her tantrum and settle right down."

"We're not safe here, Buck. We have to go. There's no telling what that kid will do."

"I've got it under control."

Buck lifted his shirt and revealed the gun tucked into his pants.

"What're you gonna do? Kill her? Don't be –"

"I ain't plannin' on killin' no one," Buck said, quieting Joe. "But if she so much as opens her mouth, I'll put the fear of God in 'er, I will."

"Buck –"

"It's late. Let's stay the night and head out first thing. I'll sleep in here with you, and if there's any sign that somethin's wrong, we'll be gone before they can say our names."

Joe didn't have the energy to fight. He was tired and his head hurt, and he just wanted to go back to sleep.

"First thing in the morning," Joe said, finally relenting.
He slid down onto the bed and put his head on the pillow.
"First thing," Buck assured.

Chapter 36

Buck's eyes opened in the night. He could have sworn he heard strange sounds coming from inside the house. He got up from the chair he'd been sleeping in and pulled out his pistol. He crept to the door and pulled it open slightly to peer out into the hallway. It seemed quiet.

Buck snuck from the room, holding the gun down low as he peered around the corner. A noise came from the kitchen. Buck put his back up against the wall.

Buck had not grown up on a farm, like Joe had, but he was no stranger to the way of life. He was, however, surprised at just how early Martha awoke that morning.

"I thought I heard something," Buck said, entering the kitchen as if nothing were amiss.

"Good mornin', Eustace," Martha said.

"Mornin'? Not even the roosters are awake. I'm certain of it."

"Roosters don't go to church on Sundays," Martha said.

"Church starts this early?"

"Me and Mr. Tucker like to walk into town in the summertime. It's a bit of a stroll, so we get an early start."

"I see."

"I was just leavin' a note for you," Martha said, holding up a piece of paper. "You spoke last night about leavin' today. I feared we might not be back in time to say goodbye."

"We were plannin' on leaving first thing."

"Randal spoke so well of you last night, Eustace. I believe he misses havin' another man around. Why, if he could write it hisself, well…"

Martha approached Buck.

"You take care of yourself. And tend to that cousin o' yours."

"I sure will, ma'am."

"Well, then," the aging woman said. "Randal is out front waitin', no doubt getting dirt on his Sunday clothes. He's not much for goodbyes, you know."

"Good luck to you."

"And to you."

Martha left Buck in the kitchen and met her husband outside. Buck watched through the door as the couple walked down the path toward the road. Martha draped her arm in Randal's.

Buck returned to the room where Joe slept. He tried to crawl into his chair without waking his cousin.

"What was that?" Joe asked, never taking his head from the pillow.

"Randal and Martha goin' to church."

"Give me another hour," Joe said. "Another hour and I'll be ready to go."

Buck closed his eyes and he too fell back asleep with no trouble at all.

When the sun came up, neither of them was any the wiser of it. They'd slept longer than the hour Joe had asked for. Buck was first to open his eyes. Joe did the same only moments later. Both had heard the rapping at the door.

Buck and Joe slunk from the room and crept to within earshot of the front door. Buck held the pistol in his hand.

"Mornin', ma'am," the man at the door said.

"Mornin'," Millie replied.

Buck didn't dare poke out his head, though from where he stood, he couldn't see the man's face.

"Sorry to bother you on this fine Sunday," the man said. "Me and my friend here were just hopin' you could help us with something."

"What would that be?" Millie asked.

"We're just out from Bethel, wonderin' if you seen two men about the area."

"Two men, you say?"

"Two men."

"What do they look like?"

"Young men, both of 'em. One slight in figure, one a little bigger. Brown hair, about so high, I reckon. One o' 'em might be wearin' a dark red hat."

"A dark red hat?"

"Yes, ma'am. Like the color of a dark rose flower."

Buck pulled back the hammer on the gun. He knew Millie had seen his hat. It had been atop his head when he'd arrived at the farm. Joe reached out and put his hand on Buck's arm, holding him back.

"Why you lookin' for them? If you don't mind sayin', of course."

"Robbed the Bethel Bank just a few days ago," the man said. "Mighta robbed another one only days prior."

"You don't say."

"Ma'am," the man said, allowing for a pause. "Have you seen anyone like that around here?"

"You know…" Millie said, allowing herself a pause too.

Buck tugged at the arm Joe held. Joe wouldn't let go.

"My ma and pa are at church this mornin'," Millie said. "Can't speak for them, but as far as I know, there's been no one around here like that."

"You're sure?" the man at the door asked.

"Look around, mister. There ain't another house for miles. If someone came around, I'd know it."

There was silence. Joe let go of Buck's arm.

"Thank you for your time, ma'am," the man said.

"No trouble at all."

"Have yourself a good day."

"And you."

The front door squeaked as Millie began to close it.

"Say," the man called out.

"Yes?" Millie said, opening the door back up.

"Might I ask whose car that is? The one parked right there?"

"That one there?"

"Yes, that one there."

"That's my brother's car. He's in visiting. Went to church with Ma and Pa a few hours back."

"Your brother's car, you say?"

"Yes, sir."

Another pause.

"All right, then, ma'am. Like I said, you have yourself a nice day."

Millie closed the door. She turned the corner and Buck grabbed her around the waist, placing his hand over her mouth to keep her quiet.

"Don't say a word," Buck said.

Buck led Millie to the front of the house. Joe put his ear to the door. He heard the sound of a car driving away. He peered through the window.

"They're gone," he said.

Buck let go of Millie.

"I knew it," Millie said with glee.

"Just settle down now," Buck said.

"Bank robbers, huh? I just knew it."

"What were the men at the door wearing?" Joe asked.

"Wearin'?"

"Yeah, what were they wearing? Uniforms, dungarees…? What?"

"Suits. Both men wore suits."

"We're leaving, Buck," Joe said. "Now."

"Not in that car, we ain't."

Joe thought. He knew they couldn't leave on foot. It would take far too long to put distance between them and whoever was looking for them, which could have been any one of several factions.

"Pa has a car," Millie said.

"Say again?" Buck said.

"Pa, he has a car. Out in the barn at the back."

"Your ma and pa are at church," Joe said.

"Walked to church," Buck said. "Left early this mornin' to make it on time. Millie, will you take us to the car?"

"That all depends…"

"Millie, please," Joe said.

Millie looked at Joe. She lost the glimmer of amusement in her eye.

"Okay," she said, surrendering. "Follow me."

Buck and Joe grabbed what few items they had in Waylon's bedroom and followed Millie out the back of the house. The trio ran across the field toward the small barn. Millie peeled back the door to reveal a black Ford pickup truck.

Buck smiled.

"Looks familiar," he said.

"Millie," Joe said, "we're gonna take your father's truck."

"I figured as much."

"He can have the Buick we left. Here's…"

Joe pulled a wad of cash from his pocket. He ripped a few bills out and handed them to Millie.

"Here's money to get it all fixed up so it's as good as new."

"Joe –"

"Don't ask it, Millie," Joe interrupted. "It ain't right. We can't, and you know it."

A tear began to form in Millie's eye. It hung onto her bottom lid, refusing to let go. Joe kissed Millie on the cheek and got into the car. Buck turned the engine and the pair of cousins pulled out. Joe looked back out the rear window. Millie had her arm up in the air. Joe turned back and focused on the road ahead.

They stopped at the Buick and loaded all their things, including the camping gear and Joe's rifle.

"Which way did they go?" Buck asked, idling at the fork at the end of the farm road.

"Can't say."

"Which way we goin'?"

Joe pulled out the map.

"Head south," he said. "That way."

Buck pulled the car onto the road.

"Any guess who those men at the door were?" Buck asked.

"Either laws or…"

"Colonel's men?"

"Could be."

"He's keepin' close," Buck said.

"We gotta find a way to get a look at *his* face, not his goons'. And we gotta do it soon."

"How do you suggest we do that?"

Joe took a moment. He shook his head.

"Only one way I can think of," he said.

Chapter 37

It might have been a record: fourteen banks in twenty-seven days. If not for one close call with a local sheriff, they might have made it fifteen. Joe's quick thinking and steady aim took out the tires of the lawman's car when they were spotted exiting the bank. The sheriff had a jump on them and would have caught them easily if he hadn't first tried to mow them down with his car. Instead the pair made it back to the truck and out of town with nothing more than a scare.

The cousins' hijinks were garnering more and more attention. The man with the red hat and his accomplice were becoming well known throughout the state. Their zigzag pattern from town to town made it impossible for anyone to predict their next hit, but that didn't stop bank managers across the state from fortifying in preparation. The duo would hit a town in the south and then one in the west. They'd show up even farther south in the next days, only to hit a bank in the eastern part of the state after that. It took many hours on many back roads, but the extra effort was a necessity for keeping them out of harm's way.

They slept in the woods, mostly. When the trail behind them felt particularly cold, though, they would stay in a local inn, sure that one of them was awake and on alert for the duration.

It wasn't their primary concern, but at the end of a month-long spree, Buck and Joe finally took the time to count their takings. They sat around a fire in the wilderness of who-knows-where, Oklahoma, surveying their bounty.

It wasn't usual for banks to have very much cash on hand in those years. They were, however, well stocked in war bonds, and the cousins found themselves flush with so many that they had to convert the tent bag into a carry case for the lot.

"We should stash this somewhere," Buck said, nose-deep in the bag of bonds.

"You're right. No sense carrying it all around."

"After the job tomorrow, we'll find a place to put it. Leave it for a day when we can come back and get it."

Not that he hadn't thought of it before, but hearing Buck speak of it aloud overwhelmed Joe that night. He didn't make his concern known to his cousin but instead kept it to himself. It was in the night, as Joe sat awake around the campfire, that he would ponder the various possibilities and outcomes. For the life of him, he couldn't foresee a time when the day Buck spoke of would come. They now found themselves in a right good mess, one they'd brought upon themselves. Joe knew his days of freedom were numbered; they simply had to be. He didn't like to think about spending the rest of his life in prison, and he certainly wouldn't allow himself to imagine being killed, but something deep down inside him knew that the end had to come one way or another.

"Good morning, ladies and gentlemen!" Buck shouted.

The bank patrons turned and gasped at the sight of the man with the gun in the air.

"There's no cause for alarm. We're not here for your lives; we're just here for the money. If you'll all kindly take a seat on the ground and place your hands under your shoes, we'll be out of here in a jiff."

Everyone did as instructed, including the two boys in the bank with their father. Joe stood watch at the door, his rifle ready in hand.

Word had spread, and the cousins' routine of meeting with bank managers had become too well known. Buck now enjoyed the smash-and-grab method more. It was quicker, cleaner, and for him at least, more fun.

"What's yer name?" someone said.

"Hush, you!"

Joe looked down to the ground.

"What did you say?" Joe asked.

The boy's father put his hand over his son's mouth.

"It's okay," Joe said. "He can talk."

Buck was overseeing the filling of the sack behind the counter.

"I just asked yer name is all," the boy said.

"Please," the father said. "We ain't lookin' fer any trouble."

"Why do you want to know my name?" Joe asked.

The boy shrugged. He looked to be in his late teens, though he had a young face. Perhaps it was the way he smiled, or the care his father showed for him, but Joe left his post at the door.

"Well, what's your name?" Joe asked, approaching the patrons on the floor.

"Marvin."

"Where you from, Marvin?"

"We're from Texas."

"Who's that?"

"That's my younger brother."

"What's his name?"

"Clyde."

"You boys go on and listen to your father there, he –"

The front door of the bank opened and a man strolled in. He stopped at the door and had a quick look around.

"What in the hell…" the man said.

He reached his hand to his hip. Buck was the first to notice the man's police uniform. He let go a shot from the back of the bank. The cop ducked and rolled onto the ground. Joe took aim but held his fire. The officer made it back to his feet and scurried back out the front door.

"You let him go!" Buck yelled.

He grabbed the bag from the bank worker and ran up to his cousin.

"Fuck. Fuck!"

Buck and Joe stood on the bank floor.

"You!" Buck yelled. "Get over here."

The woman who had filled the sack approached cautiously.

"You got a back door to this place?"

The woman shook her head.

"How the hell we gonna get outta here now?" Buck said.

"Let me think," Joe said. "Gimme a second."

"What about them stairs?" a voice said.

Buck and Joe turned.

"You could take them stairs, right there," Marvin said, pointing to a small staircase in the back corner of the bank.

Buck hurried off in that direction. Joe soon followed after one last look at the young man.

The staircase led to offices on the second floor. The offices were empty and looked to have been that way for some time. Buck snuck a peek out one of the windows at the front. Two cops were taking shelter behind their car, guns pointed at the front door of the bank.

"They're out there," he said.

"We gotta get outta here. More will be on the way."

"The roof," Buck said. "We need to get up to the roof."

They reached the back wall of the building and pried open one of the windows. Buck was first to climb out onto the windowsill. He held onto the bricks above and looked upward.

"I think I can grab the edge," he said. "I just need a few more inches."

Joe sat in the open window and cupped his hands together. Buck looked down at his cousin and then to the narrow alley below.

"Go on," Joe said. "Step into my hands and I'll lift you."

Buck put his foot on top of Joe's intertwined fingers.

"On three," Joe said.

The pair counted aloud, and Joe heaved up his arms. Buck reached for the edge of the roof and grabbed on with both hands. Joe, still hanging out the window, gave Buck's shoe soles one more shove.

Buck managed to climb onto the flat roof. Joe threw the rifle up to his cousin and then stood on the sill where his cousin had. He hung onto the wooden frame with white knuckles. Buck reached an arm down and was able to clasp onto one of Joe's. Joe put his foot on the top of the open window for support and for leverage. Instead of helping him skyward, the force of his weight slammed the window closed with a bang, sending Joe outward. For a moment Joe dangled from the building with only Buck's grasp keeping him from plummeting to the ground. Joe reached up his other arm and grabbed onto Buck's hand. He pedaled his feet anxiously against the bricks in front of him.

"Hang on!" Buck grunted.

He pulled at Joe's arm. Joe was able to make enough contact with the stubbly brick to help Buck pull him up to the roof and to safety.

"Holy shit!" Buck said.

Both cousins lay on their backs, huffing and puffing.

"That was a close one."

They caught their breath and turned onto their bellies. They crawled to the front of the building to get a better view of the street. Buck raised his head over the shallow ledge. A second police car sped their way.

"Fuck!" he said. "More coming."

Joe peered over the ledge to see for himself. Just then, the front door of the bank opened, and all the people once inside came bursting out like a cloud of flies. A second police car arrived. Two more cops got out and pointed their guns at the door. Buck could see one of the bank employees talking to the cops. The cop looked up at the windows.

"They're on the second floor!" the cop shouted.

Buck lowered his head. He and Joe lay flat on the roof of the bank.

"Can you jump?" Joe asked.

"What?"

Joe pointed over to the side of the building.

"The next building over… Can you jump?

"I don't know," Buck said. "That's a story down. If my leg doesn't hold…"

"Okay," Joe said, "I got an idea."

Joe filled his cousin in.

Ten minutes passed, maybe more. Three more police cars arrived, and six more cops pointed their guns at the front door and the second floor windows. Townspeople had come out from the local shops to take in the scene, and the streets were littered with onlookers. There was little movement from the police. They knew they had the outlaws pinned inside the bank.

"Come on out with your hands up!" one of the cops finally shouted. "There's nowhere for you to run. Come on out with your hands up, or we'll open fire!"

A few more quiet moments passed. A bullet then came whizzing down the street and hit one of the police cars. It gave off a piercing thud as the tire exploded. A second bullet came, hitting a second car, this time shattering the glass of the front headlight. The police began to scurry like ants around a disturbed anthill.

"It's coming from over there," one of the cops yelled.

"How did they get out?" another said.

Two cops opened fire down the road to the right of the bank. Several more piled into their cars and took off in that direction. A bullet hit one of the speeding car's tires. It too exploded, sending the car skidding to a stop.

In the distance a black car pulled out from the side of the road and took off in front of the police cars.

The chase was on.

Chapter 38

"Hello?" Madeline said into the phone.

"Maddy, it's Nate."

"Is everything okay?"

"Yeah, everything is fine. How is Liza feeling?"

"She's a bit better. Still pretty weak."

"Maddy, can we meet?"

"Sure, I don't see why not."

"I have something to show you."

"How about the coffee shop, say... in one hour?"

"I can do that."

"You sure you're okay? You sound funny."

"I might have something more interesting than the gun."

"Really?"

Nathaniel was sitting at the same table where they had met before. Madeline arrived to an open folder and old newspaper printouts strewn about.

"What are all these?" she asked, taking a seat.

"I ordered you a tea," Nathaniel said. "I hope it's not too cold."

"Newspaper articles?"

"Your grandmother said that Buck and Joe had become quite well known in the area. Obviously we know that the names she's giving us aren't real, but that doesn't mean that the newspapers wouldn't be reporting on the slew of bank robberies going on."

"You found them."

"Take a look."

Nathaniel turned the folder around so Madeline could get a closer look.

"Cobb Gang Strikes Again," she read. "Cobb Gang Robs Citizens Bank in Yuca. Who are the Cobb Gang?"

"I looked through tons of Oklahoma papers covering that time period. If Liza's story is correct, she's talking about the Cobb Gang. She has to be."

Madeline read one of the articles quietly.

"It says here…"

Madeline's eyes opened wide.

"I know," Nathaniel said.

"But… it can't be."

"That's what I thought," Nathaniel said, passing Madeline another article. "Here, now look at this."

Madeline began reading.

"Skip to the end," Nathaniel said.

"Just outside… in a hail of… confirmed that all members of the Cobb Gang were shot dead."

Madeline looked up from the paper.

"But how can that be?"

"I don't know. But I'm more interested in this."

Nathaniel pointed back to a line in the first article Madeline was reading.

"I know, but I still don't believe it," Madeline said.

"We have to ask Liza about it."

"You think we should?"

"How can we not? This changes everything."

"I know, but…"

"You're worried it will ruin something."

"She's telling it this way for a reason. I don't know what that reason is, but there must be one."

"I know you're right. But, Maddy, this is… this is big."

Madeline took a sip from her cup. She looked up at Nathaniel.

"If you want to ask her, you should," she said. "You're a part of this too. If something isn't right, you should bring it up."

Nathaniel nodded in silence.

Liza was asleep when Madeline and Nathaniel arrived in her room. They tried to sneak back out without waking her, but their efforts were for naught.

"Come in, come in," Liza said. "I'm awake, for goodness' sake, I was simply resting my eyes.

"Are you sure?" Madeline asked. "We can come back."

"In with you," Liza instructed. "Take your seats and let's get on with it."

Nathaniel took the chair from the side of the room and brought it to his usual spot. He got out his notepad and his voice recorder.

"Before we start today…" he said as he sat down.

"Yes?" Liza said with a smile.

"There's something I have to ask you."

"I'm all ears, Mr. Bishop."

"Well…"

Nathaniel looked up at Madeline. Madeline offered a smile.

"What is it now?" Liza said. "Don't be shy."

"Well, Mrs. Meachum," Nathaniel said again, "who's the girl?"

"The girl?" the old woman asked with a furrowed brow.

"I did a little digging, and… I'd like to know about the girl."

"You did a little digging, did you?"

"You had to know he would, Grandma," Madeline offered.

"And why's that, dear? Because he can?"

"Ma'am, I assure you –" Nathaniel said.

"Now, now," Liza interrupted. "I'm not angry. Your question is a perfectly good one. In fact, I'm surprised it took you as long as it did."

"But you haven't said anything about a female," Madeline said.

"Not yet, I haven't."

"Is it something you're going to let us in on?" Nathaniel asked.

Liza smiled a giant smile. She reached over and touched Madeline on the back of the hand.

"Mr. Bishop," she said, turning her attention back to Nathaniel, "ask me your question once more."

"Who's the girl?" Nathaniel asked plainly.

Chapter 39

1924

It had been two days since the latest bank job had gone awry. A strange car pulled into the Tilley farm and drove around to the back. The car idled. No one got out.

The car's horn honked three times. The back door to the farm opened slowly. A gun pointed out.

"Put that thing away, will ya?" Joe called out.

Buck emerged from the back of the house. The cousins met outside the driver's door of the car and embraced joyously.

"You did it, you ol' son of a bitch," Buck said.

"So did you."

"Piece o' cake."

"Where's the truck?"

"In the woods. I ain't takin' no chances."

Joe and Buck hugged once more.

"Come on inside. I wanna hear all about it," Buck said.

Joe followed Buck into the house. Buck had a loaf of bread and a wedge of cheese out on the counter. Joe ripped off a hunk of bread and took a bite.

"Did you notice the plates on the car?" Joe asked.

Buck stuck his head out the back door and had a look.

"Texas? What's that all about?" he asked.

"Come on," Joe said, taking another bite of bread. "Let's go have a seat and talk."

Buck grabbed the bread and cheese and brought it with him to the other room. The cousins sat across from each other on the floor.

"So, I made it to the next building over," Joe said.

"I saw that," Buck replied, his mouth full of food.

"I was able to hang off the edge, and the fall wasn't too bad at all. The next few buildings were the same height, so I made it fairly far. One near the end of the block had a fire ladder running down the side. I climbed down and waited in the alley."

"Couldn't 've waited long. I heard the shots."

"Wasn't long. I ducked down behind a pile of empty Coca-Cola boxes for only a minute or so. Then I saw some old friends hurrying along."

"Old friends?"

"A man and his two sons getting into their car."

"The ones from the bank?"

"They'd parked out in front of the restaurant, the one I was hiding beside. One of the boys spotted me and pointed me out to his father. At first I thought the man would call out to the cops, but he didn't. He just stood there with the boys, and the three of them stared at me.

"They had a car, and I needed one. I put my hand into my pocket and pulled out all the money I had. I reached out my arm and offered them the wad. The man didn't move. It was one of the boys that finally came up to me. He took the money from my hand, put his hat on my head, and together we walked to the car. The boy handed his father the money and took the keys. The man didn't move much; I think the cash mesmerized him. I simply gave him a nod and got into the car."

"How much you give 'im?"

"I don't know, four hundred, maybe more. I turned on the car, pulled down the road. I stopped the car and hoisted myself up onto the window ledge, and that's when you heard the shots."

"They bought it. Musta thought we was both in the car because they all took off after you."

"I shot out one of the cars and then just took off."

"How'd you lose 'em?"

"Good ol' fashioned driving."

"Outran 'em?"

"Didn't need to. Led them along the road for a while, then crossed on over into Texas."

"We were that close?"

"Makes sense, I suppose. You saw the Texas plates on the car. Couldn't have been that far if the boys and their father were up there."

"You devil. How'd you know to go that way?"

"I remembered looking at the map. Got a little lucky too, I suppose. I was already heading that way out of town. I just kept on driving and prayed for the state line."

"And they stopped chasin' ya?"

"You know it. Don't know if they got a look at the plates or not, but who cares much if they did?"

"We gotta ditch that car."

"And quick," Joe agreed. "But more importantly, how long did you have to stay up on that roof?"

"Into the night," Buck said. "I lay up there on my back and heard all sorts of rumblings."

"Laws talking?"

"Laws, bank folk, all kinds o' people. I think your friend even showed up, ol' what's-his-name."

"Alfred?"

"Alfred, that's the one. They were calling him Agent Winter, real professional-like. Couldn't hear much, though, just bits here and there. I tried to stay as still as I could."

"Hear anything good?"

"Lotta chatter about a man named Marlow. No first name, though."

"Marlow," Joe repeated. "Marlow."

"You know the name?"

"I think I've heard it before."

"Where's that?"

"Back in Kansas. Gump spoke about him, I think."

"You think it's the Colonel?"

"Could be."

"Anyways, like I was sayin'," Buck continued, "there was all sorts o' folks around the place well into the night. Had to be after midnight that the last of 'em were gone. I was thinkin' to climb back down the way we came, but even if I could get back through the window, there was no way o' gettin' outta the bank once I was back in."

"You follow the way I went?"

"Had no choice. Figured if you made it down, it couldn't be that hard. Leg held up good. I didn't make it to the ladder you spoke of, though. Shimmied my way down the front of the building beside. Reached out and got a tree branch. Hung there like a monkey till I got the gumption to let go."

"The truck was where we left it?"

"Truck was still there, bag was still in the truck."

"We could've left the bag. Come back and got it after a while," Joe said.

"Then why'd I stay up there at all? Besides, strange truck stays in the same spot too long after a bank job, and people start lookin' at it funny. They take too close a look and we lose the loot *and* lead the laws back to that farmhouse where we got it. I know we're leavin' a trail, but that's a big one for the laws. We still wanna get out o' this free men, right?"

"That's the idea," Joe said.

"So now what?" Buck asked, resting his head against the wall.

"There's a lot of things we gotta do, starting with dumping both those cars and stashing the bag. It's getting to be a liability."

"Yessir."

"Then we gotta start going about things in a new way."

"How d'ya mean?"

"We got the Colonel's attention, that's for certain. But it's enough playing around. We been at this too long. I have a little idea about how we might at least find out his name."

"Do ya?"

"We also gotta come up with a new plan if we're gonna go into another bank. We can't get caught again like in this last one."

"Whatcha got in mind?"

"I might just have an idea for that too, but…"

"But what?"

"But you may not like it."

Chapter 40

It was well over a week later that Buck and Joe found themselves driving through the Oklahoma back roads again. They hadn't knocked over a bank since the debacle of their last attempt. They hadn't given up bank robbing entirely, though; they were instead biding their time to put their new plan into effect.

They pulled into a diner at the side of the road. It was night. They waited in the car until most of the patrons had left. There were a few elderly townsfolk still inside when they finally decided to go in.

"I heard you make a great pumpkin pie," Buck said from the door.

"Well, look what the wind blew in," Annie replied.

"Promised I'd stop in if we were ever back in town."

"Joe," Annie nodded.

"Annie," Joe acknowledged.

"What can I get for you tonight?"

"We ate already," Buck said, "but a little dessert couldn't hurt."

"Are you stayin' the night?"

"Most likely," Buck said.

He and Joe took a seat at one of the tables.

"Have you been over to see Ma yet?"

"Not yet, no," Buck said.

"Coffee with that?" Annie asked, cutting into a pie behind the counter.

"Sure thing," Buck said.

Annie delivered the pie and coffee to the table and then went off to serve bills to the remaining patrons. When all had left, she came back over and sat down with Buck and Joe.

"Those fellas been back?" Buck asked.

"The ones causin' trouble the night y'all were around? Can't say I've seen 'em."

"That's good."

"Where you two been, anyway?"

"Travelin', mostly. Went to visit some of Joe's old friends. Now we're headin' back on up to Kansas."

"Back home?"

"Back home."

"What about you?" Buck asked. "What you been up to?"

"Well, I been stayin' at Ma and Pa's place the past few nights, probably will be again tonight."

"Why's that?"

"Pa's not been feelin' hisself," Annie said. "I'm just helpin' out where I can."

"What's the problem?" Joe asked.

"Can't say for certain. Came down with a fever earlier in the week, hasn't yet regained his strength. He shouts to the high heavens that he's just dandy, but he ain't."

"Well, if you're almost done here, we can give you a ride over," Buck said. "We're headin' there now."

"You two go ahead," Annie said, getting up from the table. "I have a few things to do around here."

"It's no trouble."

"I'll find you later, when I get back."

"What do we owe you for the pie and coffee?"

Annie put a chit on the table and left with a smile.

"See you later, then," Buck said.

He left some money on the table, and then he and Joe took the short drive to the inn down the road. Bess was not downstairs when they arrived. Most of the lights were off and the place was as quiet as a graveyard.

"Hello?" Buck said into the darkness. "Mrs. Prichard? Hello?"

A few moments later a light flickered on upstairs. Bess came to the top of the stairs in her dressing gown.

"Oh, hello, boys," she said.

She held onto the railing as she made her way down.

"We were just over with Annie," Buck said. "We didn't know you'd gone to bed for the night."

"Come in, come in!" Bess said. "Just a long day is all."

"We'll be needin' a room for the night," Buck said.

"That will be no trouble at all," the short, round woman said. "Follow me this way and I'll get you all set up."

"Two rooms would do even better," Buck said.

Buck and Joe followed Bess to the counter.

"You can have your old room," Bess said, handing a key to Buck. "And there's one down the hall for you."

She handed another key to Joe.

"Say," Joe said, "any post come through for me in the past few days?"

"No," Bess said, taking a moment to think. "Can't say that it has. Mail is due in again soon, though. You expectin' somethin'?"

"Perhaps," Joe said. "I gave this address while we were traveling. I might be getting something."

"Well, if something comes in, I'll be sure to let you know. But for now," Bess said as she came around the counter, "I'm headin' back on up to sleep."

"Good night, Mrs. Prichard," Buck said.

"Good night, boys. Enjoy your stay."

Bess waddled her way from the room and headed back up the creaking stairs.

"You know," Joe said to Buck, "if Annie's staying here, she's sure to have a room to herself."

"Your point is?"

"Not that I'm complaining about having a little privacy for a change."

"We got enough money, Joe."

"I'm just saying."

"I know what you're just sayin'."

"Tell me that's not what you were thinking."

Buck looked at Joe with a sly smile.

"Help me get the things from the car," he said.

Later on, Buck and Joe got comfortable, each in his own room. Buck drew a bath and Joe found his pillow without delay. Buck was exiting the bathroom down the hall when he noticed a light on downstairs. He got dressed and went to investigate.

As he'd hoped, young Annie was sitting on the couch with a book in hand.

"Thought you said you'd come find me?" Buck said.

"Here you are," Annie said, smiling up at him.

Buck sat down beside her on the couch.

"Annie," he said, putting his hand on her knee. "I got a proposition for ya."

Chapter 41

"Any mail today?" Joe asked, peeking around the corner at Bess.

"Mornin' there," Bess said. "None today, sorry. Maybe tomorra."

"I'll just wait here for Buck, then," Joe said, entering the room.

"'Fraid you'll be waitin' quite some time."

Bess was busying herself behind the counter.

"How's that?"

"Left early with Annie. Two of 'em went into town t'gether."

"They did?"

"Sure thing. Said they'd be back in time for supper. He said to tell you to take the day off, whatever that means."

Joe left Bess to her business and walked outside. He didn't get very far, taking a seat on the front steps.

Buck had no doubt just been poking fun when he'd told Joe to "take the day off," but the suggestion rang through Joe's mind nonetheless. It had been a long while since Joe had taken any time to think about something other than next steps or new schemes or finding his way out of trouble. It had been like that since the day they'd left Kansas, it seemed. As Joe sat there on the steps of the inn on that early autumn day, he was overcome by melancholy.

It takes a special kind of moment for a person to stop and take stock. When the circumstances are right, it's something that seems quite natural, really, but in certain trying times those circumstances seem to come around less often.

Joe wondered what sort of life he had left for himself. He had no parents, no brothers or sisters, and only one cousin to whom he felt any sort of familial ties. He had no job, no woman, and no house of his own to call home. He traveled in a car that was purchased with money he stole from a bank; the clothes on his back and the food he ate were bought the same way. And since he'd returned to his state of birth a few months prior, Joe had become not only a thief but a murderer too.

These things weighed heavy on Joe's mind. Often when he went to rest his head on the pillow at the end of a day, thoughts of his old life or burdens of his new one would arise to disturb his rest. But what stood out for him on that particular morning, sitting on the steps of the inn in Bristol Falls, was that he was responsible for all of it. He could not pass off blame or shirk responsibility. He alone had done it to himself. He found himself in a fight for his life, a fight for his cousin's life, all because of the choices he had made.

Joe was not proud of himself. He feared for the future. It was not so much a fear of coming face to face with the Colonel or getting caught by the lawmen for what he had done, but something far worse. Should he one day find his way clear of all the trouble, what did he have left to live for? Robbing banks and finding the Colonel had become his entire life. It was not a long-term plan, nor did Joe want it to be. He was beginning to get an empty feeling in his gut, and he didn't like it.

Joe got up from the steps and headed to the car. He snatched the rifle from under the seat, crossed the road, and marched into the open woods. In the past he'd found peace amongst the trees, and he went looking for it again that day.

Along his hike Joe came upon a deer. He put it in his sights but didn't fire. He lowered the gun and let the animal be. Joe just walked. He walked for hours.

Joe returned to the inn late in the afternoon, his rifle over his shoulder. Buck and Annie were sitting together in the front room.

"Where ya been?" Buck asked.

"Walking," Joe said.

"We gotta talk, now," said Buck.

Buck took Joe by the arm and led him up into his room. He pulled out a newspaper tucked into the back of his waistband. He threw it to Joe. Joe caught the paper and unfolded it.

"Bladwell Gang Strikes Again," Joe read aloud.

He looked up at Buck with astonishment.

"They know who we are," Buck said.

Joe looked back down at the paper.

"Cousins Paul 'Buck' Bladwell and Joseph Bladwell..." he read.

"They got your name wrong, but it's close enough, and they got mine right. They know who we are."

Joe looked up at Buck again. He thought for a moment.

"There's only one place they could have gotten these names," Joe said.

"There're plenty o' places they could have got 'em."

"That may be, but there's only one person I can think of that would call me Joseph *Bladwell*."

Buck stared at his cousin, knowing full well what he was referring to.

"It's just starting to get dark," Buck said. "We can make it there by tonight."

"I know…" Joe said, hesitating.

"But?"

"But we need that letter."

"What's so important about the letter? You've had a thousand letters from Alfred."

"I asked him about Marlow."

"You didn't."

"I had to. I spoke about the Colonel with him before. He won't think it's unusual that I asked if his name was Marlow. We have to wait. We have to take the chance, at least for the night. If the letter doesn't arrive tomorrow morning, we leave before lunch and –"

Buck put his finger to his lips in a hushing gesture. He pointed to the bottom of the door with his other hand. Joe turned. The sun had begun to go down, and as it shone through the hallway window it illuminated the outside of the door. The beam that came in from beneath the door was not complete; two thick and one thin column of darkness impeded its way. Someone was there. Someone was listening.

The dark objects quickly vanished, first one, and then the other two. A slight creak of the floorboards whispered through the air.

"Who was that?" Buck said softly.

"Who around here has more than two feet?"

"Stay in yer room," Buck said. "And sleep with one eye open. We're outta here tomorrow mornin', with or without that letter."

Chapter 42

It was well after dinnertime when a car pulled into the inn. A man got out of the driver's side and walked around to the trunk. He opened the lid and pulled out a small suitcase. He walked up the steps of the inn and opened the front door.

The man approached Bess and spoke with her. He shook her hand. The man took a key from her and sauntered up the stairs, unbuttoning his jacket as he did. The man entered one of the rooms and shut the door behind him.

Back downstairs, Annie was saying good night to her mother.

"Good night, dear," Bess replied.

"Pa is feeling a little poor tonight," said Annie. "Perhaps you should close up early and see to him."

"Will do."

Annie turned to leave.

"Say, Annie…" Bess called out.

Annie came back around the corner.

"Yes?"

"I seen you all day with that boy. Now, I know –"

"Don't worry about it, Ma. He's already asleep in his room. Somethin' about gettin' an early start."

"Well, good. I'm just sayin'…"

"Night, Ma," Annie said, smiling.

Annie went up to her room on the second floor. She shut the door and turned off the light. The inn grew quiet.

It wasn't long after that that Bess, taking direction from her daughter, closed up the counter and slowly made her way up the stairs to her own bedroom and to her husband.

It was after midnight. The only light that burned was in the front hallway of the inn. It lit up the foyer with a yellow glow.

Upstairs a doorknob turned. The door opened slowly and very quietly. A bare foot poked out from the door. It was soon followed by another. The man who had arrived that evening glided out into the hallway. He looked around. He turned on his toes and walked toward the door beside his. He opened it slowly and turned on the light. He entered the bathroom.

The man soon exited the bathroom and turned the light out behind him. He stood on the landing at the top of the stairs. He waited.

Nothing made a sound.

The man made for his room, walking gingerly so as not to disturb the old floorboards beneath his feet. He stopped at his door and put his hand on the handle. He leaned back his head and looked at the number on the door. He looked at the number on the door beside his. He approached his neighbor's door. He placed his hand on the handle. He opened the door just a fraction, slowly and quietly. He looked in through the small slit.

The man looked over his shoulder. Still nothing else moved. The man reached into his pocket and pulled out a small revolver. He opened the door, stepped over the threshold, and approached the bed. He'd made it to a few feet from the mattress when he quickly turned his head over his shoulder, back toward the door. There stood Buck, pistol pointed straight at the man. The man turned quickly and raised his gun. Buck put a bullet into his head without hesitation. The gunshot lit up the room for a fleeting moment.

Buck stood in the doorway, his pistol smoking, his other hand holding up his unbuttoned pants.

"Buck!" Annie cried out from a door across the hall.

The front door of the inn exploded open. Buck rushed over to the top of the stairs and pointed his gun. He was about to pull the trigger when he saw Joe step into the light, his gun pointing upward at Buck.

"Joe!" Buck said.

"I heard shots."

Buck lowered his gun.

"Where were you?" he asked.

"Across the street in the woods. I must have fallen asleep."

"Annie!" Bess cried, emerging from her bedroom.

"Ma, I'm here. I'm okay."

Annie came into the hallway, a bed sheet wrapped around her otherwise naked body. Bess shuffled across the floor in her dressing gown and hugged her daughter. Not far behind her was John, limping along with his crutch.

Joe came up the stairs. He walked over to Buck's room and looked in. Bess couldn't help but look in too.

"My goodness!" she said, putting her hand over her mouth.

"What have you done?" John said to Buck.

Buck turned. He lifted his gun and pointed it at John's head.

"It was you," he said.

"Buck, no!" Annie pleaded. "What do you mean? What was him? Why are you doing –"

"You told 'em we was here."

John's back was up against the wall. He stared at the end of Buck's gun, his eyes agape, his head shaking, denying the claim.

"I told them nothing," he said. "I swear it."

"How did he know to find us here? How did he know what room I was in?"

"He didn't know we got two rooms," Joe said quietly.

"What?" Buck asked.

"He didn't know we got two rooms. He heard us talking today in your room. It's the same room we stayed in together last time we were here. He didn't know we got two rooms."

Buck took a step forward and put the gun to John's forehead.

"Buck, please!" Annie pleaded.

John dropped his crutch. He began to slide down the wall.

"John?" Bess said with fear in her voice.

"Pa!" Annie cried.

John was grasping his chest with both hands. He dropped to the floor and slumped over like a rag doll.

"What did you do?" Annie yelled to Buck.

Buck took a step back and lowered his gun. Annie ran over to her father.

"It's time to go," Joe said, grabbing Buck's arm.

Buck was still looking down at John, who was gasping for air.

"Now, Buck," Joe said calmly.

"Annie," Buck said.

Annie didn't even look his way. Buck finally turned away. He followed Joe down the stairs and out the front door.

"Who the hell was he?" Joe asked, driving like lightning from town. It was only a matter of minutes before they were gone from Bristol Falls altogether.

"Colonel's man," Buck said. "Had to be."

"But how did you –"

"Was in Annie's bed. Heard someone movin'."

"You're one lucky son of a –"

"And where were you, in the woods? What were you doin' in the woods?"

"I couldn't sleep. It didn't feel right in there."

"You left *me* in there."

"I was watching the whole time, like I told you. I must have fallen asleep."

"I coulda been killed."

"We both coulda, but we weren't."

"Lucky for you."

Joe shot Buck a harsh glare. Buck did not look over to receive it. Joe returned his eyes to the road.

"So much for the letter," he said, sardonically.

Joe soon slowed the pace of the car. The last thing they needed was a lawman coming after them for driving too fast. The car glided along the road and soon the cousins sat in silence. Joe thought to make conversation but had too much on his mind. Buck was content to look out the window, though his eyes became heavy after a while.

It was the middle of the night, and they weren't yet halfway to where they were headed. Joe pulled off the road and drove the car between two trees. The branches were full and heavy and hung nearly to the ground. He turned off the engine and the darkness of the open country enveloped the car like a hungry whale. Once again, in the wilderness, the cousins slept.

Chapter 43

It was early in the morning when Buck and Joe arrived at their destination. They parked the car far enough away so as not to be spotted, but close enough that they could return to it quickly if they had to run. Buck held his gun close to his body. Joe walked with his rifle in both hands, like a hunter. They wandered through the trees and up to the edge of a small clearing. They hunched down. The house they were after was in clear view.

"We're gonna have to find a way in," Buck said.

"Maybe we wait until someone comes out."

"Could."

"But by then it may be too late. Might get out too far ahead of us."

"Let's give it a minute, see if anything goes on in there."

Buck and Joe got down on one knee. They tried their best to peer through the windows of the house. Neither could see much of anything.

"Maybe no one's there," Joe said.

"It's still early. Probably still asleep, if anything."

"How long we gonna wait?"

Buck, motionless like a statue, stared at the house.

"Fuck it," he said.

Buck got to his feet, skulked from the tree line, and hurried across the field, staying low to the ground. Joe reluctantly followed close behind. They reached the side of the house and put their backs up against the brown wood. They waited.

"I don't hear anything," Buck whispered. "You hear anything?"

Joe shook his head.

Buck nudged his chin toward the back of the house. He and Joe walked carefully along the side wall. Buck took the first look around the back. He turned back to Joe and made a motion for him to follow. The two got down on the ground and crawled around the back of the house.

They reached two wooden storm doors leading into the basement of the house. The doors were held closed by a rope. Buck started working on the knot. Joe kept watch.

When Buck finally got the rope to give, he tore it from the handles and pulled one side of the door open. The hinges gave off a high-pitched squeak. He and Joe both cringed and held their breath.

When it was clear that no response was forthcoming, Buck shimmied into the passageway and down to the cellar door. He lifted the small lever and with his shoulder shoved at the door. Joe, looking down from above, saw it open. He followed Buck down the few steps and together they crept into the root cellar.

Like most others of its kind, this root cellar was dark and damp and musty. They walked carefully to avoid stepping on anything that might make any noise. Buck and Joe reached the staircase that led to the main floor.

"Wait," Joe whispered.

Buck turned.

"How you gonna do it?"

"I'm gonna find out the Colonel's name, and then I'm gonna put a bullet in the back of his head. If not, I'll put one right in the front," Buck said, pointing to the spot between his eyes.

The pair climbed the stairs gently to avoid making any creaks or groans in the old wood. Buck got down on his knee and turned the handle of the door. It opened with the tiniest of squeals. They stepped carefully onto the main floor. Not a sound could be heard from any direction.

Joe followed Buck from the first room to another. They kept their guns pointed outward and ahead. No one was in the kitchen. No one was in the den. Buck was preparing to make his way up the stairs to the second floor when he peeked his head around the corner into the dining room. He quickly pulled back.

"Holy shit!" he said.

Joe put his finger to his lips and with an angry face hushed his cousin.

"I don't think it'll matter," Buck said.

He looked around the corner once more, this time holding the gaze. Joe poked at Buck's side, jostling for information. Buck stood straight up and turned.

"Have a look for yourself," he said.

Joe brushed past Buck and looked around the corner.

Upright and no longer creeping, Buck and Joe entered the dining room. Sitting at the head of the table with a knife through the back of his hand to the wood beneath and a gunshot wound in the side of his head was a tall, fat, slovenly man. Someone had gotten to Gumpy first.

"Check the rest o' the house," Buck said.

Joe left the room and leapt up the stairs. If anyone remained, they too had no doubt met the same fate as Gump. Buck approached his old cohort to get a closer look. His head was slumped to the side. Joe returned.

"Woman upstairs is dead," he said. "Her face is kissin' the floor."

Joe looked away when he saw bits of Gump's brain sitting on the table beside him.

"He gave us up, and they killed him for it," Buck said, standing over the mutilated man.

"What a scene," Joe said.

"Where'd they get her?"

"All over, and more."

"Splendid."

"Hey, touch him."

"I ain't touchin' nothin'," Buck said.

"Just feel if he's warm. Go on."

Buck put his fingers on the back of Gump's neck. He shook his head.

"Cold, like raw meat," he said.

"The Colonel did this."

"Was there any doubt?"

"That means he was here."

"You don't know that for certain."

"I'd bet on it. They did some talking first, too," Joe said. "Look."

Joe pointed out the number of plates on the table. There were four in total.

"It was a meeting," he said.

"Didn't end well for Gump, I'd say."

"He's the one that gave up our names. There's no doubt of that."

"Like you said, no one else called us the Bladwell boys."

"Wonder why he waited so long," said Joe.

"Whaddaya mean?"

"Why wouldn't he give us up from the start, tell the Colonel who we were?"

"Used it to bargain, maybe?"

"Maybe. Looks like it didn't work," Joe said, turning away from the body. "I gotta get outta here. It's starting to smell, and I can't look at his insides anymore."

Buck followed Joe from the room and soon from the house. They took care walking back across the open field toward the trees. Not that anyone was around to see, but taking precaution when leaving a house with two dead bodies inside seemed an obvious concession to safety.

"Back to Oklahoma," Buck said, as the pair returned to the car.

Buck got in on the driver's side.

"You know where we're going?" Joe asked, pulling the map out and opening it up on his lap.

"I got an idea."

Buck turned on the car and pulled onto the road.

"Gonna make a quick stop first," Buck said.

"What you got in mind?"

Buck didn't answer. He just drove along with a silly grin on his face. Joe soon figured out where Buck was taking them. It wasn't difficult, after all.

Buck pulled up to the Bladwell house and stopped the car out front.

"You sure about this?" Joe asked.

"Whaddaya mean?"

"Nothing. Go on. I'll wait here."

"You ain't comin'?"

"The woman hated me."

"She did not."

"What's the matter with you? She couldn't stand the sight of me from the moment I set foot in that house. Besides, I got some bad memories of that place."

"Suit yourself," Buck said.

He got out of the car and walked up to the house. Joe sat alone for a while but grew bored quickly. He too got out of the car and began to walk down the road.

Joe thought about the day he'd arrived at the house. He thought about meeting Buck and Myron for the first time. He thought about Alfred, who had brought him there to begin with.

Alfred. *Alfred.*

It was then that it hit Joe like a train. *Alfred knows.* Alfred had no doubt put together the pieces and made the connection between Paul "Buck" Bladwell and Joe since their names hit the papers together. He must have figured out that it had been Joe robbing those banks all along. He would simply have to know by now.

Joe felt sick. He turned around and went back to the car. He got in and put his hands to his face. If only he had gotten that letter in Bristol Falls. That would have tipped him off one way or the other.

Buck had only been inside the house for twenty minutes, but Joe couldn't wait. He blew the car horn. Buck didn't come out. Joe blew the horn a few more times. Buck finally came out to the porch and threw his hands up in the air.

"We have to go back to Bristol," Joe shouted out the window.

"What?"

"We have to go back –"

"I heard you," Buck said.

He came down to the car.

"What the hell are you talkin' about?"

"I need that letter from Alfred."

"I thought we went over this already. What does it matter now?"

"I have to find out if he knows."

"Knows what?"

"About us, Buck! About me!"

Buck took a good look at Joe.

"We ain't goin' back," Buck said, pointing his finger at Joe. "We got a plan and we're stickin' to it."

Buck stomped off and disappeared back into the house. Joe was left alone in the car again. He got out and walked off in no particular direction.

Joe got to thinking. He began to work things out in his head and to plan. He began to calm down. By the time he turned around and headed toward the car again, he almost had a grin on his face. Almost. He'd come up with an endgame, a way to finish the business he'd started so long before. He was eager to share it with Buck.

More than an hour had passed, but Buck was still inside the house when Joe got back to the car. He hesitated for a moment but then opened the car door and leaned on the horn once more.

Chapter 44

Back in Oklahoma, Buck and Joe prepared for the next bank job and for the three after that. They plotted out a route that would lead them from Bright Hill to the town of Lazlo. For the first time, instead of changing direction, they were headed in a straight line from town to town across the middle of the state.

It was a little after noon in Bright Hill. Joe sat in the car on the side of the road. The rifle sat on the seat beside him. He kept his eyes glued to the rearview mirror. He was watching the door of the bank.

When the door busted open, two figures emerged and came running for the car. The ringing of the alarm filled the air. Joe turned on the car. The car doors flew open and the two jumped in. Joe took off like a rabbit down the road.

Millie was a natural. She didn't have much experience with a gun, but after Buck gave her a few shooting lessons in the woods, she grew comfortable enough to hold the thing and point it properly.

The trio made it out of town with little trouble. Buck and Joe had become adept at getting in and out fast and discouraging any would-be followers. By the time the police arrived on the scene and were tipped off about which direction the thieves had fled, the car was well on its way to the next town and out of harm's way.

By nightfall Buck, Joe, and Millie were tucked away in the wild, free to count the day's take. Joe made a fire. Buck and Millie looked over the stash.

"I've never held this much money," the girl said.

"That's nothing," Buck joked. "Give it another week and you'll need new pockets."

"How many more o' these banks we gonna hit?"

"Don't know," Joe said, poking at the fire with a stick.

"You said you had a plan for more. I didn't come along for just one."

"A few more, and then that's it."

"Why stop now?"

"I told you, Millie, we got our reasons. We're not doing this to get rich or prove a point."

"Right, right," Millie said sarcastically. "You ain't provin' nothin'."

"We told you –"

"I know," the girl said. "You're doin' it to get to the Colonel."

"And once we do, we turn away and never look back."

"Says you."

"You're free to do whatever you like, Millie. But in a few weeks we'll part ways and you'll never see us again."

"You're just gonna leave it all behind? All the money? All the –"

"How else does it end?" Joe said. "You think you can do this for the rest of your life?"

"Until I have enough money, yeah."

"How much is enough?" Buck asked.

"I'll know it when I see it."

"We're doing this because we have no choice," Joe said. "And you're here to help us."

"I know why I'm here. I ain't no fool."

"No one said you were," Buck said, getting up from the ground.

"Where you going?" Joe asked.

"If you must know…" Buck said, as he began unbuttoning his pants.

He disappeared into the darkness.

"So where to next?" Millie asked.

"Baylor Ridge."

"Never heard of it."

"That's the idea."

"Tell me again why we're headin' to Lazlo?"

"Because it's just a jump away from two borders. If things go sour and we gotta run, we need to be able to head in any direction."

"Why would things go sour?"

"Because we're inviting guests."

"The Colonel?"

"Among others."

"What others?"

"You don't wanna know."

"Hey," Millie said, "you came to get me. *You* need *me*."

"When we get to Lazlo, the laws will be there waiting for us."

"How can you be so sure?"

Joe looked at Millie.

"Because I'm gonna tell them we're coming," he said.

Buck returned to the fire and sat down with his back against a rock.

"That felt good," he said.

"Spare us," Joe said.

"Your cousin was just tellin' me that he's gonna tip off the laws that we're coming to Lazlo."

"Did he?"

"You think that's a good idea?"

"I think if you want to come along, you let us do the thinkin'."

"I think you two are crazy. That's what I think."

Millie got up and stormed off. Buck and Joe watched her go.

"Got a brass pair on her, that one," Buck said.

Joe scoffed.

"Think she'll cause us trouble?"

"She'll be fine," Joe said.

"I dunno," Buck said. "Don't know if we can trust 'er."

"She's just a kid."

"You tell her everything?"

"What do you think?"

"I think for the first time in a while, I'm gettin' nervous."

"First time in a while?"

"Yeah, why?"

Millie came back into sight.

"Hey, sorry, fellas," she said. "I didn't mean to offend."

"It's okay, kid," Buck said.

"Joe?"

"It's fine."

"Can I sit back down?"

Joe gave a nod and Millie pulled up a patch of ground.

"I'll do what you tell me," Millie said. "I know you two'll steer us right."

Joe let the fire be and took a seat on the ground across from Buck and Millie.

"Say," Buck said to Millie, "you ever hear anything about the Colonel back home?"

"Heard his name once or twice," Millie said. "Friend o' mine worked for him for a while. Drivin' booze in and outta New Mexico."

"Friend of yours?" Joe asked.

"Yeah, friend called Wayne. We went to school together when we were kids. Him and his pa helped out the Colonel. That jar you drank when you were at the farm, that was theirs."

"Where's Wayne now?"

"Can't say. Haven't seen 'im in a while."

"Think you could find him?"

"Wouldn't know where to look. His pa is back at the farm, though."

"Don't suppose you know the Colonel's real name?" Buck said, wryly.

"Marlow, I think. Henry Marlow."

Buck and Joe looked at one another.

"What?" Joe said. "You sure about that?"

"What? His name? I dunno. Pretty sure. Wayne's pa would talk about him, time to time."

"You've seen this man?"

"Can't say for sure. This once I saw a buncha men. Came by the Beethberry farm. That's Wayne's pa's name – Harold Beethberry. Three carloads showed up. They was all dressed alike too. One man did most o' the talkin'. Me and Wayne stayed outside, but we saw them come and go, sure thing we did."

"Any other names, other men you remember?"

Millie thought.

"Can't say, really."

"But you heard the name Henry Marlow."

"I thought everyone heard that name," Millie said. "Hold it," she sputtered. "I do remember one other thing. Now, this was a while back, half a year or more, but there was this one other fella that stuck out. Big guy, ugly too, looked like he was in a fight with a dog or somethin'. Had part of his ear torn off. Looked real strange."

Buck and Joe shared another glance.

"Wait a minute," Millie said. "You fellas been after the Colonel all this time and you didn't even know his name?"

"If you saw Henry Marlow, would you recognize him?"

"I might."

"Henry," Buck said, looking at Joe with an inquisitive glare. "Wasn't that the name of the fella –"

"Yeah," Joe said.

"The one that showed up at your farm lookin' –"

"Same one."

"So you do know who he is," Millie said.

"We do," Joe said.

"Met him a few times," Buck added.

"He know you're comin' after him?" Millie asked.

"That all depends," Joe said.

"On what?"

"On whether or not you can be after someone that's also after you."

Chapter 45

1995

"We're going to have to stop," Liza said, touching her forehead.

"I don't get it," Madeline said.

"Don't get what, dear?"

"Why did they bother with Millie? Why do that at all?"

"You mean why did they bring her along?"

"Right? What purpose did she serve?"

"Mr. Bishop," Liza said. "Do you want to answer that?"

"I suppose..." Nathaniel began. "I suppose because Joe was afraid of being caught inside a bank again?"

"Perhaps," Liza said. "Perhaps there were other reasons."

"Like what?" Madeline asked.

Liza put the back of her hand to her cheek.

"Joe had been going into the bank with Buck. It was quite apparent to the authorities and bank employees alike, I would imagine, that it was two men committing the crimes."

"Right."

"You have to remember too, the Colonel knew their names. By adding a third member, they would no doubt throw him off a little, don't you think?"

"So if they saw a man and a woman –"

"She was a decoy. A distraction."

"For the Colonel or the cops?" Nathaniel asked.

"Both, I imagine."

"Grandma," Madeline said. "Are you feeling okay?"

"Just a little tepid, dear. Perhaps you could get me some water."

Madeline went downstairs to fetch water. Upon her return, Liza took the glass from her granddaughter and took a small sip.

"It would seem so, wouldn't it?" Liza said.

"What would?" Madeline asked.

"Mr. Bishop here just asked if Millie was the girl in the newspaper articles. The one you asked me about."

Madeline was interested in continuing the conversation, but not as interested as she was in her grandmother's health.

"Why don't we call it a day," she suggested. "You should get some rest."

Liza nodded in agreement and rested her head back on her pillow.

"I can show you out, Nate," Madeline said.

Nathaniel turned off his recorder and packed up his things.

"I'll see you soon, Mrs. Meacham," he said.

Liza forced out a smile, though her eyes were already closed. Madeline and Nathaniel left the old woman to sleep.

They walked down the stairs, and Madeline showed Nathaniel to the door.

"I have an assignment tomorrow for most of the day," Nathaniel said, opening the door. "Hopefully I'll be done early enough to come by after."

"That sounds fine. Just call and let me know."

"I will."

"Good night, Nate."

Nathaniel didn't leave right away. Instead he held the door in his hand and looked at Madeline as if he had something he wanted to say.

"Good night, then," he finally said, choosing discretion.

Madeline locked the door behind him. She too was tired, though it was still early in the evening. As soon as Nathaniel was gone, she retired to her room.

The next morning Nathaniel's phone rang in his pocket. He pulled it out, looked at the number, and put it away for later.

The mayoral race in town was kicking off, and Nathaniel was being sent to cover the incumbent's speech. He sat amongst the press in a city hall meeting room. He was listening to the man at the podium but couldn't help but think of Liza and Madeline and wish he were there instead. He had been pleasantly surprised when he'd seen their number on his phone. If the mayor hadn't been in the middle of his speech, he might have picked up the call.

Nathaniel tuned the mayor out. When a fellow reporter asked him some detail about the speech as they were packing up, he simply nodded and smiled and shrugged his shoulders. Nathaniel's phone rang again. This time it was his editor.

"Can you make it back here in twenty?" the taciturn woman asked.

"I can try."

"We need you in the boardroom."

"Anything urgent?"

"Emergency, no. Important, yes."

"I'll see you in twenty."

Nathaniel's editor wasn't lying when she said it was no emergency. Word had come down that the mayor's chief adversary, a middle-aged man with five children, had consorted with a local prostitute. Nathaniel and a cameraman were dispatched to the man's residence to wait outside for comment.

The man was standing outside as they arrived. Nathaniel and the cameraman ran up in time to get a sound bite of the good Christian denying the claim. Nathaniel's phone vibrated. He pulled it from his pocket and looked at the number. It was a number he did not recognize. He held the microphone out in front of him, though he was more interested in the call.

As soon as the man was through and had retreated like a frightened squirrel back into his home, Nathaniel checked his voicemail.

"Nate, it's Maddy," the message played. "We're in the hospital. Call this number when you can."

Nathaniel handed the microphone to the cameraman and hurried off on his own to a quiet spot in front of a neighbor's house. No one answered his call. Nathaniel tried again.

"Hello?"

"Maddy?"

"Nate," Madeline said with relief in her voice.

"What happened?"

"I thought to call you when it happened, but it was so late."

"What is it? Is she okay?"

"I couldn't sleep last night, of all nights. I looked in on her before I went back to my room to see if she was feeling any better. Her eyes were open but she wasn't answering me. She was barely breathing. I called 911 and they brought her here right away. I thought I was going to lose her."

"But you didn't, right?"

"She's alive," Madeline said. "She's got tubes coming out of her every which way, but she's alive. It's good you called now and not earlier when I was a mess. She's awake and responding now. Tired, but awake."

"And her breathing?"

"Better. They've got her on oxygen."

"Did they tell you what happened?"

"She's just old, Nate. She wasn't feeling well, and she hid it from me. She hadn't been feeling herself for days."

"And she'll be okay, right?"

"They hope so. The doctors want to keep her here for a while."

"Of course. Can I come by later today to see her?"

"Nate," Madeline said, "I don't think we should push her more than –"

"No, of course not," Nathaniel interrupted. "I meant just to visit. We can pick up the work when she's feeling better."

"Of course. Sorry. I didn't mean –"

"Which hospital are you at?"

Nathaniel was able to escape the office early in the evening. He made it to the hospital with plenty of visiting hours to spare. He stopped at the gift shop and purchased a bouquet of flowers.

"Hi," Madeline whispered as Nathaniel crept into the room.

She pulled him back out into the hall.

"I brought these," Nathaniel said, handing her the flowers.

"Thank you."

"How is she?"

"Not too bad, actually," Madeline said with a smile. "She's not as feisty as usual, but who can say that's a bad thing? She's asleep now."

"I can come back."

"Not at all. She's due to see the doctor any minute, so she'll have to be woken. Stay. She'll be glad to see you."

The doctor came not long after, and Madeline joined him in the room. When all business had been completed, Madeline invited Nathaniel to come in.

"Thank you for the flowers," Liza said.

The woman looked different. She was wearing a nightgown of her own – one that she no doubt had Madeline retrieve for her – but her hair was unkempt, and her face showed no touch of makeup. She had a clear tube running across her cheeks and into her nostrils, and her eyes drooped as if she had aged even more overnight.

"How're you feeling?" Nathaniel asked.

"Oh, I'm fine. I don't know what all the fuss is about."

"Everyone is just making sure you're okay," Madeline said.

"So," Liza said, "where did we leave off?"

"Grandma!" Madeline scoffed.

"I think we should wait a while," Nathaniel said. "At least until you're back home."

"Nonsense," Liza said. "If they had their way, they'd keep me here forever. I'm fine enough to talk. Now have a seat."

"I didn't bring any of my things," Nathaniel said. "Besides, I've had a hell of a day."

"You too?" Liza joked.

"You heard what the doctor said," Madeline added. "At least wait until they've done all the tests and your fever is gone."

"I might not have much time left, you know. We still have much to discuss."

"Grandma…"

"Okay, don't get upset. I was just being funny. Mr. Bishop, you'll still have a seat and stay a while, won't you?"

"Of course I will."

Nathaniel and Madeline both took a seat in Liza's room.

"Tomorrow," Liza said.

"Tomorrow what?" Madeline asked.

"Tomorrow we continue. Right in this room if we have to."

"Why don't I just come by and we'll see then how you're feeling," Nathaniel said. "I don't want you to strain –"

"Come tomorrow," Liza said, "and don't forget your things."

Chapter 46

1924

Buck, Joe, and Millie sat together at a restaurant in Montrey, Oklahoma. They had finished their lunch and were preparing to get up when two uniformed police officers sauntered into the establishment and saddled up to a table nearby. The cops each ordered a coffee and a piece of cake. The three outlaws at the table dared not make eye contact with the lawmen. They kept their heads down and ordered refills of coffee so they could linger a while longer.

"This is crazy," Buck said. "It's worse just sittin' here."

"I agree," Millie said.

"We have to walk right by them if we leave," Joe said.

"If we walk out one at a time, no one'll be the wiser," Buck said.

Joe didn't like the idea, but he also didn't like the feeling of being ten feet away from men who would become heroes for taking them down.

Buck was first to get up and leave. Millie and Joe decided to go together. They walked arm in arm. One of the cops looked up as they passed by and caught Millie's eye. The young girl smiled. The officer smiled back and then simply went back to his coffee and conversation.

Back in the car, Joe put forward the idea of skipping the town bank altogether. It didn't feel right to him. Lately it seemed as though every town was on high alert, but this town felt especially bad. Besides the two in the restaurant, they had also seen a police car out on patrol as they drove in.

"I say we stay," Millie offered. "We can still do it."

"I don't know," Buck said, looking out the window of the car. "I'm with Joe. What's the sense of it, anyhow? Let's just skip ahead to Lazlo."

"It's right there," Millie said, "a hundred paces away. All that money."

Joe turned on the car.

"We're skipping it."

Millie huffed. Joe put the car in gear and pulled out slowly.

"Can I at least stop in the store before we run?"

"You need somethin'?" Buck asked.

"Why else would I ask?"

Joe pulled up to the sidewalk and let Millie out. The surly girl got out and went into the store a few doors down.

"She's got one big chip on her shoulder," Buck said.

"Don't know what it is," Joe said. "Stubborn like a mule."

"I tell ya, though, she's got guts. That's fer sure."

"Hey, have a look on that map. What else we got between here and Lazlo?"

Buck opened the map, and he and Joe had a look together.

"Not much," Buck said. "Looks like a few one-horse towns and then Cardin."

"Don't know if two banks are enough to…"

Joe stopped.

"What? What is it?" said Buck.

Joe looked up at his cousin.

"Millie said she knows those folks that worked for the Colonel," he said.

"Yeah, so…?"

"Don't you see?"

Buck thought for a second.

"You sayin'… we get her to tell 'em?"

"He doesn't know she's riding with us."

"If we keep knocking over places, he will."

"Then we don't. We go to Lazlo and make sure the Colonel knows we're coming."

"Why would the Colonel believe her?"

"We'll give her something to convince him."

"Like what? What you got in mind?"

"Like the car that's probably still parked at the Tucker farm."

"All right," Buck said. "You trust 'er?"

"I think we can trust her."

"I don't know," Buck said. "There's somethin' about her –"

An alarm bell rang through the air.

"What the hell?" Joe said.

Millie came bursting out the front of the bank. Joe turned on the car and hit the gas. The car squealed out and wobbled as Joe tried his best to gain control. A man emerged from the bank not far behind the running girl. He aimed his pistol and fired. Millie, hearing the shot, ducked her head as she and the car met in the middle of the road. The man fired again, hitting the side of the car. Millie dove into the back seat. Joe hit the gas and the car tires spun. The man was joined by a second, and both fired at the speeding car. Buck and Joe lowered their heads. Millie stayed laid out in the back.

"What the fuck 're you thinkin'?" Buck yelled.

A bullet hit the back window.

"Just drive!" Millie screamed.

Another bullet hit the back of the car.

The car soon hurtled past the "Thank you for visiting Montrey" sign, tossing up a pile of sand and dust as it did. No one was behind them, but to be safe, Joe turned off the main road at the first opportunity.

They stayed on that road for about twenty minutes more when Joe pulled off to the side in barren country. He turned to the back seat.

"Get out," he said.

"What?" Millie said, having heard the direction perfectly well.

"Get out," Joe repeated. "Your fun ends here."

"We're in the middle o' nowhere –"

"I don't care where we are. You put our lives at risk, our entire plan at risk. You need to get –"

"I'm sorry," Millie said.

"Sorry won't cut it."

"I was just tryin' ta impress you is all. Show you I could do it."

"Do what? Get caught? Get killed?"

"No, I wasn't –"

"You weren't thinking. And now it's time for you to go."

Millie looked at Buck. Buck offered no support.

"Please, Joe," Millie said calmly. "I didn't mean to make you angry. Let me stay with you a while more."

"Why? Why would I let you stay if I can't trust you?"

"You *can* trust me. Honest, you can."

"We've come too far to let you mess this up," Buck said.

"I won't mess up anything, I swear it. Just tell me what I can do to make it up to you. Here," she said, reaching into her pockets and pulling out sweaty handfuls of money. "Take it. You can have it all. Go on, take it."

"That won't do it," Joe said. "It's not about the money. Don't you get that?"

"Tell me what to do, Joe. Tell me what I can do to make you trust me."

Joe and Buck looked at one another in silence. Joe took a breath and looked back at Millie.

"Put that money away," he said.

Joe pulled the car back onto the road.

"There might be something you can do, come to think of it."

The car jerked forward a few times, sending the occupants reeling. The machine then sputtered to a halt.

"What's the matter?" Millie asked.

She got no response.

Buck got out of the car. He opened the hood and took a look inside. Joe got out to join him. They didn't spend much time looking at the engine. Instead they walked around the side of the car and stopped near the back on the passenger side. Millie, unable to contain her curiosity, stepped out of the car and joined them.

"Well," Buck said, "at least it didn't catch flame."

He and Joe were staring down at a pool of liquid drooling out from under the car. Millie stuck her finger into one bullet hole on the side of the car and then into another, and then one more.

"Yeah, it was one of those," Buck said mockingly.

"Now what?" Millie asked sheepishly.

Buck and Joe just stared at the girl.

Joe walked to the car door and pulled out his rifle. He brought it back around to the side.

"What's that for?" Millie asked, taking a step back.

"Grab your things," he said. "We're walking."

Chapter 47

They made it to the next town by nightfall. Buck and Joe sent Millie to the store for some supplies while they set up camp in the woods.

There was a small lake just outside town, one perfectly suited for drinking water and bathing and whatever else they might need it for. Millie returned with food and insisted on preparing dinner for all. Joe retired to the lake to wash up and take a moment for himself.

The stars were especially bright that night. The moon was full and lit up the lake to look like a blackened mirror. Usually a person couldn't see more than a few feet ahead in the woods without a flame of light, but this night was different. Joe could see for miles in every direction.

Joe was drying off on the shore when Millie came down to fetch him.

"Supper's on," she said, handing Joe one of his shoes.

"Thanks."

"Say, Joe?"

"Yeah?"

"I really am sorry about before."

"I know you are."

"Didn't mean to make you angry."

"Let's just look past it, shall we?"

"No hard feelin's, then?"

"We don't have time for hard feelings."

Millie lunged forward and wrapped her arms around Joe. Joe didn't know how to react at first, but he soon patted Millie gently on the back to appease her.

The three ate supper in relative silence. Having not eaten in quite some time, they polished off the food in minutes. Buck licked his fingers clean and rolled a cigarette with the fresh tobacco Millie had brought back. He lay back against a tree and smoked it. Millie came to join him. She put her back up against the same tree and Buck handed her the tobacco.

"We're going to need a new car," Joe said, feeding the fire.

"Too late to do anything about it tonight," Buck said. "We can find one in town tomorrow."

"Somethin' fast," Millie said.

"How much cash you got on you?" Joe asked Buck.

"Enough for ten," Buck said with a smile.

"You think you're okay to go into town and get us a ride?"

"I'll go," Millie offered.

"I don't think so," Buck said.

"You don't trust me on a simple task?"

Buck gave Millie a disapproving look.

"I need you with me, Millie," Joe said.

"What're we gonna do?" Millie asked.

"We're gonna find a telephone."

"Who we callin'?"

"The welcoming committee."

"Who might that be?"

"Remember that promise you made me earlier?"

"Which one's that?"

"The one to make it up to us for getting us shot at."

"I do."

"Tomorrow you're going to call Mr. Beethberry. You're going to call him and tell him that Buck and I came by your farm, and that you heard us say that we're headed to Lazlo – Lazlo Savings and Loan – in two days' time. Don't tell him anything more. Don't tell him you're with us; don't tell him where you are at all. Tell him that we mentioned the Colonel's name more than once, and that we ran off with your truck."

"You want him to tell the Colonel about it?"

"You're going to see to it that he does."

"Okay," Millie said, "I can do that."

"Settled," Buck said.

Buck took his hat from his head and lowered it over his eyes. He crossed his arms and dropped his chin to his chest.

"Wake me up when it's mornin'."

"I ain't ready to sleep," Millie said.

"Don't recall askin'."

Millie got up and stood near Joe at the fire.

"I don't think he likes me much," Millie whispered.

"I wouldn't say that."

"Then what would you say?"

"I'd say he doesn't like you at all."

"And what about you?"

"Me?"

"Yeah. How do you feel about me?"

"How do I feel about you? You mean after that stunt you pulled this morning?"

"I mean besides that."

"I'd say you're all right," Joe said. "A little wild... careless even, but you're all right."

"Just all right?"

Joe looked up from the fire to see Millie staring at him.

"What?" Joe asked.

Millie leaned in and tried to kiss Joe. Joe moved back and stopped her.

"Whoa, now," he said.

"What?" Millie asked, slightly embarrassed.

"Let's just take it easy with that."

"So you *don't* like me..."

"I didn't say that, now, did I? I just don't..." Joe paused. "Look," he said. "You got a lot of things going for you. You're young and pretty and –"

"Never mind," Millie said. "Just... never mind."

Millie turned and walked off toward the water. Joe watched her disappear into the small valley.

"She's trouble, that one," Buck said. "Like I told ya."

Joe followed Millie down to the water. He found her sitting on the shore and sat down beside her.

"What is it you want from me?" Joe asked.

"What do I know?" Millie said, trying to hide her tears.

Joe took pity on the girl. She was, after all, just a kid. He remembered what it was like to be that age, to be lost and unsure, to not know where, or if, you belong.

"What is it you're looking for out here?" Joe asked.

"Nothin'," Millie said. "I just wanted to get away from the fire."

"No, not out here by the water, out here with us. Why did you want to leave home so badly?"

Millie looked over at Joe, though she didn't hold the glance for fear he might see her cry.

"When Jervis didn't come back from the war…" she began. "I don't know."

Millie wiped her eyes with her arm.

"Everything's been different. Ma and Pa… They barely know I'm alive."

"You think that's true?"

"Everything changed when he died. Ma didn't come out of her room for a month, not for one minute. Hell, it didn't take Waylon long to have his fill of it. He was smart. He ran off to Texas. Left me there, though, alone. After a while I started runnin' off. Couldn't help it. I just had to get away."

"What about your father?"

"He didn't care much about it. He was always partial to the boys. I helped cook a bit, clean… That was all he knew."

"Where'd you run off to?"

"Wayne's, mostly… sometimes just to the old barn. I'd stay the night just to see if she'd notice."

Millie looked at Joe.

"Does that make me a terrible person?"

"I don't think so," Joe said.

"I stayed out for just a night at the start, then maybe two. Came a time where I didn't come back for a week, maybe more. She didn't care at all."

"That can't be true."

"One time, not too long ago, I was gone for what musta been a month. Went to Georgia, went to see the ocean, just Wayne and me. When I got back, she didn't mention a word about it. Didn't ask me where I was, what I'd been doin'. It was like I was never gone."

Joe and Millie looked out on the water. Joe thought about Erma. He thought about the way she'd treated him when he lived with her. He knew what it was like to feel unwanted.

"I had a mother," Joe said. "Once, a long time ago. I was young, much younger than you."

"What happened?"

"She died. I was just a kid at the time, but I remember it well."

"Was she a good mother?"

"She was."

"Did you love her?"

"I did. Very much."

Millie looked over at Joe. She didn't care that he saw her tears this time.

"Did she love you?" she asked.

Chapter 48

Buck split off from Joe and Millie at the edge of town. He went in search of a car while the other two went looking for a telephone in a somewhat discreet location. They planned to meet up in the afternoon, back at the camp.

It was in the lobby of a small hotel that Millie spotted two wall-mounted phones for public use. They waited until everyone was gone and both phones were free before they approached. Joe picked up the receiver on the first phone. He did not make a call. He simply wanted the phone to look occupied.

"Call him," Joe said to Millie.

Millie picked up the phone and through the operator was able to reach the Beethberry house. Harold was out in the shed, but his wife was kind enough to fetch him when Millie asked politely.

"This is Harold," the man said.

Millie held the earpiece out so Joe could listen in.

"Mr. Beethberry, this is Millie Tucker."

"What can I do for you?"

"I was wondering if you'd seen Wayne in a while? I haven't been able to get in touch with him."

"Wayne's off for work. Has been for some time."

"Oh," Millie said, in her most innocent voice. "Is there any way I could get in touch with him? I had a question."

"What's yer question? I can pass it on when I sees 'im."

"I don't know if... maybe I shouldn't..."

"I'm right busy today, Millie. Is there somethin' I can help you with or not?"

"I wanted to know if he could get in touch with the Colonel for me."

There was a pause on the other end.

"Lilah," the man said, "would you mind fetchin' me my old boots? They're out by the car."

There was silence.

"Mr. Beethberry?" Millie said.

"The Colonel, you say?"

"That's right. I was hopin' to get a message to him."

"And what makes you think Wayne can do somethin' like that?"

"It's just that... Well... I figured since..."

"What's the message, girl?"

"I know where he can find the men he's lookin' for."

"The men he's lookin' for?"

"The ones that been robbin' all the banks. The ones blaming it on the Colonel."

"And how might you know where those boys are?"

"They were at the farm."

"What farm?"

"My farm."

"Them boys that've been robbin' all those banks were at your farm?"

"Yes, sir. Not too long ago. Didn't know it was them till they was long gone. But it was them, all right."

"How can you be so sure?"

"I saw their names in the paper. One of the men had on a burgundy hat, like they said. They even drove up in that car the laws chased outta town. Car's still sittin' at the house now. They took Pa's truck and got away."

"Their car is at your Pa's farm?"

"That's right."

"And you know where them boys are at now?"

"I know where they're headed."

"Do ya now?"

"Yes, sir."

"Well, why don't you go on and tell me what you know, then."

"And you'll get the word to the Colonel?"

"Go ahead and tell me. I'll worry about that."

"They said they're headin' to Lazlo to stay a day or two before leavin' for good."

"Lazlo."

"That's right. Said they was gonna stick it to the Colonel big-time."

"Did they say where they was runnin' to? After Lazlo?"

Millie looked at Joe. Joe shook his head.

"No," Millie said, "they were talking about the Lazlo Savings and Loan. Said somethin' about a reserve bank with all the cash at the end of the month, or some nonsense like that."

"You don't say. And how'd you happen on all this?"

"They stayed the night. One o' them took a hit to the head and needed a place to rest. Hell if we knew who they were. I went to take them coffee in the morning and they were jabberin' on. I listened through the door."

"What else they say?"

"Not much more than what I told ya."

Joe nodded in approval.

Harold was silent on the other end.

"You still there?" Millie asked.

"Why you rattin' these boys out, anyway?"

"I know you... I mean I know Wayne's done some business with the Colonel. And, well... those men took advantage of my family. They stole my daddy's car, after all. Seemed like the right thing to do."

"Where you at?"

"I'm out at my aunt's place. Didn't want to call from home and worry Ma and Pa."

"Don't be mentionin' any o' this to your folks, ya hear?"

"Yes, sir."

"We never spoke."

"Will you be able to get the message to Wayne?"

"I'll get the message where it needs to go. Who else you told about this?"

"No one. Wouldn't know who to tell."

"Don't speak another word of it. Not to anyone, you understand?"

"Yes, sir."

"You done the right thing callin' me, Millie."

"Yes, sir."

Harold hung up the phone. Millie did the same. She looked at Joe with satisfaction on her face.

"Good," Joe said. "You did good."

"Thanks."

"Why don't you go on and get us some Cokes or something?"

"What? Why?" Millie asked.

"This next call is one I gotta make on my own."

"What for? You don't trust me to hear?"

"It's not that, Millie," Joe said, still holding the phone in his hand. "You did good just now, real good. It's just that – to tell the truth – I'm not so sure about how I'm gonna do. I'd rather make this call alone, if you don't mind."

Millie gave Joe a disapproving look but left him to make his call. She ventured off to the small newsstand at the other end of the lobby.

Joe let go of the phone he held. The receiver swung in the air like the pendulum of a grandfather clock. He picked up the other phone and placed his call.

"Hello, Marie," Joe said.

"To whom am I speaking?" Marie asked on the other side.

"It's Joe."

There was a long pause.

"Oh, Joe," Marie said, "you shouldn't have called."

Joe's head dropped.

"Why's that?" he asked.

"What have you done, Joe? Oh, what have you done?"

"Ma'am, I –"

"Why are you calling here?"

"To speak with Alfred, I –"

"You broke that man's heart, you did. Broke it in two."

"I wanted to explain."

"There is no explanation you could give. Don't you know that? Alfred works for the Governor. He's an agent of the law. What's more, he cared for you. He brought you into our house. What is it you could say to him now?"

"So he's not there, then?" Joe said meekly.

"He is not," Marie said, "but even if he were, I don't know that he would speak to you. You've done enough already to –"

"I'll be in Lazlo in two days," Joe said, interrupting.

Marie was flustered and sounded out of breath.

"What did you say?" she asked.

"I won't bother you anymore," Joe said. "I just need you to tell him that I'll be in Lazlo in two days' time. After that I'll be going away. Going away for good.

"You want him to come say goodbye?"

"He can do whatever he wants. I just need you to tell him that. After Lazlo I'll be gone. He'll never have to see me again."

"Never see you again?" Marie said. "Oh, Joe. What a sad, sad thing, that after all this time you could think that would be what he wanted."

Joe couldn't take any more. He hung up the phone without another word. He held his hand there as if he were afraid the phone would leap back to life with Marie on the other end. Joe was not one for false bravado, but he did his best to choke back the hardening lump in his throat.

Millie returned with a candy bar and a Coke. She offered each to Joe. He declined.

"I'll meet you and Buck later today," Joe said.

He began to walk off.

"Where're you goin'?" Millie asked.

"I need some time."

Millie looked around the hotel.

"Well, what am I supposed to do?"

Joe did not answer. He continued to show her his back as he left the hotel lobby.

Millie was left standing alone. She took a sip from the bottle of Coke. She smiled at a young man walking by. She looked up at the ornate ceiling of the lobby.

Then Millie turned and faced the phones. She took a bite of her candy bar and another sip of Coke. She looked around to see if anyone was near. No one was. Millie reached for the phone. She picked up the receiver and placed a call.

Chapter 49

Buck arrived back at camp. He brought Joe and Millie to the place in the woods where he'd stashed the car he'd acquired.

The car was a gray Pontiac. It wasn't a new car, nor was it particularly good-looking, but it had four wheels and, from what Joe could tell when he turned it on, the engine sounded just fine.

"How much was it?" Millie asked.

Buck just shook his head.

"What does that mean?" Joe inquired, getting out from the driver's seat.

Buck stared at Joe with a smirk.

"It means he stole it," Millie said.

Buck's smirk turned to a full-toothed smile.

Joe looked at his cousin. He thought for a moment but couldn't come up with a viable reason why the theft should matter at all.

"Okay," Joe said, "we'll leave tomorrow."

There was a feeling of stoicism in the camp that night. Perhaps it was just Joe; he wasn't in a mood to chatter. After supper he walked down to the lake on his own and stayed there until dark. Neither Buck nor Millie went down to see him. When he returned, the other two were sitting by the fire, smoking their cigarettes. They saw Joe approach but neither said a word to him.

It wasn't until morning that Joe spoke up.

"Let's get outta here," he said. "We'll get breakfast on the way."

There wasn't much to pack up, and soon they were back on the road and headed for Lazlo. Buck drove, and Millie sat in the back. Lazlo was a good half-day's drive away, but Buck was in no particular hurry. Being that they were in a stolen car, it was the wise thing to do to take it slow.

They stopped at a roadside station an hour into the journey. Joe and Millie went into the restaurant while Buck filled up the tank with gasoline. He came to join them soon after.

"I ordered you some breakfast," Joe said.

"What's gotten into you?" Buck finally asked.

"What do you mean?"

"I mean, you've been sour since yesterday. What's come over you?"

"Nothing," Joe said sternly. "Let's just eat and get outta here before we draw any attention."

"Attention?" said Buck, looking around the empty place. "We're in the middle o' nowhere. No one's lookin' for us out here. Out with it."

"Alfred knows."

"Who's Alfred?" Millie asked.

"You knew he would soon enough, Joe," Buck said.

"You shoulda heard the way Marie spoke to me."

"Who's Marie?" Millie asked.

"And you're surprised?" Buck asked.

"Not surprised, no. I don't know what I am."

"I do," Buck said."

"Who are you talking about?" Millie asked again.

A young waitress came by the table and placed three plates with fried eggs and bacon down on the table.

"Coffee?" she asked, holding the pot in her hand.

Buck held up his mug and the woman filled it.

"It ain't hard to figure," Buck continued when the waitress had gone.

"Is someone gonna tell me what's goin' on, or am I gonna scream?"

"Joe's friend Alfred, the lawman, he knows about what we been up to."

"Oh," Millie said, shoving a forkful of egg into her mouth as if the news were no big deal. "How could he not? All he had to do was open up a newspaper."

Joe looked at Millie with disdain.

"What?" Millie asked. "What'd I say?"

"Can we just eat?" Joe said.

"You need to brush it off," Buck said, pointing his fork at Joe. "This ain't gonna do you no good. So the man knows. Big deal. What did you think was gonna happen?"

"You're right," Joe said. "I know you're right."

"Good. Then eat up and let's get outta here."

Joe picked up his fork and tried his best to find an appetite.

"So who's this guy Alfred, anyway?" Millie asked. "How'd he come to be your friend?"

"Just someone I knew when I was young."

"And he didn't know about all this till now?"

Joe shook his head.

"Must not be much of a copper, then, I'd say."

"We were careful to stay clandestine," Joe said.

"What's that mean, 'clandestine'?"

"Means quiet," Buck said. "Like a secret, right?"

"In any case, he knows about us now, and things won't ever be the same."

"What makes you think they woulda anyhow?" Buck asked. "You and me, we ain't the same. She ain't the same. No one's the same. Time don't stand still and things change."

"You still have a home," Joe said. "That didn't change."

Buck put down his silverware and looked across the table at Joe.

"Get this straight, cousin," he said. "Them people you visited with might've been the last good thing you knew, but *I'm* as close to a home as you ever had and you're ever gonna get. And don't you forget that. So you can sit there and cry in your coffee that Alfred and his ol' lady don't think you're so sweet and innocent no more, but hell if I'm gonna let you feel sorry for yourself about it. Now eat your breakfast and let's get ta Lazlo and get on with it."

Buck picked up his fork, but only for a moment. He dropped it back onto his plate with a clank.

"And I'll tell you somethin' else," he said. "If I see that Alfred or any of his kind in Lazlo, and he gets in our way, I'll take him out just like the Colonel. I'll take him out and I won't think twice about it. And you shouldn't neither. Because I'll tell you this, that man won't think twice about puttin' a bullet in you, and he surely won't think twice about puttin' one in me. No matter who you think you were to him, you ain't no more. You even said it yourself."

"You don't know that," Joe said.

"Don't you doubt it," Buck said sternly. "Don't you doubt it for a second."

He picked up his fork, stabbed an egg, and shoved it into his mouth.

"That man is your enemy now. Only difference is, *he* already knows it."

Joe didn't like the feel of what his cousin was saying. It stabbed at his chest and turned in his stomach. Any appetite he might have had before was now gone without a trace. He couldn't even think about eating, and not because he was unsure what to think but because he knew that what Buck was saying was true.

Alfred Winter had been the first friend Joe had had. He'd been the first to protect him after his parents were killed. He'd been the first to show concern. He was the man he'd shared all those letters with, who'd sent him books, who knew more about him than anyone in the world besides his cousin. But now he was the man after Joe, the man whose job relied on bringing him in or bringing him down. Alfred Winter, who had helped clothe, feed, and to some extent rear the boy, was now, like his cousin said, Joe's enemy.

Millie sat in the front seat of the car as they headed back out. Joe spread out in the back and closed his eyes. He hadn't gotten much sleep the night before, and nodding off was the only thing he could think of to help ease his mind. But Joe didn't sleep. He listened to the sound of the tires on the road and to the low hum of song and static on the radio. He listened to his cousin and Millie jabber, and though he couldn't make out most of their words, he didn't care to either. But mostly Joe listened to the sounds in his head, the ones telling him that his only obligations were to himself and to Buck, and to seeing to it that they both made it out of this alive.

Chapter 50

There was a small motor lodge just outside Lazlo. It was a fortuitous find, and one that Joe and Buck had not planned on. They pulled off the road and parked within eyesight of it. Millie was sent in to secure lodging. It was agreed that all three travelers would share one room.

Millie completed her business and returned to the car. Buck and Joe used a side entrance, sidled into the long, slender building, and stowed away in the room. They brought their firearms in with them.

"I want to go have a look at the bank," Millie said.

"Too dangerous," Joe responded, without hesitation. "We can't be seen in town. There's no telling who's already watching that place."

"Maybe you can't be seen, but they don't know about me."

Joe and Buck exchanged a glance. Joe hesitated but finally gave in.

"Don't you make any noise. And don't attract attention."

"And bring back some groceries," Buck added. "If we're gonna be holed up in this room all night, we'll need somethin' to eat."

Millie agreed and within moments was gone from the room. Buck moved the shades and watched as the girl made it to the car and pulled away.

"Think it's smart?" he asked. "Her goin' into town in that car?"

"Let her check out the bank. Might not be a bad thing that she learns the streets while she's at it."

"Whatever you say."

Joe took a seat on the bed. He lifted his rifle and gave it a good inspection.

"You trust her, don't you, Buck?" he asked.

"You don't want to hear my answer."

"That's answer enough."

"You do? Trust her, that is?"

"I think we can, for now at least," Joe said. "This'll all be over soon, anyhow."

"Tell me true. You think it'll all work out?"

Joe didn't answer right away. He put down the rifle and lay down on the bed, not bothering to remove his shoes. He folded his arms on his chest and looked straight up at the ceiling.

"If things don't go as planned, we may not be around to regret it," he said.

"I have an idea about the bank," said Buck.

Joe turned his head to his cousin. Buck didn't always have his own ideas about things, but when he did, they were usually worth listening to.

Millie returned to the room many hours later. She brought a smattering of groceries back with her. Buck plunged his hand into the paper bag and pulled out a loaf of bread.

"See anything interestin'?" he asked.

"That's one big place," Millie said. "I never seen a bank so big."

"This ain't no small town," Buck said.

"Did you go in?" Joe asked.

"Don't worry," Millie assured. "I just took a quick look."

"Did you see a safe?"

"Big one, near the back. There was a man with a gun standin' right beside it. Two more by the front door, and each o' them had guns too."

"Don't worry 'bout that," Buck said.

He ripped off a hunk of bread, used a pocketknife to cut into a slab of cold roast beef, and then shoveled the food into his mouth.

"I'm not worried," Millie said. "Just thought you should know."

"What took so long?"

"Was there a hurry?"

Buck threw a wad of bread to Joe.

"Think your friend Winter is here?" he asked.

"Might be," Joe said.

"You got a friend?" Millie asked.

"Already told you about it this morning," Buck said.

"Oh… Alfred," Millie said, cocking her head to the side. "Alfred Winter," she repeated to herself. "Alfred Winter. I've heard that name before."

"You think he'll get to the Colonel before we do?" Buck asked.

"He might," Joe said. "If the Colonel's here, that is."

"He better be here."

Buck turned his attention to Millie, who took a seat by the covered window.

"You sure your neighbor there got the word to the Colonel?"

"I'm sure," Millie said.

"Doesn't mean he'll come," Joe said. "Man like that —one who tries as hard as he does to stay hidden – man like that might send someone else."

"Oh, well, great," Buck said. "That's just great. Good thing you're bringin' that up now. When everythin' we done, everythin' we're gonna do, relies on him showin' his face."

"He'll come," Millie said, confidently.

"There you go," Joe said calmly.

"You're takin' her word for it?"

"You got a better idea?"

"He'll come," Millie said again.

Buck took a look at Millie and then at Joe.

"You're both a little soft in the head, that's what I think."

"I ain't the one with bread crumbs on my face," Millie said.

Buck pointed his pocketknife at Millie.

"You know what, girl –"

"Okay, Buck," Joe said, "take it easy. We're all a little tense. Why don't you go get some air or something? Go on and check that the car is hidden away."

Buck took a moment.

"Good idea," he said.

Buck left the room in a huff.

"Don't prod him like that," Joe said. "He can have a short fuse."

"I'm just havin' a little fun."

"This isn't meant to be fun."

"I know that," Millie said. "I take it serious."

"I know you do. And tomorrow we're gonna count on you. We can't do it without your help."

Joe leaned his head back on the pillow and rested his eyes.

"Now, tell me about the bank, and everything else you saw in town," he said.

Buck returned sometime later having taken time to calm himself down. He took a seat in a chair and kicked off his shoes.

"It's quiet out there," he said.

"Quiet is good," Joe said.

"Let's go over tomorrow. Millie, you know what you're meant to do?"

"I do," Millie said.

"Joe, you good?"

"I'm good, Buck."

"Well, great. Good talk."

Buck got up from the chair and headed to the door.

"Where you headed now?" Joe asked.

"What's the difference?"

Joe smiled and sat down in the chair that Buck had just left.

Millie took out a pack of tobacco and rolled herself a cigarette. She lit it up and took a puff.

"That new?" Joe asked.

"What? This?" Millie asked, holding up the silver lighter. "Got it in town today. They got plenty o' nice shops."

"You see a bookstore?" Joe asked. "I'd sure like to go to a bookstore. Haven't been in some time."

"No," Millie said, paying more attention to her cigarette than to Joe. "No bookstore. Saw a pile o' newspapers on the street though."

"You didn't happen to pick one up, did you?"

"I don't bother with those things. Nothin' worthwhile in 'em."

"That may change by tomorrow," Joe said.

Chapter 51

1995

Liza returned home on a Saturday. She was weak and exhausted and needed help to get up the stairs to her bedroom. Madeline felt the obligation to serve as caretaker and didn't want to bother anyone else for assistance. She alone would tend to her grandmother's needs. She got the old woman into her bed, dressed her in her sleeping gown, and made sure she was as comfortable as she could be. She brought her grandmother a warm glass of lemon water and placed it beside the bed where she could reach it.

"Try to get some sleep," Madeline said.

"Thank you, dear," Liza muttered.

"Are you sure you don't need anything more? You haven't eaten much."

"I'm fine for now, thank you."

"Okay. I'll check in on you in a little while."

Madeline turned to leave.

"Oh, one thing," Liza said, turning Madeline back around.

"Yes?"

"I need you to get something for me."

Liza pointed to the side table on the other side of the bed. Madeline approached it.

"This?" Madeline asked, holding up a photo of Liza as a younger woman.

"No, no, not that," the old woman said. "Inside. You'll need to open the drawer."

Madeline put her hand on a drawer handle.

"Lower," Liza said. "The bottom drawer."

Madeline opened the drawer.

"Are these Grandpa's things?" she asked, pulling items out one at a time.

"At the bottom," Liza said.

Madeline removed some books, a small photo album, some loose papers, and finally a layer of old socks.

"There's nothing more, Grandma. Are you sure this is the right drawer?"

"Look closer, dear."

Madeline, worried that her grandmother may not be herself, still did as she was asked. She got down on her knees and looked closely at the empty drawer.

"I don't... Oh," she said, "wait a second."

Madeline reached down to what looked like a piece of beige tape affixed to the bottom of the drawer. The tape looked old and weathered. It had worn to the point of bleeding into the color of the wood beneath. Using her fingernail, Madeline began to pick at a corner of it. Once she had enough to grasp between her fingers, she pulled the piece up and off the wood.

The tape came away in one shot. There, stuck to the bottom of the strip, was what Liza was clearly after.

"It's… a key," Madeline said, removing the metal artifact from the tape.

"Keep that in a safe place," Liza said, "and don't show it to anyone."

"What's it for? What's it meant to open?"

"You'll have to wait and see. "

"Grandma," Madeline said, getting up from the floor, "is everything okay? You're acting funny."

Liza laughed.

"Oh, my love," she said, "come sit here."

Liza tapped the bed beside her. Madeline sat down.

"You worry too much. You know, your mother worried like that too. Just promise me not to speak a word about that key to anyone."

"You're talking about Nate, aren't you? You don't want me to show this to him."

"You're right. Not yet."

"Why not?"

"He's too curious. He'll pester and prod to no end. You have to have patience."

"You want me to wait."

"You must wait."

"Yes, but for what?"

"You'll know it when you see it, dear. It won't be long now."

"What won't be long? Grandma, you're talking as if –"

"Now, now. None of that," Liza said, taking Madeline's hand in hers. "Do you remember what your mother told you before she died?"

Madeline and Liza locked eyes.

"I don't want to talk about it," Madeline said.

"She told you she'd always be here with you."

"I remember."

"Do you think it's true? Do you think she's here with you?"

"I don't know sometimes."

"You don't? Why not?"

"It's just that…" Madeline choked up. "I haven't been able to find the place where I'm at peace with it all. That place where I can forgive her for everything and just let it all be."

"There's nothing wrong with feeling conflicted, dear. It happens to the best of us."

Liza took the key from Madeline. She brought it close to her face and had a good look at the thing. The small, round key, once newly minted brass, was now brown and stained. It was heavy in her hand and felt ancient from years of being shielded at the bottom of a drawer. She squeezed the key tightly in her palm. Liza then lifted Madeline's hand and placed the key inside, closing Madeline's soft, young fingers around it with hers.

"You know," Liza said, looking up at her granddaughter, "sometimes it's when you stop looking for the things you're after that they come up and find you all on their own. Sometimes you just might find them in the darnedest of places, places you didn't even think to look. And sometimes… sometimes, my sweet dear, you end up finding things you didn't even know you were looking for. And those are the best things of all."

Chapter 52

It was well after midnight when Buck and Joe snuck out of the room and climbed into the car. Buck drove into Lazlo at a safe and steady pace. They roamed the streets in the dark, in no hurry at all, eventually coming upon the block where the Lazlo Savings and Loan stood. Instead of stopping to get a closer look, Buck simply circled. Both he and Joe paid close attention to the buildings and laneways that surrounded the bank. Buck slowed to a near crawl as the alleys between the buildings were revealed. Against their better judgment, Buck then took a second pass of the block. Joe carefully noted very particular things.

Lazlo was a larger town than the ones Buck and Joe were used to. Most of the buildings in the center, where the bank was, were at least two stories tall. Many of them were more. Directly across from the bank was a building housing a tailor shop, a pharmacy, and a women's clothing boutique. All had apartments above them. Joe took a close look at the structure of the bank and at the stores across the way.

A car approached, going in the opposite direction. It too drove slowly. Buck turned to look at the driver as they passed. The driver looked back. Buck didn't like the look of the lone man. He felt the man held his glance too long for a random citizen out for a late drive. Though Joe could do with yet another pass, they settled for the two and headed back to the motor lodge without hesitation.

Millie was asleep when they returned. Neither Buck nor Joe made a sound. They were left to sleep the rest of the night away. Neither had an easy time doing it.

In the morning Buck opened the window and a cool breeze washed over him. Fall was in the air. When Millie returned from the bathroom, Joe gathered the trio and began to go over the day's plan.

By the time the sun hit the middle of the sky, it had become another hot day. Joe, Buck, and Millie got into the car and drove the short ride into town with the windows rolled down. When they arrived on the city streets, Buck pulled over to the side of the road. He left the engine running.

Though the bank was still more than a block away, it was easily visible from the car. It was a grand building, adorned with tall columns on both sides of the door and a large white clock over top of it. The clock showed ten minutes past one.

Millie was first to exit the car. She didn't need to say a word to Buck or Joe. They all knew their roles well, and they were prepared to play them. When Millie was out of sight, Joe prepared to get out of the car next. He waited until the street emptied and then made his move.

Though it was warmer than he'd expected, Joe kept his large brown overcoat on. This was to hide the rifle strapped to his back. He closed the door of the car, nodded to Buck, and ducked behind a building into an alleyway. Buck reached into the back seat, pulled up a Tommy gun, and placed it on the seat beside him. He pulled away from the curb and made his way into the distance.

Joe tried his best to walk down the narrow alley as if he was just out for a stroll. He hoped he wouldn't come face to face with anyone along the way, a wish that nearly came true. As Joe neared his destination, however, a man in a white apron, filthy with brown and red stains, opened the side door to a building to bring out the trash. His eyes met Joe's. Joe's stomach dropped when he saw the man's suspicious gaze. But the man's face grew friendly and he offered a smiling nod as Joe passed him by. Joe returned the gesture without a stutter to his stride. Joe turned back after a few paces and saw the man going about his business, paying no mind to the stranger in the overcoat on a humid day.

Joe reached a four-way intersection in the alley. He turned swiftly to his left and approached the back of a building. Cars passed on the road ahead of him. None turned down the alley. Joe stopped. He looked about to see if anyone was watching. No one was around. Joe grabbed the bottom rung of a hanging ladder and hoisted himself up.

The black ladder led to a fire escape balcony on the second floor. Each subsequent floor of the four-story building was connected by a metal staircase. Joe reached the second floor landing. Peering carefully into the window of the apartment, he saw a small, pristine reading room, devoid of any persons. Joe made his way to the third floor. The shades of the windows were closed. He reached the fourth and final floor. With his back up against the brick wall, Joe stuck out his head to look through the window. Inside, a young boy sat on a rug, playing with tin toys and eating a sandwich. The boy wasn't facing the window directly, but he wasn't exactly facing the opposite direction either.

Joe waited.

Every minute or so, Joe would peek back through to see if the boy had turned his back to him or, better still, left the room altogether. Joe stood on the balcony for what felt like ten minutes before the boy busied himself with his finger in his nose. When the boy got up to wipe his find on the wall, Joe made his move. He slowly crept toward the ladder that led to the roof, keeping his eye on the boy all the while. He began to climb. Nearing the top rung, Joe felt an urgency and couldn't help but reach for the ledge and yank himself upward.

Though he thought to crawl over to the other end of the building, the unkind gravel bits atop the flat roof's layer of tar made it painful on his knees and hands. Joe got up on his feet and pranced to the far edge, his back hunched over as if he were ducking an invisible wire.

Reaching the front of the building, Joe got down on his stomach. After a moment's rest he removed the overcoat, pulled the strap over his head, and pried the rifle from his back. He laid the gun down beside himself and raised his head up. He had a clear view of the front of the bank. Now all he had to do was wait and hope that Buck and Millie were as successful as he had been.

Joe looked down to the large clock above the bank doors. He had plenty of time to spare. He turned and rested on his back. He found a comfortable position with his head on the prickly gravel and looked upwards. If not for the sounds of people on the street and of the cars clanking and stammering as they drove by, Joe could have been out in the woods, looking up at the same skies. A few wisps of white hovered above him, too thin to block out the sun. Joe stared up and watched as one at a time they distorted and dispersed before his eyes. He marveled at the timeless precision each had, able to change shape so dramatically in just a few moments, without any noticeable movement.

Joe's next check of the clock revealed that only a few minutes' peace remained. He reached for the rifle and shuffled onto his belly. He took position against the edge and pointed the long barrel at the door of the ornate building across the way.

Joe waited. The sun beat down on the back of his neck. He felt a bead of sweat drip past the back of his ear. He wiped it away, returning his hand promptly to the grip of the gun.

Joe took his eye off the door and glanced up at the clock. It was time.

He closed his eyes, took in a deep breath through his nose, and blew it out his mouth as if he were expelling smoke from a cigarette. If he was ever going to be ready, now was the time.

A faint crunching noise lilted through the air, but Joe's attention was too focused to break. He took dead aim at those doors.

He glanced up at the clock once more. Buck was late. Joe grew nervous and impatient and squirmed in place.

"Come on, come on," he whispered to himself.

It wasn't Buck or Millie who finally broke Joe's iron-like concentration. Instead it was the faint sound of a hammer being pulled back, and the feeling of a gun barrel resting on the back of his head. Joe dared not move, other than to slowly take his hands off the rifle and hold them out to the side.

"Hello, Joe," an unfamiliar voice said.

Chapter 53

Joe got up off his belly and turned to face the man who had found him. The man with the gun took a step back and smiled at him, never lowering the pistol.

"Who are you?" Joe asked, his hands in the air beside his shoulders.

"This way," the man said, waving the gun toward the back of the building.

Joe walked over and climbed down the ladder to the balcony below. The man with the gun followed. Joe looked down into the alley. There, waiting for them, was a second man, with a second gun, standing beside a car. The back door of the car was open, no doubt in anticipation of Joe's arrival on the ground.

Joe and the man with the gun made their way down to the alley, and the second man guided him into the car and closed the door behind him. The second man looked like a boy. He couldn't have been any more than twenty years old, if that.

The older man got into the driver's seat. The younger got in on the other side. The car was already running, and the man began to drive toward the road ahead. He reached the city street and pulled out in front of the oncoming cars.

They drove past the bank. Joe looked out the window as the building came and went from his sight. Still Buck was nowhere to be seen. Joe worried for his cousin.

"Who are you?" Joe asked.

The younger man turned around in his seat and pointed the gun at Joe's head.

"No questions," he said. "No talkin' at all, come ta think of it."

The car drove through the city. The streets looked foreign to Joe. He tried his best to notice certain signs or buildings or markers along the way, but his mind was racing, his heart was thumping, and his captors were making too many turns.

The car finally came to a stop in front of two large, arching wooden doors. The driver honked the horn. After a moment the doors began to open. The car pulled in and the doors closed behind it.

"Get out," the older man said, stopping the car inside a giant room.

Joe did as he was told.

"Now walk."

The older man held the gun at Joe's back and pushed him forward.

The indoor space they were in was abnormally large. The ceiling was at least three stories high and covered with steel crossbeams. They were in some sort of factory.

The younger man walked ahead and opened a door. Joe and the older man walked through. The boy caught up and opened a second door, and the three walked through that one too.

The room Joe now found himself in was dark. One small window covered by black bars was the only source of light from the outside. Two chairs faced one another in the middle of the room, with nothing much else in sight.

"Take a seat," the older man said.

Joe sat down in the chair that faced the door.

"Now don't get up," the man said.

Both he and the younger man left the room and closed the door behind them.

Joe looked around. If there was any way to escape, he couldn't see it. The door he'd entered through was the only possible exit. Joe was confined.

Minutes passed. Joe knew they were keeping him waiting to make him nervous. He tried his best to stay calm and think of what he was going to do or say when someone, anyone, returned.

An hour passed, maybe more. Joe thought about Buck, and about Millie. He wondered where they were and whether they were okay – if they were even still alive at all.

A noise came from behind the door. Joe sat up straight in his chair.

The door opened. His two captors reentered and stepped to opposite sides of the door, revealing a third man, who walked behind them into the room. The man took the seat across from Joe.

"Hello, Joe," he said.

"Hello, Henry."

"It's been a while."

"I see your face has healed."

Henry touched his cheek.

"Good as new," he said, smiling.

"Where's my cousin?"

"Oh, we've got him. He's in the other room right now, actually."

"I want to see him."

"In due time, in due time," Henry said calmly. "I wanted to talk to you first."

"About what?"

"About all the things you two have been up to, of course. You didn't think you'd get away with it, did you? Hell, if it was up to me, you'd already be dead."

"Is that right?"

"It is."

"Then let me talk to whoever it's up to," Joe said.

Henry smiled. He turned to look at the two men by the door. They joined in his jollity.

"You're the one that killed Arland," Henry said, looking back at Joe.

Joe didn't respond.

"That's okay, you don't have to answer. I saw it with my own eyes."

"He deserved to die," Joe blurted.

Henry laughed.

"That may be true," he said. "That may be true."

Henry's demeanor turned. An angry look took over his face and the hand resting in his lap transformed into a fist.

"You tried to kill me too, though, didn't you?"

Joe just looked away. He glanced around the room.

"Doesn't matter," Henry said, instantly returning to a jovial state. "That's all in the past now."

Joe looked back at the man.

"What do you want?" he said.

"I already told you what I want."

"Why am I here?"

Henry didn't answer. He just looked at Joe with a silly smile on his face.

"Have you met my friends?" Henry asked. "How rude of me."

He turned in his chair.

"That there is Michael, and that's Wayne. They were the ones good enough to bring you here."

"Wayne?"

"That's me," the younger man said, tipping a cap he wasn't wearing.

"What's your last name?"

"What's that your business?" the boy said.

"You know him, do ya?" Henry said.

"He don't know me," Wayne said. "He may think he do, but he don't."

"I know who you are," Joe said.

"Good. Then we're all acquainted," Henry said.

"Where is she?" Joe asked.

"Where's who?"

"You know damn well who. Where is she?"

"You should calm yourself, Joe."

"I want to see her. Bring her in here."

Henry shook his head in disappointment.

"They told me you were a clever one," he said. "Not all that clever now, though, are ya?"

Joe did everything he could to hold back his emotions. He was overcome with anger, with disbelief, and also with fear. But Henry could see it in his eyes.

"Okay," Henry said, "bring her in."

Wayne opened the door and disappeared into the other room. Joe and Henry just looked at one another.

Wayne returned soon after. Millie followed him in.

"You," Joe said.

It was all the words he could muster.

"What can I say?" Millie said.

"Why? Why would you do this?"

"They had my folks, okay? Besides, you were playin' me like a fool the whole time. You were just usin' me. And don't say you weren't."

"We weren't."

"Like hell," Millie said.

"When did you –"

"I did what I had to do," Millie blurted. "Okay? I did what I had to do."

Millie turned to Henry.

"Can I go now?" she asked.

"No," Henry said. "Stay. I want you to see what comes next."

Chapter 54

A man in a brown suit walked into the room. He walked up to Henry, leaned over, and whispered something in his ear. Henry responded with a single, muted nod of his head. The man exited the room without another word to anyone.

"Why am I here?" Joe asked.

He was close to exhaustion.

"This is where you wanted to be, isn't it? You've been trying to get our attention for months now. So here you are, and here we are."

"You haven't said what you want from me. What is it you want?"

"It's not what *I* want," Henry said. "Like I told you, I would have put a bullet in your head a long time ago. But someone else had other plans."

"Who? Who had other plans?"

"You don't know?"

"If I knew, I wouldn't have asked you."

"The Colonel, of course. The Colonel had other plans."

Joe looked at Millie. Millie offered nothing in the way of explanation.

"But I thought…" Joe began.

"You thought what?"

"I thought you were the Colonel."

"Did you now? Well, I hate to be the one to disappoint you, Joe, but I suppose you should count yourself lucky that I'm not, or we wouldn't be having this conversation at all."

"You told me it was him," Joe said to Millie.

"I thought it was," Millie said, shrugging her shoulders.

"Sweet girl, isn't she?" Henry said. "But it seems your pretty young friend there has been misinformed, Joe. Though it's no big surprise. The Colonel rarely introduces himself to the simpler kind. I often get mistaken for the man, as a matter of fact. Well what can I say?" he said with a smile, holding up his hands in mock humility. "Who am I to correct them?"

"So who is it, then? Who is the Colonel?"

"I bet you're just dyin' to know, aren't you? 'Specially after all this time. It must be eatin' away at you."

Joe had grown tired of Henry's magnanimous tone, but he knew if he was ever going to meet the actual man he was looking for, he would have to play along with his underling's little game.

"Alas," Henry continued, "you are in luck. The man wishes to meet you too."

Henry got up from his chair and brushed his thighs with his hands. He began to walk out of the room. He turned and looked at Joe once more.

"I'd thank him if I were you," he said.

Wayne opened the door for Henry. The three men exited, followed by Millie, who offered Joe a mournful look before Wayne closed the door. Joe was left alone again.

Joe could hear soft mumbles from behind the door. He tried to listen in, but the sounds were more like the hum of machinery than human voices, and he couldn't make out a single word.

The voices subsided. He could hear a door in the distance opening and closing again, and then footsteps approaching. The latch of the door rose. Joe watched the door intently as it opened. He was at a loss for words when a man entered and stood there, looking down at him.

"Hello, Joe."

Joe couldn't think of a thing to say. His tongue was stuck to the back of his teeth. He felt a heavy pang of anger and of heartbreak. His eyes never left the man's face as the man walked toward the chair. Calmly, Alfred Winter sat down.

"You're probably a little confused," Alfred said, taking off his hat and placing it on the floor beside him. "Had I known it was you that day you came by the house, well, it might not have come to this."

Joe still did not say a word.

"I have to say," Alfred continued, "I really would have preferred to keep you out of all this. I wanted better for you. You have to know that. I wish you'd never found out at all."

"How?" Joe managed to get out.

"How what?"

"How is this possible?"

"I hate to say it, but it's all quite simple, really. You have to remember that I get paid to dispose of all my competition. After that, it becomes all too easy."

"But... why?"

Alfred sat back in his chair.

"Well, now, that's a different story altogether."

He closed his eyes and rubbed his brow.

"One that I never imagined talking to *you* about."

"I trusted you."

"You, and many others," Alfred admitted, a small look of shame on his face. "But they're the real crooks and thieves, Joe. They steal people's lives away."

"Who?"

"The ones that take what we've earned, that tell us what we can and can't do with our lives. The ones that send us to war to watch our friends and our brothers get their limbs torn off, their heads ripped off..."

Alfred stopped himself.

"War does terrible things to a man," he said, apologetically. "Terrible things. Unspeakable things."

"I don't understand."

"I couldn't help any of them, Joe. I couldn't even help my own daughter."

"How did you find out?" Joe asked.

He wanted to bring Alfred back from the depths he was entering.

"Find out what?"

"That it was me. How did you find out?"

"Your friend in Kansas, the fat one, he started talking to anyone that would listen. It wasn't long before word got to me."

"And then you killed him."

"Henry killed him."

"But you didn't stop him."

"He had a big mouth. Henry did what was necessary for all of us."

"But you stopped Henry from killing me."

Alfred looked up at Joe.

"Are you comparing your life to his?"

Joe had no answer.

"He sent a man to kill you, Joe. Your cousin put a bullet in that man's head in a motel room, as I recall."

"Where is Buck?" Joe asked.

"He's here."

"I want to see him."

"You will."

"What's going to happen to him?"

This time it was Alfred who didn't answer. He just looked into Joe's eyes, carefully, thoughtfully, and with remorse.

Alfred got up from the chair. He walked to the door behind him and opened it up.

"Bring him in," he said. "And get Henry. Send them both in."

Alfred closed the door. He returned to his seat.

"You're disappointed, I know," he said. "You thought I was a better man, someone you could look up to."

Alfred picked his hat up off the floor and put it back on his head.

"It's funny," he said. "I tried to be that for you. I never wanted you to see me like this."

"See you as you really are?" Joe said.

Alfred smiled, though there was pain in his eyes.

"You know who I really am, Joe. You may be one of the few."

The door opened, and Michael and Wayne carried a man with a brown burlap sack over his head into the room. His hands were tied behind his back. He muttered nonsensical sounds through whatever held his lips together. They threw him to the ground.

Henry entered. He held a gun in his hand.

"Alfred, no," Joe pleaded.

"This was the price," Alfred said.

"Take the bag off," Henry said, lifting the gun.

Michael ripped the sack from the man's head.

"On your knees," Henry commanded.

Alfred gave Joe a moment to take one last look at his cousin. Henry put the pistol to the man's head. Loud, muffled sounds spewed from behind the gag wrapped around his mouth and neck.

"This is for Arland," Henry said.

"Wait," Alfred snapped.

He raised his hand as if he were halting traffic. He looked back at Joe.

"Wait for what?" Henry asked. "This is what we agreed. The cousin first."

Without taking his eyes off Joe, Alfred responded.

"We need to leave," he said. "We need to leave now."

"What for?"

Alfred looked at Henry.

"Because that's not his cousin," he said.

Chapter 55

Michael and Wayne led the way. Alfred took Joe by the arm and pulled him from the room. They passed through the second room and entered the large factory floor.

Millie was leaning against a car next to a man Joe had not yet seen. She held Buck's burgundy hat in her hand.

"We're leaving," Michael said abruptly. "Get in the car."

The man waiting with Millie opened the door and held it open. Millie, spooked by the hasty retreat, looked around for direction. She peered over at Joe and then the man being led out by Henry.

"Who the hell is that?" she said.

Shots began to ring out. The first missed Millie by inches and entered the chest of the man holding open the car door. He dropped to the ground with a thud. The second bullet hit Michael in the head, killing him instantly. Everyone scurried as bullets began to ricochet off the ground and off the steel beams. Joe dropped to the cold floor and landed on his back, the perfect vantage point from which to watch the bullet hit Alfred in the gut.

"Alfred!" Joe called out.

Wayne pushed aside the gagged man and lunged toward the front of a parked car, where he ducked down for cover. Henry hurried to the side and hid behind a wide steel post. Alfred, having fallen to the ground, crawled slowly back into the room from which they had all just come.

Wayne began to return fire from behind the car. Henry shot back too.

Joe, left with scarcely any other option, dove through the open door of the parked car and covered his head.

Millie, like Wayne, had run to the front of the car and got down low to escape the bullets.

"Where's he at?" Wayne yelled out.

Henry did not answer. He just continued to fire in the direction of the gunshots. The sound of gunfire echoed through the open space. Joe kept his head down as bullets came in through the back windshield. He managed to turn around and got a glimpse of the dead man who was holding the door ajar. Joe slid along the seat. He reached out and pulled the pistol from the dead man's holster and then took cover again inside the car.

Joe tried to look inside the second car without raising his head too high. He was unable to see much, but he did notice something unmistakable. Sitting on the front seat of the second car, like a passenger, was Joe's rifle.

Wayne lifted his head from the front of the car to look out. Joe saw him out of the corner of his eye. He pointed the gun and put a bullet into Wayne's forehead without vacillation. Millie screamed out as her friend slumped down in front of the car, his lifeless eyes wide open and staring straight at her, a bullet hole gaping in his brow.

The man with the gag still in his mouth got up from the ground and started to run. Bullets from both directions cut him down in seconds.

The shots momentarily subsided. Then Joe heard the faint sound of bullet casings jingling as they hit the concrete floor. Only Henry held a revolver.

Joe rolled out from the front seat, yanked open the door of the second car, grabbed his rifle and made a mad dash toward the front doors of the factory.

Shots began to ring out again. Joe dove for cover behind a stack of thick, black metal machinery. He put his back up against the bumpy exterior and held his rifle close to his body.

The shots subsided once more.

Joe looked around the factory. His eyes darted like a hummingbird.

"Buck!" he yelled out. "Buck, where are you?"

Buck did not answer.

Joe thought to poke out his head. He popped it out and then back in, like a jab.

"Buck!" he yelled again.

Too much time had gone by. Joe grew fearful that Buck had been hit.

"Come on out, Joe," Henry called. "I've got what you're looking for."

Joe hesitated but then stuck his eye out ever so slightly. At first he didn't see much of anything, but then he caught a glimpse of Henry. The man was shuffling out from behind a pile of old wooden boxes at the far end of the floor. He had found Buck. He had him in his clutches and was using him as a shield. Buck's arms were up in the air as Henry dragged him into the open.

"I'll give you five seconds to come out before I put a bullet in his head."

Joe put his head back against the machine.

"One," Henry called out.

Joe squeezed his rifle and gritted his teeth.

"Two."

"Don't do it, Joe," Buck yelled out.

Joe looked out just in time to see Henry whack Buck on the side of the head with his gun. Joe emerged from behind the machine, his rifle primed at his shoulder. He stared down the sights at Henry and Buck.

"Put the gun down, Joe," said Henry. "Put it down now!"

Joe did not waver.

"Alfred!" Henry called out.

Alfred did not answer.

"Alfred, I'm going to kill your boy!"

Still there was no answer.

"Hey, kid!" Henry yelled.

No one responded.

"Wayne!" Henry shouted.

"He's dead," Millie squealed.

"Who's there?"

"Millie," the girl said, remaining out of sight.

"Get in there and find Alfred," Henry said. "Tell him I got 'em both here."

Millie finally emerged from in front of the car and scampered off to look for Alfred in the rooms off to the side.

"Put the gun down," Henry said.

"He's been shot," Millie said, bursting back onto the factory floor.

"How bad? Is he alive?" Henry asked.

"I don't know. He's not movin'."

Joe took a single step forward. Henry took the gun from Buck's temple and pointed it at Joe.

"Don't you move," he said.

"We need to check on Alfred," Joe said.

"You need to put the gun down," Henry said.

Still clutching Buck, Henry began to shuffle over to the door of the room. Millie got out of his way as he approached. Henry looked through the open door into the room.

"Buck!" Joe said. "Buck, is he alive?"

Buck tried his best to look through the door, but Henry's grip around his neck was too tight.

"I can't see," Buck yelled back.

Henry smacked Buck on the side of the head with the gun once more, opening a wound. Blood ran into Buck's eye.

"Alfred!" Henry shouted. "*Alfred!*"

Henry got no answer. He tugged Buck back out to the floor and stood by the cars.

"Put the gun down now or he gets it," Henry said, returning the pistol to Buck's head. "Last chance."

Joe stood frozen. He knew that if he put down the gun they would both be dead.

"You think I don't mean it?" Henry said.

"I think you want to get out of here alive, and if you start shooting –"

Henry turned the gun and fired at Millie. The girl's hands flew up to her stomach. She stumbled backwards and hit the wall. She slid down it, slowly, to the ground. Blood began to seep through her fingers.

The light sounds of sirens wafted through the air.

"They're coming, Henry. Do you hear that? They're coming."

"I'll give you five seconds," Henry said.

"What was the deal?" Joe said, anxiety building in his stomach and in his fingertips.

"What?"

"What was the deal you had with Alfred? For my life."

"Don't fool yourself, Joe. There was no deal."

"Then let's make one now," Joe said. "You're a business man, right? You can have me. Let him go and you can do whatever you want with me."

Henry thought about it for a moment. He stared across the room at Joe.

"You'd do that for him?" he asked.

The sound of sirens drew closer.

Joe stared back at Henry, whose revolver was aimed at Buck's head.

"I would," he said. "I'm the one that killed Arland, not him."

Joe couldn't read the look on Henry's face, but he hoped it was one of reason, one of mercy, one of compromise, for whatever that meant to him.

"Do we have a deal?" Joe asked.

Henry took his time. Time neither of them had. He looked across the room at Joe.

"No deal," he said plainly.

Henry pulled the trigger and put a bullet into Buck's head.

"No!" Joe yelled out, but it was too late.

Buck's body crumpled to the ground like a pile of wet clothes.

Henry turned the gun on Joe and fired. He was able to get one poor shot away before Joe sucked in a breath, pulled the trigger, and lodged a bullet in Henry's head, sending the man off his feet and into the backside of the car behind him.

Henry was dead.

Joe ran over to Buck and knelt down beside his cousin. He leaned in to get a better look but had to turn away when he saw the better part of Buck's skull was missing.

Joe turned to Millie. Her body was lifeless; her head slumped over to the side. Her eyes stared blankly across the room.

As the wailing of the sirens swelled, Joe rushed into the room at the side of the factory floor. There on the ground with his head against the wall was Alfred. Joe got down beside him.

"Alfred?" he said, as he shook the man's body.

Joe surveyed the damage. Blood had soaked Alfred's midsection. Joe didn't have time to find the wound, only to see if Alfred was still alive. Joe was no doctor, but nothing about Alfred's condition suggested he was.

The sounds of the sirens were upon him. With no time left to linger, Joe left Alfred where he lay and dashed from the room. Whoever was coming had not yet breached the doors. Joe had to take his chances the other way. He dropped his rifle down beside Henry's dead body, scuttled between the two parked cars, and ran for the far end of the factory. He dodged and weaved his way through piles of old boxes, giant rusty machines, and discarded paraphernalia littering the ground.

He soon heard the sound of the large wooden doors bursting open but didn't stop to look back.

Chapter 56

"Everyone was dead," Madeline said.

"Everyone but Joe," Liza replied.

"Where did he go?" Nathaniel asked. "Joe, I mean. Did he make it out of the factory?"

"He did. He made it out fine."

"And he ran?"

"Like the wind. And he never looked back."

Nathaniel reached over and turned off the voice recorder. He sat back in his chair.

"That's some story," he said. "So the girl in the newspaper, the one they found shot dead, was Millie."

"Indeed."

"And how did Buck escape being captured?"

"And who was the man they brought to the factory instead?" Madeline added.

"It was part of their plan that neither Buck nor Joe would enter the bank that day. It was far too dangerous, and they knew it. It would have been like walking into a lion's den, had they even made it in. No, Millie and another man were meant to walk in that day. Joe never could get the details from Buck before he was killed, but he was meant to pay a man to wear his hat and coat and to deliver a written message to a girl named Millie inside the bank. Buck no doubt told the man a wonderful story, one of a shy courter, or a father surprising his daughter. No matter. I'm sure the fifty dollars he offered was incentive enough for a man to wear a hat and hand a lady a note, don't you think? Either way, it would seem that man never made it into the bank anyhow. The poor man got snatched up before he even made it near the doors."

"And what about Millie?" Nathaniel asked.

"She most likely never intended to arrive at all. She no doubt had the plan foiled before the day even began."

"Who was he – the man posing as Buck?" Nathaniel asked. "Did anyone ever find out?"

"That's something you'll no doubt be able to uncover, Mr. Bishop. Now that you have the information, you'll know what to look for."

Liza took a deep, unsettling breath. Madeline reached out her hand.

"Grandma?" she said. "Are you okay?"

"Fine," Liza said. "I'm fine, dear."

"Why don't we continue this tomorrow?" Madeline offered.

"Mr. Bishop," Liza said, trying her best to muster more strength. "You do remember our deal, now, don't you?"

"That I'm not to print a word of this until you say."

"You mustn't even speak of it."

"I understand."

"Then, until tomorrow. I will answer any questions you have when we meet again."

Nathaniel got up, and as he had done so many times before, he returned the chair to where it belonged.

"I'll make us some tea," Madeline said to Liza, patting the back of her hand.

Liza smiled and shut her eyes.

Madeline left Liza's room with Nathaniel and showed him to the front door. They looked at one another as if they had just disembarked from a transatlantic flight, worn out and weary. The weight of Liza's story was not lost on either of them.

"I'll be by tomorrow," Nathaniel said.

"Do you have much more to ask her?"

"A few things," Nathaniel said. "But I guess I've just become so used to coming…"

"It's been nice."

"It has, hasn't it? That's one interesting woman."

"You're telling me."

"I have some work to do in the morning. I'll be looking through old papers and records and things. But why don't we meet for lunch? Say one o'clock, at the diner?"

"I'll see you there," Madeline said, smiling.

"Good."

Nathaniel opened the door and made his way out. Madeline stood in the breach and watched him walk out to the street.

"Say," Nathaniel said, stopping a few steps away. "You think there's anything she's not telling us?"

"What do you mean?"

Nathaniel paused.

"Never mind," he said. "It was just a thought." Pulling his car keys from his pocket, he said, "I'll see you tomorrow."

Madeline was a whisper away from stopping Nathaniel and telling him about the key her grandmother had given her, but she did not. Something held her back. Even when Nathaniel reached his car and was nearly out of earshot, Madeline struggled with the notion of running to him and telling him.

Nathaniel was soon gone. Madeline closed the door. She brewed a pot of tea and prepared a platter to deliver to Liza's room. She reached the top of the stairs and stopped in front of Liza's door. She gently placed the tray on a hutch in the hallway and walked to her own bedroom. Madeline opened a drawer in her desk and pulled out an old ring box. She opened the box, took out the key, and held it in her hand.

Madeline liked holding on to the secret. Though she knew that Nathaniel would one day become privy, for now it was something between her and her grandmother, and no one else. It was a part of her grandfather that only she knew about. What the key meant, or what lock it opened, she almost didn't care. There was a reason her grandmother had given it to her without speaking a word of it to Nathaniel. It was the same reason Madeline was going to shield it and keep it safe – it, and whatever it protected.

"Maddy?" a small voice called out.

Madeline returned the key to the box and put the box back in the drawer.

"Coming, Grandma," she said.

Chapter 57

Madeline and Nathaniel met at the diner as planned, only they didn't talk much about Liza. Instead they spoke about books and movies, and what it had been like for them growing up years before.

When they were done, Nathaniel accompanied Madeline back to the house to visit with Liza. He had several questions to ask the old woman, but something kept the three of them from broaching the subject at all that day. Still they talked for hours. Liza was happy to be the one listening for a change. She shut her eyes several times and just listened to the sound of the younger people's conversation.

Liza's health began to deteriorate more in the weeks that followed. Nathaniel would still visit every few days, though, and he found that Liza answered all his inquiries with nothing but candor. He was satisfied with the results. And when he had all the information he needed for the time being, he continued to visit just for the sake of being in the room with Liza and Madeline.

In the evenings Nathaniel would listen to his recordings of Liza's story. He would read over the careful notes he had taken as she spoke. He made more notes as he listened again. If any questions came up, he would be sure to bring them with him on his next visit. They would get those questions out of the way early and convene on lighter matters for the duration.

After a few months Liza lost the ability to speak more than a few words at a time. Madeline provided her grandmother with a pad and pencil for her to jot down anything of importance, but only a few more weeks had passed when Liza didn't even have the energy to write.

It was a very cool morning when Liza was taken to the hospital once again. The ambulance responded to Madeline's call after Liza was unresponsive and couldn't be woken up. Liza opened her eyes later that day in the hospital bed but did not speak or write another word thereafter.

Madeline was able to take her grandmother back home after only one day. The doctors said there was nothing more they could do for her. Madeline was told to make the old woman comfortable and see to it that she at least tried to eat and take her medicine.

Nathaniel continued his regular visits to the house. Upon listening to the recordings yet again, he found he had even more questions for Liza, but he knew the time for answers was over. He would have to make do with what he had. She had told the story as best she could, and now he would have to do the same.

It was over tea in the kitchen with Madeline one afternoon that Nathaniel raised the matter.

"I think I've gotten just about all I can from the recordings," he said. "I've listened to them so many times, I almost know them by heart by now."

"And what do you think, now that you've heard the story from beginning to end so many times?"

"I think…"

Nathaniel paused. He wanted to choose his words carefully.

"I think there's something missing."

"Missing? Like what?"

"I don't know. I can't put my finger on it. Anyway, I'll have to work with what I have. I've started writing, you know."

"You have?"

"Just a few bits and pieces. I know I'm meant to wait, but… I still don't know for what."

"Yes, you do," Madeline said. "You've known since the start, and so have I."

Nathaniel looked into Madeline's eyes.

"I won't tell her I've started," he said.

"Good."

"I'm sure it will take me years to put it all together anyhow."

"That long?"

"There's still a lot of research to be done. I'm certain I can find out more. Once I figure out a few pieces, the rest should fall into place. Names, dates, events… There have to be records of it all."

"So you believe the story, then?"

Smiling, Nathaniel answered, "How can you ask me that now? After all this?"

"What was it that convinced you?"

"The newspapers. I haven't been able to connect all the dots yet, but those articles were persuasive."

"For me it was finding the gun. Not that I didn't believe her before, but holding it in my hands made it feel so real."

"I just hope..." he said.

"What?"

"I was going to say that I just hope I can do it justice."

"I'm sure you will, Nate," Madeline said.

She reached across the table and touched Nathaniel's arm.

Liza held on for weeks. It was as if the instinct to survive was so deeply ingrained in her that even in her direst state, her mind wouldn't let her body go. Madeline found her grandmother dead on a Monday morning in the winter. She simply didn't wake up that day. At least, Madeline liked to think that Liza had passed away gently in her sleep, and for all anyone could tell, she had.

The funeral was sparsely attended and brief. Being of such advanced years, Liza didn't have many friends remaining. Likewise, her family consisted of only Madeline, who was subsequently left with the house and all of Liza's other earthly belongings.

Of course, Nathaniel attended the funeral. He offered the eulogy for the few who came.

After the service Nathaniel escorted Madeline back to the house. Madeline invited him in for a drink, which he graciously accepted. Forgoing their usual tea, Madeline poured them each a glass of Scotch, and they sat on the couch in the living room instead of in the kitchen.

Madeline didn't say much. She took tiny sips of her drink and lost herself in thought. Nathaniel didn't mind the quiet. He was content simply to keep her company.

When Madeline finished her drink, she got up for a refill and offered Nathaniel the same. He declined, having half of his drink still remaining in the glass.

"I'm not much of a drinker," he said.

"Me neither."

But Madeline poured herself another. She put the bottle down on a long wooden bookshelf. She looked over the book titles as she took small sips from the glass. Her gaze came upon a framed picture of her grandparents. She lifted it from its perch.

"How old were they then?" Nathaniel asked.

Madeline turned the frame over, as if the date would be scribbled somewhere on the back.

"I'm not sure," she said, turning it back around. "They look so young."

"When did they meet? Your grandparents?"

"I don't know exactly…" Madeline said.

She looked up to the sky.

"She was thirty-four when she had my mom. Grandpa was a year older, so… I would say they were both around that age. Thirty-three, thirty-four."

"That was late to start a family in those days."

"I guess," Madeline said.

She put the picture back down, and her hand shuffled across the shelf. She picked up another frame and held it in her hand.

"Who's that?" Nathaniel asked.

Madeline didn't answer. She stared at the picture. She put down her glass and held the picture with both hands.

"This is my mother," she finally said.

"What happened between you two?" Nathaniel asked.

Madeline turned away from the photo. She looked up and smiled at Nathaniel, but he saw something much different in her eyes. Nathaniel wanted to get up and embrace her. He wanted to, but he didn't.

"You know," he said, "I *will* have another."

He held up his glass. Madeline didn't move right away. She looked across the room at Nathaniel as if there was something more that she wanted too.

"I've got a better idea," she said.

"What's that?" Nathaniel said, lowering his glass to his lap.

"Come on, I have something to show you."

Madeline walked over to the couch, took Nathaniel by the hand, and led him from the room.

Nathaniel waited momentarily in Liza's room for Madeline to return. When she did, she held out her closed fist. Nathaniel figured out quickly what she wanted and opened his hand like a child waiting for candy. Madeline dropped the key from her grandfather's drawer into his palm.

"It's a key," he said, looking down at the item, unimpressed.

"It was in my grandfather's drawer. Grandma gave it to me a while back. She told me not to show it to anyone, not even you, until the right time came."

"What does it open?"

"That's just it," Madeline said. "I don't know."

Nathaniel looked around the room.

"You think it's something in here?" he asked.

Madeline looked around too.

"I've never seen anything here with a lock on it," she said.

She opened and closed the top drawer of her grandmother's armoire and then the one below.

"Help me look," she said.

Nathaniel walked over to the closet and opened the door. He searched inside. He looked up on the top shelf, down underneath the hanging dresses, and even in between the racks of clothing.

"It doesn't look like there's anything in here," he said. "I don't feel right about moving too much around."

"Nate!" Madeline called.

Nathaniel turned. Madeline was standing beside Liza's bedside table. The top drawer was pulled wide open, but Madeline wasn't looking inside. She had found something else of interest. She was peering down at the envelope she held in her hands.

"It's addressed to you," she said, looking up at Nathaniel.

Nathaniel walked over and took the envelope from her. The front simply read, "Mr. Bishop."

"Open it," Madeline urged.

Nathaniel tore open the envelope and pulled out its contents. Inside he found notepaper, covered front and back in pencil markings.

"That's the paper I gave her," Madeline said. "What's it say?"

"It's about Joe," Nathaniel said, his eyes scrolling the text.

"Read it to me."

Madeline sat on the edge of the bed. Nathaniel sat down beside her.

Chapter 58

1924

Joe had escaped the factory through a broken window at the back of the building. He carefully navigated the narrow laneways so as not to be detected by the fleet of lawmen who were scouring the area. He made it back onto the city streets, but he was still not in the clear.

Joe walked briskly but did not run. A police car with its siren blaring approached, sending Joe's heart into his stomach. The car sped past. Joe had no idea where he was or how to get back to the meeting spot that he and Buck had arranged for their getaway. Buck must have parked the car nearby, but Joe had no idea which direction that area was in.

A local bus roared to a stop across the street from Joe. He hurried across the road and leapt onto the vehicle just before it closed its doors. Joe paid the fare and took a seat near the front as the bus started rolling.

"Looks like something's goin' on over there," an elderly woman said.

"Must be some trouble," the driver replied.

The bus drove up to the street on which the factory stood but did not turn there. Instead the driver kept on through the intersection.

Within a couple of minutes Joe was clear of the immediate area. He rode the bus for quite some time before approaching the driver.

"Excuse me, sir," he said. "I'm looking to get to the Treasure Cinema."

"You're a long ways from there," the driver replied with a chuckle. "It's across on the other side of town. Your best bet, if you ask me, would be to hail yourself a taxicab."

Upon arriving at the bus station, Joe took the driver's advice and hopped right into a waiting taxi. He told the driver his destination. The man made no acknowledgment of Joe's request other than to put down his newspaper and start the car. He pulled out of the station and headed out onto the streets.

When the cab arrived on the other side of town, Joe paid the man and got out onto the sidewalk. He approached the box office of the Treasure Cinema to avoid any suspicion. Once the cab was gone from sight, Joe smiled to the box office attendant and changed his tack.

He walked along the sidewalk. He glanced up ahead and could see the Lazlo Savings and Loan, poking its ornate corners out onto the street not very far from where he walked. He did not see the car.

Joe reached a side street at the end of the block. The street was lined with cars, but Joe spotted the Pontiac in seconds. It was parked only a few spaces in.

Joe hurried to the car. He reached under the running board and pulled out the key. He opened the door and got right in. Joe's things were already stowed in the back, as were Buck's. Joe turned on the car, pulled away from the curb, and headed toward the outskirts of town. It wasn't long before he'd left Lazlo in his rearview mirror.

Joe headed northwest. He did not stop to eat or to relieve himself. He drove that car until it was running on gas fumes, at which point he pulled into the next service station he found.

A quick stop into the restaurant and Joe was back in the car with a bacon sandwich already in his stomach. He headed into the Oklahoma Panhandle.

Left with time to ponder, he ran through the events of the day many times. In his mind's eye he watched Buck get shot over and over again. He thought about Alfred.

Joe had been on the road long enough for the sun to go down. Though it was not late in the night, he began to grow tired. With Alfred and Henry both gone, he knew it would be unlikely that anyone would be after him. Joe pulled off the road into a small town and rented himself a room for the night, but he had trouble sleeping. He couldn't shake the urge to cry, nor would the tears come.

It was approaching lunchtime the next day when Joe finally emerged from the room. He sat in the car, the same old tattered roadmap on his lap.

Joe had choices to make. Alone now, he had only himself to satisfy. Colorado, New Mexico, or Texas? Kansas was out of the question.

Joe turned on the car and hit the road once more. As he neared the state border, he stopped at a station to fill up one more time and to get something to eat for breakfast.

He was waiting at the lunch counter when he noticed a man abandon the afternoon newspaper a few seats away. Joe got up and took the man's seat and his paper. The headline he was looking for was near the bottom of the front page. "Bladwell Gang Shot Dead. Agent Winter Hero," it read. Joe flipped the paper open and found the main article inside. He began to read as quickly as his eyes would let him.

Among other things that caught his eye early, Joe couldn't help but read one sentence over again. It was the line that confirmed that Alfred Winter was still alive.

Alfred had survived the gunshot wound and was recovering in a hospital nearby. The legend that prompted his nickname in the war would continue into his life back home. It would seem that the Colonel simply couldn't be killed.

The article went on to detail the events that had brought down the elusive bank robbers and listed the names of the deceased: Paul "Buck" Bladwell, age twenty-three, was chief among them. The others mentioned included William Taffit, age thirty-seven, Wayne Beethberry, age twenty, Michael Birch, age twenty-eight, and the lone female member of the gang, Mildred Tucker, age eighteen. A special mention was made of the demise of the man known around the state as "the Colonel", Henry Marlow, age fifty-one.

There was no mention of Joe's name at all. Joe read the article over again just to be sure he hadn't missed it. It was during his second pass that a light came on in Joe's head. He understood now what Alfred had done.

By implicating his own cohorts, Alfred Winter could maintain his innocence and no one would be any the wiser. More than that, he made himself the hero for eradicating a large and menacing contingent of the Oklahoman criminal element. And true criminals they were, the lot of them. Alfred was just doing his job as an agent of the state. He'd been shot in the line of duty. Accolades from the Governor would certainly follow. A genius plan, to be sure.

Joe's order was ready. He took his food out to the car and ate it there, reading the newspaper article yet again.

When Joe reached the state line, he pulled the car over to the side of the road. He wasn't ready to cross just yet. He picked up the newspaper to look at the headline once more. Under the paper on the passenger side of the car sat the old road map.

Joe thought about Buck. He pictured him sitting in the seat beside him, both of them gleeful from a plan perfectly executed.

Joe picked up the map and held it in his hand. He gave the front of the map one last good look. "Oklahoma," it read simply in large red lettering. Joe wadded the map in his hand. He looked out into the expanse outside the car and saw the wide-open fields of grass. He looked at the trees out in the distance. He looked at the road that lay ahead, and that's where his gaze remained.

Joe waited no longer. He heaved the map out the window and onto the dirt. The wheels of the car spun on the sandy ground and took hold of the road beneath.

There was one thing that ran through Joe's mind as he crossed into Colorado. He couldn't help but smile when he thought of why Alfred had left his name off the list of Bladwell bandits, and out of the story altogether. Sure, Alfred might have done it so that no one would think to track down the only other person to make it out of the factory alive, the only one who could finger him as the true Colonel. But Joe preferred to think of it another way. He chose to believe that Alfred did it because he loved him, and he wanted to finally buy Joe his freedom, once and for all.

Chapter 59

1995

Madeline and Nathaniel continued to look through the house for something the key might open. At first they focused on Liza's bedroom, but after several scans they moved the search to the other areas of the house.

It was in the basement that they found the items that seemed the most promising. They went through what remained of Madeline's grandfather's things together. Each box they opened brought new hope that they might find something, anything, that might require the key.

They stopped after a while to look through old photo albums they found. Madeline regaled Nathaniel with stories of her childhood as she pointed herself out in pictures.

They eventually gave up for the day when both grew hungry. They were tired of opening boxes of old clothes and books and knickknacks that Liza had refused to throw away. Madeline offered to prepare something for the two of them there, but Nathaniel insisted on taking her out for dinner.

They were becoming regulars at the small restaurant at the end of the street – so much so that the waitress waved to them across the room as they sat down at their usual table. She came by to say hello and to take their orders.

"So what are you going to do with your afternoons now?" Madeline asked, once the waitress was gone.

"There's still plenty to do. Besides, I have a lot of work at the paper I've been putting off."

"Have you fallen behind?"

"It's nothing unmanageable. What about you? What are you going to do now?"

"I really don't know," Madeline said, forlornly. "I was thinking about maybe going back to school."

"Going back to school? What would you study?"

"All this storytelling has gotten me interested in writing again."

"Again?"

"I used to like to write, a long time ago. I did it a lot when I was younger."

"Is that so? Do you have anything kicking around that I might read?"

"I have a few old notebooks with some stories, but you wouldn't want to read any of those."

"Of course I would."

Madeline took a moment to ponder the request.

"I'll think about it," she said. "I haven't looked at them in years. They're probably really embarrassing."

Madeline and Nathaniel finished their meals and walked together back to the house. Upon Nathaniel's incessant urging,

Madeline finally fetched a notebook of her stories and allowed him to read it. Nathaniel sat among the boxes in the basement and read as Madeline continued to peruse the old items her grandmother had stashed years before.

"Maddy," he said, interrupting as she dug into a box. "These are really, really good."

"You're just saying that."

"If I was just saying that, I wouldn't have used two 'reallys.' But these are *really, really* good. You've actually got something here."

"You think so?"

"I do."

Madeline and Nathaniel retired to the kitchen for tea. Nathaniel brought the notebook of stories with him. They had finally gone through all the boxes and so had given up looking in the basement for something that the key might open. They had turned the place upside down and hadn't come close to an object or artifact that might suggest they were nearer to their goal.

"Is it okay if I take this with me?" Nathaniel asked, holding up the notebook.

"Sure," Madeline said. "Just don't show it to anyone."

"You're going to have to get over that if you're going to be a writer, you know."

"I never said I was going to be a writer. I just said I was interested."

Madeline smiled through her embarrassment.

"Speaking of which," Nathaniel continued, "I'd like to take your grandmother's letter home with me too."

He took one last sip of his drink and got up from the table.

"Is it still up in her room?"

Madeline accompanied Nathaniel to Liza's bedroom. Nathaniel stood among the old woman's things and took it all in. The sweet smell that permeated from the perfumes on her dressing table, the look of her old pictures and pieces of jewelry, and the feel of the rug, worn in the spots most trampled over the many years.

"I'm going to miss this," he said, putting his hand on Madeline's back.

Madeline smiled a painful smile and nodded her head in agreement.

"You're going to miss *her*," Nathaniel said. "Aren't you?"

Madeline turned and finally embraced him.

"I should get going, I think," Nathaniel said moments later, letting go of the teary-eyed woman.

"Okay," Madeline responded.

Nathaniel took the letter from the bedside table and folded it into the shape in which he had found it. He opened the envelope to place it back inside.

"Maddy…" he said.

Madeline was smoothing over the cover of the empty bed with her hand. She looked up to see what Nathaniel wanted and was taken by his demeanor.

"What?" she asked. "What is it?"

Nathaniel reached his hand into the envelope and pulled out a small piece of paper, ripped from the corner of a larger sheet.

"Look at this," he said.

He handed the sliver to Madeline. Nathaniel shifted and looked over her shoulder.

"It looks like an address," Madeline said, turning her head to meet Nathaniel's eyes.

Nathaniel nodded broadly.

"Do you recognize the street name?" she asked.

"I don't. Do you?"

"I've never heard of it before."

Madeline stared at the paper.

"We have to look this up," she said.

Madeline brought her laptop down to the kitchen, where she and Nathaniel sat at the table together. They pushed aside their teacups and wasted no more time. Madeline punched in the number and the street in an online mapping service.

"There's no address like that in Charleston," she said.

"Try all of South Carolina," Nathaniel offered.

Madeline did as directed.

"Okay," she said, "there's a street with that name in Columbia… but the numbers don't go up that high. Not even close. It's a tiny street."

Madeline looked up at Nathaniel. He was sitting back in his chair, pondering the problem.

"Could it be something other than an address?" she asked.

"Let me try something," Nathaniel said.

He leaned forward, turned the computer toward himself, and began to type.

It only took a few seconds for him to get his results. He turned the screen back to Madeline and sat back in the chair. Madeline's eyes opened wide.

"It's in Oklahoma," she said, turning to see Nathaniel's response.

Nathaniel had a coy grin on his face as he nodded in self-satisfaction.

Madeline dug into her pocket. She pulled out the small key and held it in her hand.

"What do you think?" she said.

"Wanna take a trip?" Nathaniel asked.

Chapter 60

They waited until the weekend to leave for Oklahoma. Setting off early in the morning, they drove until very late that night. They were both exhausted when they pulled into a motel just outside Tulsa. The address to which they were heading was still an hour or so away, but sixteen hours in the car was more than enough for one day. Nathaniel procured a room and carried Madeline's bag from the car to their lodgings.

Nathaniel was already asleep on his bed when Madeline returned from freshening up in the bathroom. She did her best not to disturb him. Though she too wanted and needed to get some rest, her thoughts kept her awake for a while longer. Eventually she too nodded off for the night.

In the morning they found a restaurant, had a quick breakfast, and were soon back on the road. They arrived in Nowata, Oklahoma, just after ten a.m. and kept on driving until they had passed through the small town. They drove by a smattering of farms and a few roadside gas stations and fast food restaurants, but the pastoral road was mostly pristine country otherwise. When they finally reached the road they were looking for, Nathaniel struggled to master his excitement as he turned onto it. Madeline, also quite eager, looked out the window for any signs marking address numbers as they drove.

"It must be coming up," she said, pointing to a small post on the side of the road that showed a number only a few away from the one they were after.

Nathaniel slowed the pace as they both peered out ahead.

"You think that's it?" he asked, pointing to a building in the distance.

"It has to be."

Nathaniel pulled the car into the driveway of a green building.

"It looks like… a store of some kind," Madeline said.

"Look," Nathaniel said, pointing out the front windshield. "The number is on the sign."

They had reached the address to which Liza had pointed them.

"This is it," Madeline said.

"It's… a fishing store?"

"Looks like it."

Nathaniel parked the car in the small lot, and he and Madeline headed for the front door. The one-story building was painted bright green with red trimming, no doubt to catch the attention of passersby, but the colors also gave it a festive look.

They entered the store together.

"Mornin'," a man welcomed as the bell on the front door jingled.

"Morning," Nathaniel returned.

Madeline and Nathaniel stood near the front and looked around.

"Anything I can help you with?" the middle-aged man asked, approaching the pair.

"Um, not right now, thanks. I think we're just going to look around."

"Let me know if you need anything," the man said.

Nathaniel and Madeline headed off in separate directions and walked the floor of the shop. They couldn't help but eye all the wares on the shelves, but they both knew that was not why they had come.

"I don't get it," Madeline said, convening with Nathaniel near the back.

"Neither do I."

"What is this place? Why would she send us here?"

"Excuse me?" Nathaniel called out.

The man who had greeted them came to the back.

"What can I do for you?" he asked.

"Has this always been a fishing store?"

"Has been for as long as I can remember. Might have been some other kinda shop prior, but that was before my time."

"Are you the owner?"

"Yes, sir," the man said. "Was a store just like this when I bought it."

Madeline and Nathaniel looked at one another.

The man put his thumbs into holes in his fishing vest.

"I know that once upon a time it was all farmland up here. But that's the best I got."

"This used to be a farm?" Madeline asked.

"I can't say for sure, miss, but considering everything around here was, I don't see why not."

"Thank you," Nathaniel said.

"Was there anything else?" the man asked, looking a bit perplexed.

"No, thank you."

"Okay, then. Well, I'll be around if you need me."

The man turned to leave.

"Say," Nathaniel said, "you wouldn't mind if we took a walk around outside, would you?"

The man shrugged.

"Be my guest," he said with a smile. "Not much to see, but you're welcome to it."

Nathaniel and Madeline walked back to the front and exited the store. They looked out across the land ahead.

"What're you thinking?" Madeline asked.

"Could have been a farm. Like he said."

"Whose farm?"

"Your grandfather's?"

Madeline looked around.

"Come on," Nathaniel said. "Let's go take a look around."

They walked around the side of the store, looking about for any sort of clue. It looked like any old store might. There was nothing much interesting about it.

At the back of the building they stood and gazed at the back door. Madeline pulled out the key her grandmother had given her and tried it in the lock. To the surprise of neither of them, it didn't fit.

Nathaniel took a few steps back to get a better look at the building. Madeline came to join him. They stood facing the green structure. Nathaniel crossed his arms.

"What are we missing?"

Madeline walked back a little farther so that she could get the whole area within view at once. Nathaniel joined her.

Again they stood and stared.

"Oh, hey," Nathaniel said, "I can't believe I forgot to tell you. I got Alfred Winter's real name."

"What was it?"

"Thomas Gains. And you wanna hear something else?"

"Sure."

"Only two years after the shootout in the factory, he fell on some ice up in Chicago and hit his head on the sidewalk. Died a day later."

"You're kidding."

"I guess the legend wasn't all that accurate."

"What was he doing up in Chicago?"

"Beats me," Nathaniel said, lifting his shoulders. "Maybe he was looking for your grandfather."

"Yeah," Madeline laughed, "wouldn't that be funny?"

Nathaniel's phone chimed. He pulled it out and had a quick look. What he read didn't interest him much, so he stowed the phone back in his pocket. He made an audible sigh.

"Want to try inside again?" he asked.

Madeline looked down at the key in her hand.

"Okay," she said unhappily.

They stood there a few seconds more, this time in silence. Madeline finally made a move to go.

"Hang on," Nathaniel said.

He reached out and grabbed her arm.

"What?"

Nathaniel lifted his finger and perked up his head. Madeline followed his line of sight, trying to get a sense of what he was thinking.

"Do you see something?" she asked.

"Shhh," Nathaniel said. "Don't say anything."

Madeline remained motionless.

"Do you hear that?" Nathaniel asked. "Sounds like…"

Madeline listened carefully.

"Sounds like… water," she said.

They both turned and faced the other way. They looked at one another for a few seconds before they both started walking toward the trees.

"Sounds like a stream," Nathaniel said, entering the thickly wooded area behind the store.

Madeline picked up her pace to match his. It wasn't long before Nathaniel and Madeline could see the flowing water. The sound of it lapping against the rocks became clearer and then unmistakable. They reached the shore and stopped.

"This is it," Madeline said, her eyes shifting about.

"Look," Nathaniel said, grabbing Madeline's arm and pointing off to the left. "Look there."

Nathaniel took Madeline by the hand as they walked along the rutted, uneven edge of the stream and came upon a small decline. At the bottom a rocky wall face protruded from the ground. They approached the rocks. Nathaniel let go of Madeline's hand and rubbed the rock with his palm.

"Do you see anything?" he asked.

But Madeline had already spotted what they were looking for. On the western edge of the short rock face was a small, dark opening partially covered by thick brush.

"It's a cave," Madeline said, looking through.

"Can you fit in?" Nathaniel asked, joining Madeline in front of the opening.

Madeline contorted her body and managed to wriggle through the hole. She found herself on the other side. Nathaniel couldn't help but follow her in, though he managed to catch his shoulder and tear his shirt in the process.

The inside was large enough for them to stand, though they both had to hunch over just a bit. The cave was not deep, but it was just spacious enough for them to maneuver without bumping into one another. Even in the diminished light, it only took a second for both of them to take notice of the faint white chalk marks on the walls. Nathaniel rubbed at the markings with his hand.

"I can't believe these have lasted all these years," he said.

"What's that?" Madeline said, pointing at the ground between them.

"What?" Nathaniel asked, turning away from the wall.

There was something poking out from the dirt.

Nathaniel dropped to his hands and knees and began to paw at it. Madeline got down beside him.

"It looks like…" he said.

Nathaniel unearthed the rest of the object. Together they took it in. Poking out of the small hole Nathaniel had dug was an old, dirty, black rabbit's foot.

Nathaniel went to pick up the charm, but it was held down by something. He dug some more and revealed a length of twine attached to it. The twine led farther down into the ground.

"It's down there," Madeline said.

Nathaniel dug with his hands at the protruding string. Madeline joined in and helped. Both were building piles of sand and dirt beside them like children at the beach. They dug and dug until Madeline's fingernails scraped against something unnatural. It was a material of some kind. They kept on digging.

"I think it's a bag," Nathaniel said, pulling up even more dirt and sand.

He found a piece of a handle and tugged at it. It did not come up easily, but with both arms and Madeline's help, they yanked the bag topside.

"Let's get it outside," Madeline said, looking down at their find. "It's too hard to see in here."

Madeline was first from the cave. She pulled the bag out after her and then helped Nathaniel squirm from the opening. They both got down on their knees. Nathaniel reached for the rusty zipper and pulled the bag open. Both he and Madeline stared down at what was inside.

They had found a sack full of immaculate war bonds. The thick material of the bag had kept them safe and dry over many, many years below ground. Madeline picked up a stack and flipped through them with her thumb. Nathaniel did the same.

"There must be hundreds of them in here," Nathaniel said, unpacking even more.

"This is where he stashed the bag. When he came back to the farm after they were caught inside the bank, he stashed all the money here."

"Maddy..." Nathaniel said, solemnly.

His hands were deep in the bag. He pulled out a small, metal box. He turned around to show her. The front of the box had a small hole, begging for an old, small key.

Nathaniel placed the box atop the bag as Madeline fished the key from her pocket. She tried the key in the slot. It slid in with ease. She turned the key. The lid of the box popped up a few inches. Madeline lifted the lid and fingered the contents.

"Letters," she said, rifling through the papers at the top.

Nathaniel shifted his position and knelt beside her to see for himself.

"They're all signed 'Thomas,' " she read.

"Thomas Gains," Nathaniel said. "It's Alfred."

In the middle of the pile of letters was paper of a different kind. It was a single, weathered, brown sheet, torn and ragged at the edges. Madeline touched the tips of her fingers together after feeling it.

"This one has some sort of sticky goop on it," she said.

Nathaniel looked at her with surprise. Madeline clued in quickly.

"Oh my God!" she said, opening the folded paper. "Pictures."

The old photographs were not in good shape. The figures weren't easy to make out, but one was clearly of a young man, standing with a young woman. The second looked like the same pair, but on this one, there was a toddler on the man's knee.

"You think these are them?" Madeline asked.

"I think there's something on the paper," Nathaniel said.

Madeline turned the delicate paper and removed the photos carefully, trying not to cause them more damage. Though the inside too had a film of sludgy residue, the better part of the text could still be read.

" 'Oklahoma Certificate of Birth,' " Madeline read, "from 1903."

Her eyes shifted to the bottom of the paper.

"For…"

"Oh, wow!" Nathaniel said.

He couldn't help but take the paper from Madeline's hands. He lifted it to his face to get a better look.

"I don't believe it."

Madeline looked up at Nathaniel with utter shock.

"It was her," he said. "It was her all along."

Nathaniel read the name on the birth certificate aloud: "Josephine Tilley Eliza Decamp."

"It was her," Madeline repeated, at a loss for emotion.

"Joseph… was Josephine."

"It was her."

Nathaniel handed the paper back to Madeline. He took a seat beside her on the ground.

"I don't…" he started.

"Nate," Madeline said.

Nathaniel looked over.

"It was her," she said yet again.

Chapter 61

Nathaniel and Madeline returned to the car with the bag in tow. Nathaniel placed the bag in the back seat, and he and Madeline got into the front. They both took a moment in the parking lot to let recent revelations sink in. Nathaniel finally pulled out the keys and turned on the car, and the two travelers headed for home.

Madeline looked out on the horizon, but she had something else in her mind. She was picturing her grandmother coming upon her father's important things in the basement of the Tilley farmhouse. She was just looking for candles to light the abandoned house and found her birth certificate and photos of her family along with the other items.

"Of course she left it out of the story," Madeline said, breaking the silence. "She had to, right?"

"It makes sense," Nathaniel said, off on his own tangent of thought.

Madeline looked over to him.

"So many little things in the story…" he continued. "It makes sense that it was a woman. *That's* why they went back to get Millie. She was a decoy, like your grandmother said. The police were looking for a man and a woman going into those banks. Joe – or Josephine – was using Millie as a stand-in. It's probably also why Alfred made a connection and tried to protect her when they first met. She must have reminded him of his daughter."

"But…" Madeline began after a moment's pause.

"But what?"

"Why wouldn't she just tell us from the start?"

"What? That it was her? I don't know. Maybe she thought I wouldn't believe her. It is a crazy story, after all. Especially if she's at the center of it."

"I don't know. I don't think that's it."

"Maybe she thought she couldn't trust me? Like I would go to the cops or something. I can't blame her, really. She didn't know me."

Madeline looked out her window. She simply wasn't satisfied with Nathaniel's reasoning. There had to be something more to it.

"Or maybe…" Nathaniel said. "Maybe it wasn't about me at all."

He looked over at Madeline.

"Maybe it was about you."

"Me?" Madeline said, tearing her eyes from the trees outside her window.

"Yeah, maybe it was all about you."

"How?"

"Okay… what about this. Maybe she didn't want to see how you'd react if she told you it was her from the start. She knew she didn't have much time left, right? Maybe she didn't want to change the way you saw her or thought of her, or treated her, even."

Madeline remained quiet.

"Think about it. You had a very particular relationship with her, a close one, a good one, of course. My guess is she didn't want to do anything to change your impression of her."

"But she had to know I would find out. She *wanted* me to find out eventually."

"She waited until the very end to give you that key. And she didn't even tell us about that address until after she was gone."

"It wouldn't have changed anything between us," Madeline said.

"Can you be so sure?"

Madeline was silent again.

"I mean, think about it," Nathaniel said. "Now that you know, you have to admit, things seem a little different."

"In what way?"

"There's a whole side to the woman you knew nothing about. That can be jarring. It jarred me, and I've known her for less than a year."

"But I wouldn't have loved her any less."

"She was old, Maddy. And as strong-headed as she was, she probably didn't want to take that chance. You were the most important thing to her in the world. You were the last of her family. Imagine what it would have done to her if something changed between you, if *anything* changed."

"You could be right."

"She was protecting herself, and you. Besides, I think she got a kick out of leaving it a mystery."

Madeline smiled. Nathaniel looked over his shoulder to change lanes. He caught a glimpse of the back seat.

"So, hey…" he said. "What do you think you're going to do with all that money?"

"Me?"

"Sure. It's yours now, isn't it?"

Madeline looked into the back seat.

"I don't know if it's mine, Nate. It's stolen money."

"You think anyone's looking for it after all this time? Besides, you didn't steal it, you found it."

"Yeah, but my grandmother stole it. There has to be some sort of law –"

"No one knows your grandmother stole it, Maddy. And there has to be some sort of statute of limitations. Besides, banks were already insured back then. It's found money, literally."

Madeline looked at the bag again.

"How much do you think it's worth?" she asked.

"Grab me a bundle," Nathaniel said.

Madeline reached into the back seat. She unzipped the bag and pulled out a stack of bonds. She handed it to Nathaniel, who did his best to keep his eyes on the road as he calculated.

"Four and a quarter percent a year on $100 since 1918…" he said. "I'm not great at math, but I think that really adds up."

"Some of them are $50 bonds," Madeline said, pulling another stack from the bag.

"What a shame!" Nathaniel joked.

"I don't know," Madeline said. "Either way, it's our money. We found it together."

"Maddy, no."

"If I have to, then you have to. We're in this together."

Nathaniel reached over and took Madeline's hand. He held it in his and rested them both on the armrest that separated the two.

"Why don't we worry about the money later on?" he said. "There's another issue we have to discuss."

"What's that?"

"Now that we know the truth, how are we going to tell the story?"

"That's a good question."

There was a pause in the conversation, but neither Nathaniel nor Madeline let go of the other's hand.

"New evidence aside, I've put some thought into it, actually. I have an idea."

"Okay…"

"Well, first of all, I think it needs to be a book."

"Agreed."

"And there's one other thing…"

"What's that?" Madeline asked.

Nathaniel took his eyes off the road and looked at Madeline. She returned his glance, and his smile. She squeezed his hand in anticipation.

"You're gonna be the one who writes it," he said.